Prisoner

Heath Gunn

ISBN: 978-1-9162957-0-4 (E-Book Kindle)
ISBN: 978-1-9162957-1-1 (Paperback)

A CIP catalogue record for this book is available from the British Library

Any references to historical events, real people, or real places are used fictitiously. Names, characters, and places are products of the author's imagination.

Front cover image by Stuart Bache, Books Covered.

First printing edition 2019.

Page Turner Publications 20-22 Wenlock Road London, N1 7GU
www.heathgunn.com

For my Dad
Who never got to see me published

Thank you to my family for their endless support and encouragement

ACKNOWLEDGEMENTS

A special thank you to Hilary Woodward who turned my hand written scribbles into something I could work with.

Also to Elinor Mary Clarke who worked at The Titchfield Mill and whose name I asked to use for a victim.

Prisoner

1

'Hell' was the one-word description Detective Inspector Lomas Baxter used to describe his day as he sat with his phone pressed between his left shoulder and ear, the awkwardly shaped hard plastic digging into the top of his ear. He had a mountain of paperwork to get through, which he detested, and little chance of leaving his desk for the whole of his shift. As he spoke, his wife listened sympathetically to Lomas summarise his day on the other end of the phone. He knew that it didn't matter how bad his day might have been, after fifteen years as a policeman's wife, Heidi would let him rant, wait until he'd finished, and then, if his mood wasn't too bleak, she would talk about whatever she had called for. He paused to take a breath and realised that Heidi hadn't said much.

'Sorry I've been ranting, everything OK at home?'

'Yes, all good, I literally just called to see how your day was going, on the off-chance that you'd be there.'

Lomas hadn't been sleeping well for a few days and he guessed that she'd felt him shuffling restlessly in bed. He knew that even though she was used to it, Heidi still worried about the toll some of the cases took on him.

The red light on the base of Lomas's phone flashed to indicate an internal call from the control room and he hastily rounded off the conversation with Heidi.

'Good morning Lomas. I thought you might want to know, someone's found an arm,' said the almost robotic voice on the internal line.

'Shit, really? OK, tell me more, Jim, where and when?' asked Lomas, thinking that this wasn't a good way to escape his desk and certainly not the way he would have chosen to avoid the mountain of filing and reports he had to check through. He glanced at the half-read report in front of him on his swamped but ordered desk, piles of neatly arranged reports stacked and grouped in case order, the downside of preferring to read printed reports instead of on a screen. Lomas dropped a crisp, stapled sheaf of papers onto the relevant pile, it landed askew as he reached for a pad to take down the information from the desk sergeant, who delivered the details in the same monotone voice as his opening line. DI Baxter scribbled down the location of the find along with the name of the person who had reported it. He finished the call, grabbed his coat from the back of his chair and made his way quickly down to the carpark at the rear of the station.

Lomas could move swiftly when he needed to, a

habitual gym rat, who'd spent most of his adult life throwing weights around a local gym. He was tall and athletically built, with broad, muscular shoulders and slightly greying, neatly cropped hair. He had warm, dark-brown eyes and a healthy glow to his skin and was dressed in an immaculate navy blue suit and white shirt.

He jumped into his car, started it and spun the wheel with the heel of his right hand, firing the vehicle left onto the main road, glancing at the large hotel that stood across the road from the station. Lomas cast his mind back to when the city was a quieter place, without the seedy, sometimes stomach-churning crimes he was called to these days, or, he wondered, was it that he was just less involved in the early days? His years on the force had desensitised him to the horror and gore, and little shocked him now as it had done in years gone by.

With the light fading, he eased his car up behind a row of police vehicles parked alongside the tree-lined road, muted the gentle rumble of the engine, blipped the key fob to click the locks into place and ventured into the woods – leaves and twigs cracking underfoot as he strode towards the hive of activity that awaited him.

On entering a small clearing, he glanced around at the rotten hollowed-out logs strewn around the periphery, as if left long ago by youngsters enjoying a campfire. Lomas was greeted by a young, fresh-faced officer to whom he introduced himself as they walked through the clearing and went deeper into the woodland. He made a special effort to be courteous to the younger, more inexperienced police officers he encountered, taking the time to listen to their sometimes nervous and elongated explanations of events and situations, remembering how insignificant he was made to feel when he was new to the job. They continued through to another smaller clearing and Lomas was led over to Tom Anderson, a foppish-looking dark-haired man in his early thirties who stood in an uneven circle of flattened grass, where he'd been shuffling and crouching to fuss the glossy black Labrador that sat obediently by his side as Lomas approached.

'Mr Anderson, I'm DI Baxter,' Lomas began as he squatted to rub the back of the canine's head. 'I understand you, or rather your dog, recovered some remains from the stream. Can you tell me how you came to be here and where you found the arm… and please, take your time.'

'Yes, certainly,' replied Tom, clearly quite shaken by his dog's grisly find. The air of confidence with which Lomas conducted himself seemed to make Tom feel immediately at ease.

'We were walking through the woods, which we do quite often. I was off in a world of my own, daydreaming I guess, when Max jumped into the stream. Again, there's nothing unusual about that, he loves the water – sometimes it's a struggle to get him out of it when it's time to go home.' A slight grin sneaked briefly across Tom's lips as he looked down at Max. 'Anyway, the next thing I know, he's bounding out of the river with what I thought at first was a branch hanging from his mouth. It wasn't until he stopped in front of me and dropped it so he could shake that I realised what it was.'

As the university lecturer explained, Lomas listened intently, noting Mr Anderson's body language as well as his account of events leading to the rather unsavoury discovery. His face blushed and his head lowered slightly as he continued.

'I'm a little embarrassed to say that I threw up when I looked more closely and realised what Max had dragged from the water.'

'It's OK, Mr Anderson, there's no need to be embarrassed. It's not every day you're confronted with this kind of situation. Tell me, you said you walk in the woods often – how often, would you say?'

'Nearly every day. Max loves it, and I get to spend some time on my own with my thoughts.'

'Now there's something I'd love to be able to do – escape for a while with my thoughts,' Lomas said, empathising.

'I know it sounds a bit *Buddhist monk*,' the lecturer said, mocking himself with a wry smile. 'But having the time to immerse myself in the tranquillity of nature, with the sounds and smells of the woods, is invaluable to me.'

'No, it sounds great to me, Buddhist monk or not.' Lomas pressed his palms together in mock prayer.

'So, if you're in here nearly every day, Mr Anderson,' continued the detective, bringing Anderson back to his line of questioning, 'can you tell me if you noticed anything different about the area where Max came out of the water, or any of the other parts of the wood you regularly walk in?'

'When you say different…?'

'Well, are there any areas that have been cleared recently, or have you seen anything that doesn't belong here… items of clothing, someone's personal belongings, anything that's stood out as being out of the ordinary.'

The lecturer looked thoughtful for a few seconds and the black Lab nuzzled at the side of his leg, eager to play. He reached his hand down to the top of Max's head, instinctively messing up the sleek black mop of hair.

'One of the things I love about the woods is that they change on a daily basis – nature evolves and regenerates, you know? These woods are a complex microcosm of life and change that exists with little outside interference from mankind, except for walkers and the odd mountain bike rider. But, to answer your question more directly, no, I don't recall seeing anything recently that looked either man-made or not of these woods. Sorry, that's probably not very helpful.'

'On the contrary, Mr Anderson, everything you've told me has been very helpful.' Lomas placed a reassuring hand on Tom Anderson's shoulder and led him back to the younger officer, who had stayed on the opposite side of the clearing while Lomas had spoken to Tom. A sharp cool breeze cut across the clearing as they moved and the light visibly dimmed, as if the woods were mourning the passing of its watery victim.

'If you could leave all your contact details with the officer, please, Mr Anderson, we'll be in touch in the next couple of days. Thank you for taking the time to talk to me.' Lomas turned to the officer.

'Could you take a full statement from Mr Anderson, please, but first could you ask everyone else to come here?' he requested politely.

'Speak to you soon, Mr Anderson.' Lomas waved them off as the young officer led Tom away from the scene, his canine companion bounding along beside him, lapping at his hand, hoping for a treat.

The other officers, ready and waiting for the ensuing search, appeared in the clearing as requested, the long grass folding silently under the weight of their heavy boots.

'OK, listen up. I want the whole of the woods and surrounding area for two miles up and downstream cordoning off. I want no one in or out unless I authorise it.'

His commands came as no surprise to the team, who had already begun cordoning off the area from the roadside. A nearby car park had already been sealed off and they stood awaiting further instructions clad in protective equipment so not to contaminate anything they came across.

'One more thing,' he continued before they dispersed. 'Let's try and get it sealed off before dark. I want a detailed ground search. Mobilise the dog teams. We have an arm and have to assume for now that the rest of the body is out there, hopefully in close proximity. Any questions?' – A brief pause – 'Thank you, carry on.' He made his way over to the arm as the team he'd just dispatched began to set about carrying out his instructions.

Lomas was no stranger to the grotesque and often savage acts committed by the perpetrators of the crimes he had the misfortune of investigating. But every time he looked at hacked and dismembered bits of bodies, or the mutilated remains of whole ones, the first thought through his mind was that this was what was left of someone's daughter, son, mother or father, a thought that hovered a while as he cast his eye over the stretched and bloated skin that covered the dismembered limb. He took a torch from his pocket and shone a thin beam on one end of the arm, which had been neatly and very precisely cut from its shoulder. There were widely placed finger-sized marks visible around the biceps and lower triceps. The ways in which people disposed of human life as if it were the week's rubbish appalled Lomas, and this in itself was enough to fuel his desire to see the animals who carried out these acts caught and caged. The elbow was beaten and gouged and the thumb was twisted backwards against the wrist, exactly opposite its natural position. Both injuries could have been caused by the arm's journey down the rock-littered stream, but Lomas knew that this probably wouldn't be the case. The hand and fingers were relatively well preserved, nails well tended and unabused, except for the dirt and mud packed under them. Lomas hoped that when the forensic guys had finished with it they would uncover some clue to aid in the identification of the killer, either fragments of skin under the nails, or small traces of blood for DNA matching from the marks which scarred the skin of the victim – anything would help.

He mulled over the victims of an ongoing double homicide he was investigating in which limbs had been precisely removed and all other parts of the bodies had been found within a two-mile radius of the first. Both murders had been in the last six weeks and both had been young women; Lomas didn't much believe in coincidence.

The next morning, as throughout the night, a team of fifty officers and a handful of local volunteers combed the woods, the stream and the roadsides. They systematically turned every rock, probed through the vast swathes of brambles and searched the dense bushes and hedges. Yet again, it was the stream that released the next mutilated and severed limb from its watery grasp. Tucked under an overhang on the bank, about half a mile from where Tom Anderson's dog had made his gruesome find, a leg was discovered, removed just below the hip, again very neatly cut through both flesh and bone.

As Lomas arrived to join the search team, the scene at the woods was a slightly more frenetic one than he had left behind him the previous night. A transport was waiting to take the leg away, and search dogs yapped and jostled each other as they were moved towards the next search area. Alongside the dogs, a myriad of police officers gathered in groups in readiness for being dispatched to various parts of the woods. Lomas nodded a greeting to a team who were facing him as he made his way through the larger clearing, where he was joined by an older officer, tall and rotund, with a thin white beard and a ruddy complexion.

'Morning, Lomas.'

'Morning, Barney, how's it going?' Lomas glanced sideways at the copper. 'I thought you were shaving that thing off completely?'

'What can I say? The missus loves me having a bit of hair around my face.' Barney Joyce fired a wide grin back at Lomas.

Lomas smiled in return and retorted, 'Well, I suppose it looks better than the full Santa look you had going on.'

They arrived by the side of the stream, the smiles dropping from their faces. Lomas crouched by the side of a carefully preserved lower limb, its colour and distortion similar to that of the arm, with the exposed flesh at the top of the leg discoloured to a blue-ish hue. The method of removal looked at first glance to be the same, with the bone being precisely and cleanly severed. Lomas could see from the pallor of the young officer that had discovered the grisly remains that she was in a slight state of shock. She leaned her hand against a nearby tree and breathed deeply.

'First time?' enquired Lomas, a distinct tone of compassion echoing in his words. His thoughts quickly raced back to his first time, like the flash of a camera in his mind's eye, an instant image of him as a young officer, keen to impress. He'd been involved in what ended up being one of the largest manhunts in the formative years of his career. He'd been under the wing of a stocky old-school copper called Bruno, who had used a similar compassionate tone, which at the time Lomas remembered had been unexpected as Bruno generally took the piss at every opportunity. He'd spent two days solid combing through undergrowth, scouring the countryside for a missing mother of three, until, beside a seldom-used railway line, he had seen the woman's head, eyes wide open, with a look of fear that had burned itself into his memory and had haunted his dreams ever since. He blinked himself back from his recollection with a tiny shake of his head.

'It does get easier,' he reassured the young woman.

She looked at him, red marks on her face from wiping away tears that had flowed freely with the sleeve of her jacket. A sadness he had seen before welled in her eyes. She pushed against the tree and stood upright.

'Thank you, sir. I'll be fine.'

'If you're sure you're feeling OK, can you show me where you found it, please?' requested Lomas. The woman nodded and started walking towards the stream, wiping invisible tears from her eyes and cheeks.

A scene of crimes officer followed the pair without a word and joined a colleague who was wearing a forensic protective suit and conducting a detailed search of the surrounding woodland. The air hung heavy with moisture and the earthy scent of the mossy undergrowth filled each breath.

'Any ideas, Sherlock?' Lomas enquired of the Forensic Pathologist, so-called because in his twenty years of forensic detection he had uncovered some completely damning evidence in cases everyone else thought were hopeless. Lomas had the greatest respect for Sherlock, real name Doctor Alan Paisley, as he was meticulous in his work, leaving nothing to chance. The small, round-faced, balding man had added vital information to Baxter's cases on more than one occasion.

'Same guy as the other two?' Lomas added quickly, wanting to know exactly what he was dealing with and if his gut feeling was taking him in the right direction.

'I would think so, but I can't be positive until I've done more,' replied Sherlock, his warm brown eyes a gateway to an immense bank of knowledge. Sherlock's noncommittal answers were strangely reassuring to Lomas; he only ever stated facts when he had absolute proof, and the detective liked that, as he knew that when Sherlock was sure, there would be no room for contradiction.

'I do know that both limbs have been cut with something different to the other two bodies. Possibly a meat cleaver or a large sharp knife, but definitely not the surgical saw that was used on the others,' he added. As the two men spoke, there came word via an out of breath officer who had run to find Lomas – the next grim find was the right foot and ankle. Both were disconnected from each other; both were in similar condition to the earlier finds.

'The deep, dark lines found just above the ankle bone indicate a ligature of some description. This dent in the back of the heel will probably show that she had been tied tightly to a chair, judging by the depth of the indentation,' said Sherlock to Lomas upon examination of the foot, motioning to a concave indentation in the heel.

'The apparent dislocation or breaking of the joint is similar to the other two, Lomas,' added the doctor.

'So, it's a serial we've got then, Doc, you think?' asked Lomas.

'It does look that way. I'll try and give you more later, OK?' said Sherlock in a tone which Lomas was only too familiar with.

'I know, I know,' replied Lomas, holding his

hands to his temples. 'Let's get this one caught quickly, before we have a long line of body parts for you to examine.'

'Do you think it could be Titia Matthews? she's a woman in her thirties, been reported missing for a little while, so far nothing on her.' Titia had been the subject of a missing person investigation for nearly four weeks and despite trying to track her through friends and relatives, and retracing her last known steps, Lomas's colleagues hadn't come up with anything.

'Yeah I heard about that. It could be, maybe when we find more of her, we'll have more of an idea.'

The other body parts followed in quick succession over a three-day period. All had been removed in the same fashion at various joints, with ankles and wrists broken, all in similar states of decomposition, slowed down by the cool freshwater stream. The last piece of the victim to be found was the head, uncovered from undergrowth three-quarters of a mile from where the first arm was fished from the stream. It revealed, as Sherlock had predicted, a woman, in her late thirties. She had blonde hair, and deep blue eyes set back into what was now a battered and decaying face. Her top front two teeth had been viciously ripped from her skull with what Sherlock observed as being something like pliers, and there were sharp fragments left behind in the victim's gums. Most striking and prominent of all was the word 'PRISONER' neatly engraved in the forehead of the woman. In large capital letters, the word started from the left temple, arcing across the head, and ended at the right temple. After a detailed examination, Sherlock reported that it was highly likely that the victim was alive during both the dental extraction and the engraving.

'The press are having a field day with this hatchet man, Lomas, I really need some kind of progress,' was the first sentence that greeted him on the forty-sixth day of what had now become a triple murder investigation.

'Three in six weeks, Lomas. What are we doing?' The voice was cold and demanded respect, and an answer. Marie Carlton had been a police officer for the same length of time as Lomas and had been his DCI for two years. A tall slender woman with short-cropped dark hair and steely blue eyes, which penetrated even the hardest of criminals when she interviewed them. She was well spoken and extremely well educated, and she carried herself in a surefooted manner, commanding the respect of her staff and peers.

'Well, ma'am,' began Lomas, as his focus moved to DCI Carlton, 'we have an ID on the third woman, and downstairs they're prepping her for a formal ID.'

'Relatives here?' asked Marie.

'Yes, her husband – I'm talking to him in an

hour.'

'Does he know yet?'

'No, not yet, but I'm sure he suspects. The name hasn't been released to the press yet, but they've been giving regular updates through the local news. How do you want me to use the press on this one?'

'Speak to the husband. Then, as long as he gives consent, let's get some pictures out there and descriptions of where and when these women were killed and disposed of, but not full disclosure. See if we can shock up a public response, with the detail retained for later.'

'OK.'

'Do you have any more leads?'

'No, not as yet. Sherlock's full report will be with me by one o'clock. I'll have him get a copy to you, yes?'

'Yes, please, can you keep me informed? I'll arrange a press conference for tonight – you'll be there, Lomas?'

'Yes, of course I will.' It almost went without saying that he would be present at the press conference. He'd been told he had a calm reassuring air, which relatives found comforting and colleagues found supportive, it also meant he rarely escaped a press conference. With that, Lomas turned on his heels and went on his way to the incident room to give a briefing.

'Right, people, listen up,' he began. 'We now have three dead women, all dismembered and, it would appear, tortured pre-mortem. He's starting to enjoy himself. We know this because the level and type of torture is escalating and becoming more inventive. He's starting to experiment with different means of dismemberment, and our latest victim has an engraving on her forehead, which is a word, not just the patterns as on the heads of the first two women, who both had symmetrical shapes scraped into their skin.' He motioned towards two pictures, both of battered heads, one with intricate squares and the other with star-type shapes carved into the skin.

'Now we have the word "prisoner" engraved across the forehead. In six weeks we have had three women brutally murdered and we have no reason to believe he won't do it again. Now, what do we know about these women? Well, they were all young, attractive, professional white women, aged between twenty-three and thirty-eight. They were all of a slight build and they were all tortured and partly dismembered while still alive, then completely within a four- to eight-hour window post-mortem.'

'Pete…' Lomas signalled towards one of the officers sitting at the front of the briefing. 'How are we doing on background?'

'Well, we have no known drug or gambling habits or connections. All the friends and relatives of the first two check out, and I'm just waiting to get started on the latest victim's family and friends, sir.'

'OK, what about regular habits – pubs, clubs, visits to the gym?' enquired Lomas.

'Nothing unusual so far, but we're checking all the people they came into contact with, daily, weekly and monthly.'

'OK, good. Any questions?'

'Just one, sir,' said a calm, quiet voice from the back of the room. 'Do we have any ideas about the kind of man we're looking for yet?' The question came from DC Drew Taylor, a petite woman in her early twenties; she was a talented young officer with an enquiring mind who had contributed a great deal to the case so far. Her background checks were assiduous and the interviews she'd carried out with members of the victims' families were sensitive yet thorough and searching. Lomas viewed her very much as a growing asset to his team and a voice worth listening to.

'Yes, Drew, we have an idea.' He motioned to a tall, thin, ghostly looking figure, who until now had stood silently in the corner.

'Doctor Redman, one of our forensic psychologists, has been analysing the evidence we have so far and has built up an initial profile of our man. Doctor Redman…' Lomas said, prompting him.

'Thank you.' The doctor cast an intense gaze over the people gathered before him in the briefing room, the bright fluorescent light glinting from epaulette numbers. He lowered his chin towards his chest, tilting his head forward, his deep-set, dark eyes almost overshadowed by his high brow and thick, dark eyebrows. His lank dark brown hair, which framed his face, brushed the collar of his brown suit, which seemed to hang as if two sizes too big all the way down to his scuffed and unkempt shoes.

'From the evidence you have gathered to date, I believe the man you are looking for is likely to be in his mid to late thirties, as he has a level of patience we would be unlikely to come across in a younger man, this is coupled with the physical strength needed to carry out the attacks. He may be unemployed, which allows him the freedom he needs to move around at times that suit him, will likely be intelligent and well read, with some kind of medical training, and possibly has a history of maternal abuse. He has an interest in a less mainstream or traditional religion, as some of the shapes carved on the heads of the first two victims are believed to be of pagan origin. One in particular' – he gestured towards the first picture on display – 'is similar in shape to a symbol called the Elven Star. This was a seven-pointed star found in some branches of the faerie tradition of Wicca and serves as a reminder that seven is a sacred number, representing seven pillars of wisdom. Similarly, in Kabbalah, seven is linked to the sphere of victory, so while there is nothing definitive here, it does give us some idea of the likely spiritual leanings of our killer.' Dr Redman paused and looked out on a combination of intrigued and blank faces that stared silently and attentively back at him. He continued. 'The word "prisoner" is often used as an expression of one's own feelings of repression, or possibly a message regarding the control and power he has over his victims. He will, without question, strike again, and the frequency and severity of the attacks will increase as he gets better practised and more accustomed to his work.'

'His work?' asked Drew.

'Oh yes, he now sees this as his work. Just as your work takes up the vast majority of your waking thoughts and attention, so his endeavours do for him.' Redman left the end of his sentence dramatically as if for maximum effect on his audience and then slid back half a step and eased his head back slowly, like a tortoise retreating into its shell.

'Thank you, Doctor,' Lomas said as he stepped forward to retake control of the briefing, which he wound up with a list of instructions and his usual clap of hands. The team dispersed quickly with a purposeful rumble of conversation as officers exited the briefing room.

'Drew.'

'Yes, sir.'

'I'm going to inform the third victim's husband in about half an hour. Can you be in the car park ready. I'd like you to come along for this one.'

'Yes, sir.'

2

Louis Matthews stepped from the shower refreshed but far from ready to face the day. He stood motionless and oblivious as the water dripped from his body into pools around his feet.

His thoughts both day and night had been plagued by the disappearance of his wife four weeks previously and the apparent lack of progress, or interest, he believed the police had in finding her. This had changed over the course of the last few days as he'd seen reports in the papers, and on TV, about body parts being recovered from nearby woods. He had repeatedly played out in his mind how the conversation with the police would go, if the woman they had found turned out to be Titia. On top of this, the other thing distracting Louis from functioning normally; was that there were seemingly innumerable rows and half-finished discussions that forced their way into his thoughts, only to queue up one after the other, as if seeking conclusions to distant and insurmountable problems. They jostled for his conscious and unconscious attention, vying for space in his cluttered psyche, making the most mundane task a chore and clarity of thought an unattainable nirvana. He made his way barefoot to a brass Buddha, where he lowered himself slowly into a cross-legged position, exhaled in a steady controlled breath and began to chant, praying for the presence of mind to aid in the safe return of his wife, or the strength to deal with her death.

His daily habits had become obsessively centred on the return of his wife and were littered with new rituals, such as sitting in front of the brass Buddha, which he did regularly throughout the day and continued during the small hours. This from a man who, throughout the whole of his adult life, had denounced all forms of faith and religion as merely a crutch used by the weak in times of trouble.

His marriage to Titia had been far from idyllic, and they had developed somewhat of a chasm between them in terms of their personal interests. While he enjoyed his work as a recently semi-retired stockbroker, he also loved his weekend football and the obligatory drinking sessions which followed. She, in contrast, had grown to detest football and used his good fortune on the stock market to further her wardrobe or extravagant taste in jewellery, often coming home from shopping trips laden with bags which Louis knew would sit unopened in her dressing room. Louis had tried to bridge the growing gap with candlelit dinners at their favourite restaurant, Pines, an excellent place to dine, down by the water with wonderful countryside views. They also had regular dinner parties at home, when Titia's family would gather round in their ornate dining room, being entertained by Louis and Ben, their brother-in-law, as they reeled off tales of their childhood together in a small rural village. Having grown up together and eventually married two sisters, Louis and Ben had always stayed very close.

It was during the last four weeks that the strength of their friendship had really been evident. Ben and Coline, Titia's sister, had been a reassuring influence for Louis and had tried to make him feel welcome at their home as often as possible. Coline too was desperate with worry as to the whereabouts of her elder sister. They had a very close but competitive relationship and always had, ever since they were children. Their parents had encouraged competition as a healthy, character-building tool, and both girls had been high achievers, not only academically but also in both the gymnastic and track-and-field arenas. Sports accolades and trophies filled a room in the home of their now elderly parents, with pictures of smiling young girls they could barely remember, standing beside the trophies. Louis knew that Coline had a great belief in her sister's imminent reappearance, and she had the first moments of seeing her again planned out to the finest detail. However, her parents required constant updates and reassurances that everything would be fine. Both now in their early seventies, they were ageing all the more rapidly since Titia's disappearance. They sat in front of their TV, convinced that the miracle of modern technology would reveal some clue as to where their beloved daughter could be. The knock-on effect of Titia's disappearance was that her parents now phoned Coline four to five times a day to check where and how she was. This, Coline had told Louis, was very wearing, and she feared she might add to their worry by snapping or saying the wrong thing. The frailty of her parents concerned Coline hugely, and she was wary that any news, good or bad, might be too much for them to handle. They too had become increasingly concerned due to the recent TV coverage of the grim discoveries made in the woods, concern that had resulted in Coline and Ben having to go to see them, offering hopeful assurances.

Louis stood, silently immersed in a battle between his memory and conscience. The fight that was playing out in his head almost as clearly as watching a video replay, was set around the arrival of yet another gargantuan credit card bill. Dropping on the mat on a cold winter morning, igniting a storm of screamed insults, the ensuing row ended in the usual slamming of doors and silent tears from Titia, the plastic currency one of many abused cards that she had held and he had paid.

This minor point, although one that featured heavily in their rows, no longer seemed significant to Louis. Instead, the battle Louis faced was the open-ended and non-conclusive fashion in which their arguments had always finished. Nothing was ever resolved only stored away to be whipped up at the next opportunity and hurled like shards of glass, aimed to inflict maximum pain. Now he might never get the opportunity to resolve this or any other issue they had.

He broke from his trance-like pondering long enough to make a coffee and then ambled aimlessly from window to sofa and back again. The vast expanse of his large, uncluttered living room felt like an ocean, an ocean that he was forced to navigate from time to time, as and when unwelcome interruptions such as the phone or doorbell, called him away. A longer than was entirely necessary ivory leather sofa sat in the centre of the room. At either end of this, as if guarding it, stood two tall, thin African carvings. One was of a curious witch doctor with a scythe in one hand and a pestle and mortar in the other. The finer details of clothing and headdress had been observed and the face looked old and weathered by years of grief and tribal disagreements. Every nuance of the fabric of the tribesman's clothing was etched into the dark wood; so subtle were the contours, it looked as if it might sway in a slight breeze. The other figure was that of a young woman holding a wrapped baby close to her chest, clutched as if protecting the youngster from a harsh African sun. Again, the minutest features of her and her child's faces were engraved into the dark, warm wood. Along the floor, pale interlocked timber stretched in all directions. The focal point of the room was a monumental fireplace, above which sat a picture of Louis's ideal country retreat, a perfect scene of undisturbed tranquillity: a small log cabin tucked into a clearing, beside a gently flowing waterfall, cascading down and collecting in a crystal clear pool that reflected shafts of sunlight across the beautiful floral clearing into which you could quite easily lose yourself.

Louis stood in front of large French doors that opened from the living room onto his patio. This in turn led to a garden of four and a half acres of greenery and mature trees, complete with wild rabbits and the occasional deer. He opened the doors and stood gazing out at the grass, lightly covered with fallen leaves. The sun cast huge shadows of the trees, as if to plot where they would one day fall. He stayed for a moment, his blonde wispy hair blowing in the gentle breeze, reminding him of the reasons why, on one of their good days, they had decided on this house. He could almost hear her laughing the first time the snow had fallen. They had played in the snow like young children, balling up fists full of fresh white powder, hurling them mischievously at each other. Then they created the biggest snowman he'd ever seen, which Titia had decorated with a new scarf of his and an old walking stick she'd dug out of a cupboard.

As he gazed over to where the snowman had long since melted, a cloud came across the sun, and simultaneously his thoughts clouded too. Once again, he turned from the garden and retreated to a large armchair. He skipped through the morning papers, scouring the pictures, hoping to maybe see a picture of Titia in a crowd somewhere. The pages of the papers were dominated by the slaying of a third woman, found in woods near a stream. He briefly thought the worst and then struggled to dismiss it from his mind, trying desperately to not allow himself to be tortured any more than he was already.

3

Imposing black iron gates greeted them as Lomas and Drew drove up to the home of Louis Matthews. An impressive sight, the house stood some 250 yards in the background, a distance which didn't diminish the scale or grandeur of the property. As they passed through the gates, the gravel crunched under the wheels of Lomas's car. Either side of the driveway, sloping up and away, was a vast expanse of well-kept grounds, with lush green grass broken occasionally by a cluster of brightly coloured late flowering blooms, edged with fallen leaves. Mature oaks and chestnuts towered over the striking landscape and the driveway wound a snaking path up to the house. The home was built from sand-coloured stone, darkened in places with age. Several roof levels and large sweeping bay windows which were separated into a multitude of smaller panes, each one spotlessly clean and edged in crisp white paint, adorned the façade. Four chimney stacks stood out at various points along the roof, giving an almost majestic air to the grand home.

'How the other half live,' said Drew, quite in awe of the surroundings in which she found herself.

'Yes, and die,' replied Lomas emphatically, as if

to bring Drew back down to earth and focus her on the grim task at hand.

They approached a large white door and Lomas pressed his thumb against the bell push to announce their arrival.

The door opened slowly, and a man stood on the other side. He had a thick mop of mousey-blonde hair, green eyes and a tanned complexion that Drew thought would probably make him quite a good looking guy, if it wasn't for the fact that he looked as if he hadn't slept for weeks. He was medium height and build and had clearly looked after himself, from the way his thin white t-shirt hung close to a mildly athletic musculature.

'Mr Louis Matthews?' said Lomas.

'Yes.'

'Are you the husband of Mrs Titia Matthews?'

'Yes, that's right. Who are you?'

'I'm Detective Inspector Baxter and this is Detective Constable Taylor. Could we come in please, Mr Matthews?'

'Yes, of course... please come through.' Louis motioned towards the living room, his eyes wide and staring.

The inside of the house took Drew's breath away; the vast floor space and high ceilings were all impeccably presented. Paintings that occupied huge areas of pale off-white wall were nothing like the prints and copies that the walls of her own apartment offered.

'Would you like to take a seat, Mr Matthews?'

Drew quickly reset her focus, drawing her attention back to the task at hand.

'Have you found her?' Louis asked anxiously as he sat down. 'Is she all right?' The panic in his voice was clear, and his attention darted from one officer to the other, unable to hold a constant gaze.

'Mr Matthews, I'm sorry to tell you that we've found a body we believe to be that of Mrs Matthews,' began Lomas.

'A body… you said a body. Oh my God, she's dead. She can't be dead. She just can't.' Again his gaze darted from one of them to the other, searching for reassurance.

'I'm sorry to tell you, Mr Matthews, that if it is your wife, she is dead.'

A silence unlike anything Drew had encountered before fell upon the room, like an enormous, ponderous cloud that none of them could lift, casting a blanket of gloom across the vast lounge. She watched intently as Lomas allowed this news to sink in and as Louis Matthews dealt with the realisation of what were probably his deepest fears.

Matthews slumped back into the deep leather armchair. His hands rose to his face and his whole body shook uncontrollably as silent tears fell from his intense green eyes. Drew felt drawn to put a comforting arm around this broken man's shoulders. Lomas nodded his approval for her to do so.

After a compassionate pause, Lomas broke the silence.

'We need you to formally identify the body, Mr

Matthews – as the next of kin.'

'When?' the shaky voice retorted.

'As soon as possible.'

'Give me a few minutes and I'll go with you now, if that's OK?' Louis asked, his sobbing easing.

'There is something else I think you need to know, Mr Matthews,' Lomas continued. 'The body, although laid out under a sheet, is dismembered.'

'It's what!' Louis's now bloodshot eyes locked on to Lomas. 'She's the one in the paper, the body they've found in pieces all over the woods, isn't she? Oh my God, my dear sweet Titia, hacked and butchered by some… fucking psycho. No!'

His voice strained and morphed into a wail as he broke down. Louis fell to his knees, his face buried in his hands, his sobs and animal-like wails filled the room. Drew felt powerless to help the man before her and looked to Lomas, silently pleading for him to say something to stop Louis Matthews' pain.

Lomas stood, speechless. He had no reply, no pre-planned words or phrases. He caught Drew's eye as he glanced away from Matthews. *They don't teach you how to handle this*, he thought. He could only look on at the grief and agony Louis Matthews was experiencing, a bystander with nothing to offer but, like Drew, an arm of comfort and a shoulder to cry on.

4

Louis and Drew stood in the cold clinical environment of the morgue. The smell of disinfectant and cleanliness filled the air. A white sheet was all that covered the body, and she had been laid out carefully, put together like a life-size jigsaw. Calmer, but now nauseous, Louis Matthews nodded as the sheet was pulled back and revealed the face of his wife, a face he'd only seen in his dreams and nightmares for the past four weeks and a face that would burn in his memory for all eternity.

A long white bandage was draped across her forehead and her eyes were closed, her once stunningly attractive face now covered with cuts and bruises. Louis thought how she would never have approved of the way her blonde hair had been scraped back. A feeling of calm came over him, almost like a shroud of peace. His worrying and wondering where and how she was, was at least now over. He felt cold and numb, struggling to tear his gaze from the expressionless, dead face of his wife.

Louis glanced to his left, and there stood Drew, eyes welled up, obviously choking back tears. How strange, he thought, that someone so young, who, until his wife's body had been identified and pieced together, had no knowledge of either of them, but who now stood so deeply touched by his loss.

'Thank you, Detective,' he said to Drew in a calm and sensitive voice. 'Thank you for your compassion and for showing me the human side of police officers.'

Drew looked puzzled but somehow calmed by his words.

'Would you like to go now?' she enquired.

'Yes, please, if there's nothing more you need me to do.'

Lomas joined them as they walked out into the late afternoon sun.

'When you feel up to it, I'd like to talk to you about the last time you saw your wife, Mr Matthews.'

'Certainly, will tomorrow be all right?'

'Yes, fine, if you feel up to it?'

Louis nodded at Lomas, turned, and made his way down the grey stone steps to the street.

Drew, her eyes glistening in the sun from the tears which she had managed to stop from flowing, looked on, unable to imagine the pain and anguish that Louis Matthews was feeling. She glanced at Lomas, and he too was consumed by his thoughts as they watched Louis silently until he was out of sight.

5

The next day, an overpowering stench of urine, sweat and alcohol hung under Louis's nose as two police officers dragged a drunk through the station doors and passed him in the foyer.

'DI Baxter will be with you shortly,' the desk sergeant reassured him.

'Thank you.'

Louis had preferred to speak to Lomas at the station. His home now seemed cold and unwelcoming. *'The less time I have to spend here the better,'* was how he had described his feelings towards his home to Lomas on the phone earlier in the day. Lomas had agreed readily for Louis to come to see him.

The station buzzed with a sense of urgency. Telephones ringing, raised voices, the arrested drunk hurling abuse as he was guided to a cell to sober up. All these things momentarily diverted Louis's thoughts from the misery into which he had been so deeply plunged the previous day. The stark reality of what had happened to his wife had plagued him all night. He had relived the scene that had greeted him in the morgue over and over, each time more grotesque and explicit than the time before, his imagination wild with ideas of what was hidden beneath the white bandage on Titia's forehead. A recurring nightmare had gripped Louis each time he slid into the lightest of slumber. Titia lying in the morgue, under the white sheet. The morgue attendant eased back the sheet from the top of her battered head. As it reached her neck her eyelids flicked open. Titia's intense blue eyes fixed on Louis, and with a stare that burned deep into his soul her pain fed into him, the pain of a thousand piercing needles, accompanied by a phrase that shrieked through his head. 'You did this to me, all of this. You drove me away. You didn't find me. You didn't save me!'

At this point he had woken, shaking, with every pore of his body oozing a cold sweat, still able to hear Titia's taunting echoing in his head.

A tap on the shoulder wrenched him out of his thoughts and dragged him back to reality.

Lomas stood before him. 'Mr Matthews, are you sure you're OK?'

'Yes, yes, I'll be fine, thank you.'

The cold sweat covered Louis once more and the colour had drained from his face.

Lomas guided him towards an interview room. Once inside, Louis felt the quiet to be reassuring. The room was uncluttered, safe and calming. Here, he could be free from his demons, even if it would only be for a short while.

'Do you want a tea or coffee, Mr Matthews?' Lomas enquired.

'Tea, please.'

Lomas leaned out of the door.

'Drew, could you get two teas please, and then join Mr Matthews and me?'

'Yes, no problem, I'll be a couple of minutes,' Drew replied eagerly.

Drew was becoming immersed in the case, more so than anything else she had worked on to date. Maybe it was the sheer scale – three murders, a huge manhunt – maybe the momentum the investigation was gathering, or yesterday with Louis Matthews in the morgue. She felt as though she was on a steep curve and felt compelled to know more about the Matthews. Titia was so different in some ways from the first two victims – the other two were a decade younger – although from the photos Drew had seen of Titia she certainly didn't look her thirty-eight years. The first two victims had lived relatively mundane lives compared to the opulence that surrounded Titia Matthews.

She finished making the drinks and headed for the interview room.

Lomas had waited for Drew's return. On her entering the room he dispersed with the formalities of the interview and moved quickly and concisely to his questions. As Louis wasn't being flagged as a likely prime suspect, Lomas intended this to be as painless as possible.

'Mr Matthews, in your own time, can you please tell me about the last time you saw your wife, and also about her routines – where she went, who she saw – to help us build up a picture of set patterns she may have had, places she may have been easy to follow to or from, that sort of thing.'

'I'm not sure where to start. Titia was a beautiful, intelligent… bitch!' Drew's eyes widened in amazement. 'Shocked, Detective?' Louis enquired, noticing Drew's reaction. 'Don't be. It was no secret. She thrived on it. But I did love her. We had our ups and downs – more downs recently, if I'm honest. Two years ago, Titia stopped practising law, something she'd dedicated herself to, as I had with the stock market. As with many things she surrounded herself with, Titia grew bored. Bored with the daily rituals she had to endure, bored with the clients she represented, bored with the lack of challenge she found within the law. We had many rows over that one subject alone – her constant need to be entertained by new things. But no matter what, I still loved her.' He paused, as if waiting for someone to stop him.

'Please go on, Mr Matthews,' Lomas prompted. Louis nodded, took some tea from the cup in front of him and continued.

'The last two or three months leading up to her disappearing had been the worst. She spent more, she drank more, and because *she* drank more, so did I. At least, that's how it seemed at the time. We were in different places, our interests were poles apart. I love football, she hated it. A common game, she used to say. So, after football I used to go out, you know, with the boys, have a few beers. Anyway, she hated that too. Don't get me wrong, it wasn't all her. I disliked her friends with a passion – self-obsessed, preening, vain women who seemed to do little of value, unless you include lunch. But when we were alone, and on a good day, we had fun.' Louis composed himself and took another sip from his tea, cradling the cup in his hands and slowly breathing in the steam from the brew through his nose.

'Like I said, the last two or three months were the worst. In fact, the only time she seemed happy was when we were out with other people. So, we went out – a lot. The regular habits you asked about? There's a restaurant called Pines, a lovely place. We went there two or three times a week with various friends and her family. Like I said, she was happiest then, and if Titia was happy and smiling, I got less grief.'

The tears were rolling freely down his face, but he made no effort to wipe them. His haunting green eyes fixed on a central spot on the desk.

Lomas watched intently, listening to every word, trying to pick up something, anything, which would help him find out where or when Titia Matthews could have been taken.

Louis's reminiscence continued, and several arguments, dinners and social gatherings were described in great detail. The underlying theme in each was his obvious distress at the loss of his wife, and the ferocity with which the pair had argued.

‘The night Mrs Matthews disappeared, tell me about that please?’ Lomas asked gently.

‘That night, that fucking, awful night. We’d had a huge row during the early evening, and by the night, she was gone.’ Louis seemed to cut his account short. His gaze shifted for the first time since he’d been talking from the centre of the table and shot, briefly, up to the far right corner of the room.

‘What was the row about, Mr Matthews?’ Lomas enquired.

Louis drew in a deep breath and sighed, his hands moving to the sides of his head, pressing his palms flat against his face.

‘You might as well know. You’ll find out sooner or later anyway.’ He paused again, eyebrows raised, forehead wrinkling, this time hanging on to the silence as if he himself was just about to admit to murder. ‘For four and a half months, Coline and I had been having an affair.’

‘Coline Carter, Titia’s sister?’ Lomas almost choked on the question, in a very rare moment of surprise.

‘Yes, her sister.’ Louis paused, shaking his head. ‘It started out as nothing, a drunken one-off, but as Titia’s drinking and shopping got worse, so the comfort that Coline offered seemed more… needed, and somehow easier to justify.’

Lomas sat motionless, remaining non-judgemental. The affair did offer a layer of complexity to the Matthews’ relationship, one which he hadn't anticipated, but he had a murderer to catch. The affair, he thought, was a matter best left to Louis Matthews' conscience.

6

Drew clicked her key into the lock of her weathered black front door. She stepped inside her flat, hanging her bag on a neatly arranged hat stand as she simultaneously flicked on the lights, casting a short shadow against the inside of the door. A modest one-bedroom apartment, tastefully adorned in pastels with unpretentious accessories trimming the various shelves, she had prints of Monet classics hung around the walls. Glancing at a couple of them, she mentally graded them against the huge canvases that hung in Louis Matthews' grand entrance. Drew draped her jacket over the back of a chrome dining chair and made her way into the kitchen. Without the need for extra lighting, she reached into the fridge and produced an unopened bottle of white wine. Down to her left she retrieved a bottle opener and then carefully began to remove the cork – the shiny, cold glass sliding in her hand momentarily as she tightened her grasp. The young detective lit the wick of a yellow candle in a jar and took a second to smell the first warm waft of lemon, as the candle began to work its magic on the air in the apartment.

Confused and somewhat bewildered by the day's events, she sat holding her wine glass, gently swirling the sweet, golden liquid. As she did, she replayed the revealing and adulterous statement that Louis Matthews had given earlier in the day, her head swimming with questions that would have to remain unanswered, for now at least. Questions of the moral bearings of the man and, to an equal extent, his dead wife's sister.

It seemed that every day Drew discovered a new side to human nature, and nearly every time it was a more astonishing trait, or act, than the one before. She enjoyed her work and the revelation of each new discovery, and she found herself in awe of Lomas and the calm, calculated and confident way he conducted the team and the investigation. At times, she felt a bit out of her depth, unsure whether she belonged amongst the ranks of detectives she found herself in. Sometimes she not only felt out of her depth, but as if she was swimming against a current and one that at any moment would take her under – but if Lomas ever felt like this, he never showed any signs to her or to the outside world; he was always so in control.

She changed into jogging bottoms and a baggy T-shirt, her firm, well-toned body hidden by the shapeless, but comfortable garments. As she put her shoulder-length copper hair into a loose bunch behind her head, she glanced in the mirror. *You look so tired*, she thought. *Oh well, come on, Taylor, work to do*.

Drew sat cross-legged on her living room floor, statements and paperwork spread around her. With a half-empty glass of wine close to hand, she set about preparing for tomorrow. After two and three quarter hours of sorting out who to speak to and when, she filed the documents back neatly into her bag and went to bed, keen to be fresh for the morning.

7

The reaction of Lomas to Louis Matthews' adulterous confession was in complete contrast to that of DC Taylor. He had reached a stage in his long career where very little shocked him. Occasionally, as today, a case would take an unexpected twist, but shock wasn't how Lomas would have described his reaction.

On his way home, Lomas called in to the gym for his ritual workout. As he walked through the door of the small but well-equipped gym, the familiar smell of old weights and benches hung heavily in the air. It was a real spit and sawdust place, with its fair share of huge, freakishly out of proportion guys. Lomas had been training here for over twenty years and was a well-known face. After ten minutes or so, greeting and chatting to various people on his way in, he began his workout. He warmed up well and began with a light set of bench press. Gradually and deliberately the weight was piled up on the ends of a thick, heavy knurled bar. Two of the regulars stood at the ends of the well-loaded bar waiting for Lomas to nod for them to lift it in for him. As he lay on the wide padded bench and gripped the cold steel, his mind emptied of everything except for the three gut-busting repetitions he was about to grind out. He focussed on a spot on the ceiling, took a deep breath and nodded. His two spotters eased the bar slowly over Lomas's chest, and at arm's length he took the whole weight and they released it. He lowered the massive bar slowly towards his chest and with well-practised form drove it back up. The second rep was an exact replica of the first. He started on his third, a deep breath in and once again Lomas lowered the bar until it touched his chest. The press back up was long and slow, every blood vessel in his face filled and flushed with the gargantuan effort Lomas was putting in, his chest, shoulders and triceps straining with every ounce of power in them until he locked out his arms, his spotters racking the bar with a loud metallic clang. Lomas nodded his thanks to his spotters. Unable to speak for a few seconds, he sat at the end of the bench exhausted but with a huge sense of achievement as the blood pumped through his veins. He completed the rest of his workout in the same fully committed manner and left the gym, heading for home.

As he arrived home, the light just behind the front door was on. Lomas stepped into the hallway of his house and was, as always, greeted by Heidi. Her eyes lit up as she turned and saw him entering the house. Their love affair, it seemed, was everlasting, even after being married for fifteen years.

'I'm just off out,' Heidi said hesitantly.

'Night school, isn't it?'

'Yes, but I'll be back in a couple of hours. There's some chicken, potatoes and veg, just needs popping in the microwave.'

'OK, thanks, I'll see you a bit later. Be careful.'

'Yeah, OK, I will.'

They kissed briefly and Heidi pulled the door shut behind her as she left. Lomas was tired from his endeavours in the gym. He mixed himself a protein shake and ate his lovingly prepared dinner, then showered and changed. He donned a dark green towelling robe, which hung on the back of their bedroom door, and made his way back downstairs barefoot. The house was unusually quiet. It was a little before 9.00 p.m. and his children Antonio and Eve were due in any minute. Their son and daughter were twins, but despite this they were both completely different. While Ant was tall, loud and outspoken, Eve was petite and demure. They both shared various facial features, recognisable as being Lomas and Heidi's kids. Well educated and both very sure of their direction in life, Lomas and Heidi were very proud of them both. An inseparable twin-bond between them meant that they shared a lot of the same friends and at times were reticent towards their parents. Lomas wasn't accustomed to not knowing everything, but in the case of his two maturing fourteen-year-olds, he had learned to accept their need for privacy and their tight-lipped state at times. He heard the click of a key in the lock and within seconds, the sound of juvenile banter swept through the house as Antonio and Eve came bundling through the door.

'Hi, Dad!' they both shouted in unison. Lomas glanced round from his chair to greet them. Ant, as he was now known, stood to Lomas's right, already touching six feet tall; he was sure to take after Lomas when he filled out. Having an almost uncanny resemblance to his father around the eyes and mouth, he was a good-looking boy with thick, dark hair. Similarly, his sister was stunning and growing quickly into a young woman – far too early in Lomas's opinion.

'What have you been up to?' Lomas enquired.

'Not much,' shouted Ant, who had moved through to the kitchen and was rummaging his way through the fridge.

'Have you eaten, Ant?'

'Yeah, ages ago. I'm starving now.'

'What about you?' Lomas turned to Eve.

'No, I'm fine,' she replied, quietly compared to her brother.

Ant arranged himself a plate of various savoury bits and pieces and disappeared to his room.

'You OK, Dad?' Eve enquired.

'Yes, just tired thanks love.'

'What's happening at work? You're working on the murders that are in all the papers, aren't you?'

'Yes, I am, but you know about as much as I do at the moment.'

'Will he do it again?' she asked inquisitively.

'I don't know,' Lomas said, sighing. He and Heidi had always made sure not to gloss over things for the benefit of the kids, a rule that had made for some difficult questions at times, but at the same time both children knew that the truth was sometimes something they didn't want to hear. Not entirely satisfied, but sensing her father's reluctance to discuss the case any further, she kissed him on the cheek and said goodnight and headed up to her room.

The room once again fell silent except for the mumble of the kids' TVs as they settled down for the night in their rooms. Lomas smiled a self-satisfied smile, pleased at the way his kids were growing up.

By ten forty-five, the sound from upstairs had subdued and Heidi's key clicked in the door. Lomas felt himself warm when he heard her footsteps on the wooden hallway floor, and as she made her way into the living room, Lomas stood to greet her. Heidi wrapped her arms around Lomas's thick strong neck, and he reached around her back and pulled her close.

'How was it?'

'It was a good night,' said Heidi, 'but forget about that, I've missed you.' She looked into his dark brown eyes and kissed him full and deep. He moved his fingers softly up the length of her spine, running his left hand through her soft, sweet-smelling hair. He took in a deep breath of her scent and they sank to the lounge floor. Lomas nudged the door closed with his toe as they gently lowered themselves, their bodies intertwined.

8

A panic-stricken caller attempted in vain to describe her daughter to the desk sergeant.

'Now, madam, please try and calm down and tell me again,' Sergeant Roper said in as calm and reassuring a voice as he could manage.

'OK, right,' the woman said, sobbing. 'It's my daughter, she's missing.'

'OK, what's her name?'

'Anna-May Appleby.'

'How old is Anna-May?'

'Twenty-seven. She's a nurse, you know, only she's not been home since yesterday and I just know she's in trouble.' Her words quickened and her voice worked its way back up to a shrill overpowering wail.

'Now, Mrs Appleby…'

'Yes.'

'You must try to stay calm for me. Can you try to talk me through a few details?'

'How can I stay calm with the papers full of these awful murders? I just know something terrible has happened.'

'Mrs Appleby, I think it's best if I send someone round to speak to you. What's your address?' The sergeant realised that he wouldn't get the information he needed from Mrs Appleby over the phone and so took the details down to send out an officer to see her.

As he put the telephone down, a voice from behind him said, ‘Is that a missing woman I just heard being reported, Sarge?’ Sergeant Roper turned to see Drew standing by the edge of his desk.

‘Should I have a quick word with DI Baxter, Sarge, and see if he thinks it could be something he’d like us to pick up?’

‘Yes, sure. Be quick though, she’s in quite a state.’

Drew hurtled down the corridor, stopped outside Lomas’s office, composed herself and knocked.

‘Hello,’ Lomas shouted from inside. He looked up and looked at Drew, who was burning with a need to tell him. ‘Good morning, Drew. Well, what is it? You look as if you’re about to burst.’

‘Sergeant Roper just had a missing woman reported. A twenty-seven-year-old nurse, missing since yesterday, I thought…’

‘You thought right,’ Lomas interrupted. ‘Come on, let’s go.’ He grabbed his jacket from the back of his chair as he and Drew left the room.

They got the information from Roper on their way from the station and hurried to the Appleby residence, which luckily was less than five minutes from the station.

The home of Miss Anna-May Appleby sat in a quiet cul-de-sac of no more than twelve houses, all of which were surrounded by white picket fences and flower borders. It was like stepping onto the set of a quaint TV show. All were built in a very similar fashion, constructed of a light-coloured brick and grey slate, with lead-effect windows reminiscent of country cottages. There were also some individual flourishes of creativity that highlighted the personalities of the owners.

Drew studied the perfectly edged flower borders and neat lawn as she and Lomas made their way down the short path to Mrs Appleby's door. Lomas knocked firmly on the frosted glass pane and took half a step back, with Drew stood just behind his left shoulder.

A frail woman with short greying hair and red rings around her eyes answered his knock. Mrs Appleby was impeccably dressed but obviously distressed by the disappearance of her child. She showed them through to a similarly immaculate lounge where the smell of furniture polish hung in the air, as if Mrs Appleby had been cleaning constantly in an attempt to occupy her mind.

'Mrs Appleby, could you start by telling us when was the last time you saw Anna-May?' Drew began quietly.

'It was yesterday morning, just as she left for work. She was in a wonderful mood, singing as she walked out the door.' Mrs Appleby sobbed gently as she recounted this last sighting.

'Have you checked with friends and relatives to see if she's stopped over?' DI Baxter asked. Drew watched as Lomas crouched next to Mrs Appleby's chair, taking her hand between his. The woman nodded in answer to his question, releasing her right hand to sob into a white handkerchief but leaving her left hand resting in Lomas's.

'Now, Mrs Appleby,' he continued, 'this is quite difficult but we need to ask. Can you think of anyone who has a reason to hurt your daughter – any enemies or unwanted admirers?'

'No, no one, she's a lovely girl. She hasn't got a bad word to say about anyone.' The tears flowed freely now, and Lomas stopped his questioning for a while, moving sideways to the chair beside Mrs Appleby.

'Why doesn't DC Taylor here make us all a cup of tea, Mrs Appleby, and then you can try and give us a list of Anna-May's friends and family, if you can?'

'Which way is your kitchen?' Drew took her cue. Mrs Appleby pointed in the direction of the kitchen, and on his request told Lomas which room was Anna-May's bedroom.

Lomas took a brief look round the room – it looked untouched. Pictures of Anna-May, her friends and her mother, sat on a neatly ordered and arranged dressing table. Alongside which were an assortment of half-used make-up, hair brushes and a set of hair straighteners, the cable snaking its way down to a black plug that rested beside a white extension lead on the thick well-vacuumed carpet.

The bed was perfectly made, and even the small collection of cuddly toys were sat in size order, the largest at the back. Lomas picked up a picture of Anna-May playfully pointing a large water gun at whoever the photographer was. Behind her, in the distance, he could see the highest point of a large rollercoaster peeping over the canopy of thick trees. He tipped the picture slightly to remove a reflection of the window, which cast itself across the glass, obscuring his view of the shot. He saw a pretty girl of slight build with long dark hair tied loosely in a ponytail. She had bright, happy eyes and a beaming smile, was dressed in denim shorts, a loose-fitting white vest and flip-flops. With the exception of the hair colour, Anna-May had a similar look to the other victims, Lomas thought.

Baxter made his way back through to the lounge to Drew and Mrs Appleby, where he asked Mrs Appleby a host of routine questions, all the while watching carefully, not wanting to push her too hard as she was clearly distraught, but keen to get as much information as possible.

'Is there anyone who can come round to be with you for a while, Mrs Appleby?' Lomas enquired.

She nodded, now slightly more composed and drinking her tea. 'My sister, she only lives round the corner.'

'OK, well, we have everything we need to start looking for Anna-May. Try not to worry. Most women her age turn up after a few days as if nothing has happened,' Lomas said reassuringly.

Drew smiled. ‘We’ll be in touch soon, Mrs Appleby.’ With that, they made their way to the door and made a quiet exit.

‘What do you think?’ Drew asked Lomas as they closed the car doors.

‘Well, let’s look at what we have. A young woman, twenty-seven, white, slight build, pretty, who works as a nurse with no known enemies. I think we’d better find her quickly – that’s what I think!’

Back at the station, the briefing room, which was also doubling as the incident room, had filled to capacity. A new board had been erected with photographs and a description of Anna-May – her work, habits, and friends all mounted with space around them for comments and lines of enquiry to be linked to the other victims.

‘OK.’ Lomas interrupted the rumbling of twenty or more separate conversations.

‘We have a missing woman, Anna-May Appleby, a twenty-seven-year-old nurse from Glasshouse Close. Now, there is every possibility her disappearance is linked to our three victims, who you’re already familiar with. I cannot stress highly enough how important it is that we find Anna-May, and quickly.’ He paused and scanned the room. Everyone was listening intently, as was required, some taking notes, others just taking in every word and committing them to memory.

‘I want every friend, colleague, or acquaintance

of Anna-May Appleby finding and spoken to, and I want it done within the next twenty-four hours, Drew has details. I want to know where she drinks, where she walks, talks and who with. Now, you all know how our man operates – he abducts, tortures, kills and dismembers. If she is number four, let's find her before the torture starts. Any questions?'

Everyone remained silent.

'OK, get to it, and good luck.'

Drew walked between people in the briefing room handing out lists of names, numbers and places of work for all Anna-May's friends and colleagues. Her family list was short, just her mother and aunt. Her father had left when she was eighteen months old and had been killed in a plane crash when she was six. Her grandparents were all dead too, two from natural causes and two in an accidental house fire when Anna-May was fifteen. Her mother's grey hair and frail looks could probably be attributed to the sadness and loss she'd experienced through the years. Drew had felt a pang of sorrow for the timid-looking Mrs Appleby as she and Pete had pulled the information together that made up the lists she was handing out – such plight, such grief, and now her only daughter was missing.

9

Three days had passed since Anna-May Appleby had been reported missing and still there was no sign of her. Police resources were being stretched to the limit and Lomas was under increasing pressure to find something.

'Lomas, could you come to my office please?' The sharp tone in Marie Carlton's voice was unmistakable. Lomas knocked and waited. Twenty-seconds felt like twenty minutes – he knew what DCI Carlton wanted to know and had all the facts and figures prepared.

'Come in.' The silence was broken as Marie Carlton completed a call and dropped the handset onto the base of her desk phone. 'Lomas, come in take a seat. OK, what have we got so far?' Marie demanded.

'Not a great deal unfortunately. Anna-May left for work as usual on Thursday morning but never arrived. All her usual routes have been searched, all her friends and work colleagues have been interviewed, but no one has been able to shed any light on her whereabouts. There are no recent arguments, no jealous boyfriend, no complex love life that may have thrown up any suspects.'

'Do you think it's him?'

'Yes, ma'am, I do. Her description fits with the other three, and so does the way she vanished. I think if we don't find her soon, she'll be number four.'

'OK, Lomas, I want you to talk to her mother. Tell her I'm going on TV tonight to ask for the public's help in finding Anna-May. If she could bring herself to be there, it might help.' She paused.

Lomas knew how this was to be played. Mrs Appleby was to go on TV with Marie Carlton and make an emotional plea for Anna-May's safe return, together with pictures of the ever-smiling Anna-May. This would serve two purposes: firstly, it may jog someone's memory who had seen Anna on the morning she disappeared; secondly, if the killer did have Anna-May, the sight of her mother crying for her return on TV would hopefully humanise Anna, making her captor see her as a person rather than just another trophy to add to his collection.

When Lomas left her office, Marie picked her phone back up and started to arrange the press conference for 8 p.m. that night. Everyone from the local and national media had to be there if she was to have the kind of impact they needed, and she didn't anticipate it being a difficult task to get them there given the profile the case was quickly gathering. She only hoped that Lomas could talk Mrs Appleby into appearing on TV. From what Marie had been told, Mrs Appleby wasn't handling the disappearance of her daughter well at all, and the thought of having to plead for her return on national TV might prove too much for her. She was sure, however, of Lomas's ability, and positive he would be able to help Anna-May's mother see that it would be for the best if she could bring herself to sit in front of the cameras; even for a short amount of time it may help.

The stage was set, and at 7.45 p.m. Lomas didn't disappoint. He arrived with Mrs Appleby and Drew, who had spent most of the afternoon with the missing girl's mother, preparing her as best she could, along with a brief visit from a press liaison officer. There was time for a quick introduction to Marie and a chance to gather her thoughts before it all began. The introduction came with the reassurance that they would all be with her throughout the conference and that if she found it too difficult they would call a halt to proceedings.

All afternoon a camera crew had been working on a reconstruction video of Anna-May's route to work with an actress who bore a slight facial similarity to Anna. This was to be broadcast before Mrs Appleby took to the floor, and she would speak before Marie Carlton.

At four minutes past eight Drew watched Mrs Appleby walk nervously into the large blue room. A long table with microphones and small glasses of water was ahead of her and beyond that was a sea of press and photographers. As soon as Mrs Appleby came into view the cameras started snapping, and what seemed like a hundred flashes all zapped at once. Her first reaction was to clutch the handkerchief she held to her face and hide. Lomas, one hand in hers and an arm across her back, spoke softly and reassured her of their best intentions. He cast a steely glare across the front row of eager photographers and they quickly ceased snapping, nudging each other as they did.

She sat down slowly, flanked by Drew, Lomas and Marie. The room fell silent, and Mrs Appleby anxiously started to read from her prepared statement.

'If anyone out there has seen Anna-May or can give the police any information whatsoever regarding my daughter's disappearance, please, please contact them. Anna-May, if you're watching…' She had to pause. Her eyes welled up, her voice cracked and everyone watched in silence. Mrs Appleby broke down. The press didn't prompt her or try to break the silence, and the officers who sat beside her reassured her in hushed tones.

'You don't have to carry on if you don't want to,' said Lomas quietly.

'No, no, it's OK. I came here for my Anna-May. I will finish what I have to say.' Then, with a deep breath, she continued. 'Anna-May, if you're watching, please, if you can, let me know you're safe. Finally, to the person or persons who might be stopping my Anna-May from contacting me, please don't hurt my Anna. She's all I have. Please let my girl come home, I beg you.' She could do no more.

She stood up and quickly left the stage.

Drew followed behind her. 'Are you all right, Mrs Appleby?'

'She's not coming back, is she? I'm never going to see my baby again, am I?' Mrs Appleby wept uncontrollably onto Drew's shoulder. Drew was touched deeply by her cries, and a huge lump grew in her throat. Choking back her own tears, she tried to reassure Mrs Appleby, without giving an assurance of her daughter's safe return.

'We're doing everything possible to find Anna-May, and what you've just done in front of the TV and press will be invaluable in drumming up public awareness and support, Mrs Appleby.'

But the biggest comfort Drew could offer was just being there at that moment, for at that moment Mrs Appleby needed someone, anyone, to lean on, to cry on, to be allowed to let out every emotion that she felt. Her sorrow, her sadness and the huge longing she felt for Anna-May's safe return. As they sat out of sight of the prying eyes of the media, Drew couldn't help thinking that maybe this was all for nothing. Maybe Anna-May was already dead – a fourth victim of this evil monster. A great feeling of helplessness surged over her, like a huge tidal washing away all her usual positive thoughts. Drew struggled with this thought for a few moments and then tried to dismiss it from her mind and focus instead on the voice of Marie Carlton, who was rounding up the press conference in her self-assured, controlled manner. Marie was a great source of inspiration to Drew. A professional, female, career officer with an outlook on which to mould her own.

Marie concluded, 'I would like to thank you for coming at such short notice, and I look forward to the public's response, for which our officers are waiting, thank you.'

Lomas and Marie left the stage and joined Mrs Appleby and Drew.

'How do you feel, Mrs Appleby?' asked Marie compassionately, following quickly with 'you did really well, that's a really tough thing to do, thank you.'

'I'll be fine, thank you.' Mrs Appleby smiled through her tears. Marie returned a warm smile and turned to Baxter.

'Lomas, I have to go. I'll see you first thing and we'll see what kind of response we've had.'

'OK ma'am, goodnight.'

10

Five days earlier

A starling sat on the sill outside Anna-May Appleby's bedroom window. It sang a bright chirpy song which almost lifted the young nurse out of bed a touch before six o'clock. Her mother could be heard busying herself in the kitchen. They lived on their own and enjoyed each other's company immensely. Six o'clock struck and, simultaneously, Anna's alarm clock radio sprang into action. 'Good morning, this is the six o'clock news,' said the rather dull tone of the newscaster.

'I don't think so,' Anna said, as if to try and stop the newscaster speaking. She quickly shuffled through the radio's channels until she found a familiar tune, then her usual morning ritual began. Like a whirlwind, she flew round her room making the bed, arranging her teddies in size order, with a little pink pig at the front nestled between the legs of a large fluffy white rabbit. She went across the hallway and into the bathroom for a quick shower, where she sang at the top of her voice. From the shower, she continued singing back to her room and donned a neatly pressed pale blue uniform that had been laid on the bed by her mother while she was showering. With her hair clipped in a neat bun, she made her way to the kitchen, attaching a shiny silver fob watch as she walked, present from her Auntie when she completed her nurse-training.

Anna and her mother sat and chatted about Anna's night out the previous night, the weather, and what plans Anna had for later in the day. They tidied up after breakfast, and after giving her mother a small peck on the cheek, Anna-May left cheerily for work.

Anna-May set herself a brisk pace for her two-mile walk to the hospital where she had worked for five years. Her walk began, as usual, up to the end of Glasshouse Close and out onto the main road. It was a busy morning and the road hummed with a variety of cars, buses and motorbikes. After about a hundred yards Anna-May turned into an alleyway which led into the park. She used this route every day as it cut some ten minutes off the alternate journey around the roads and cycle paths. The alley was overhung on either side by large overgrown bushes, which seemed to grow out of the top of the six-foot-high fences that lined the cut-through. In the corners where the fence panels met the path, leaves were starting to collect in great numbers as autumn took its grip. Anna-May scuffed her foot through a pile of leaves, wafting up a fresh, early morning scent from them as they scattered.

The secluded alleyway wound for about fifty yards, and then the path split in two directions and an expanse of grass fanned out before Anna, broken only by the imposing sight of a cricket pavilion made from white wooden panels. The cricket ground itself was off limits, and one of the forks in the path led away to the left of the ground to stop people straying over there when out walking. A children's play park stood at the far side of the stretch of grass. The brightly coloured climbing frames and slides always brought a smile to Anna-May's face, even on the coldest and bleakest of days.

She momentarily lapsed into an only too common daydream of bringing her own children, four in total, to the park, pushing them on swings and cheering as they ascended to the top of the climbing frame for the first time. She even included wiping away their tears when they fell and grazed their knee from running too quickly across the park. However, for now it would have to remain a daydream. 'You haven't even got a boyfriend,' she mumbled to herself, 'never mind four lovely children.' Anna had dumped her last serious boyfriend after finding him in bed at a party with her supposed best friend.

'Oh, don't stop because of me' she had said when she opened the door on them. 'And to think, another twenty-seconds and he would have finished,' she had added sarcastically, turning and walking away and closing the door behind her. She had neither seen nor heard from either of them for months now. The first few days they had bombarded her with calls and text messages on her mobile phone, but they'd given up when attempts to justify their behaviour had fallen on deaf ears.

A paperboy on a fast-moving BMX snapped her out of her reflections and back to reality when he cut across the path about two feet in front of her. She gasped, stopped to avoid him and then carried on out of the park. The quiet road led steeply uphill and around to the rear entrance of the hospital.

Nurse Appleby looked round at the houses. As usual, some of them had their curtains still closed, the residents lucky enough not to be up and awake as early as Anna. As she looked at the cars parked neatly in their driveways, she noticed a large figure getting out of a dark red van a little way up the hill. They took a quick look at their wrist, presumably checking the time, and then slammed the driver's door closed. Birds in a nearby tree took to the sky, fleeing from the loud metallic bang. Anna carried on watching as the figure walked round to the back of the van, they were the only two people out and about on the quiet street. As Anna-May came level with the back of the van a large spanner fell from the rear door and clanged loudly as it struck the ground.

'Shit!' a voice said from inside.

Anna crouched to pick it up, and as she turned to stand and return it, a huge black leather-clad fist hit her full in the face, its devastating impact driving her down onto the ground. Dazed and unable to regain her footing, she felt a hand grip her throat and another on the back of her head. Anna-May's hair clips dug into her scalp and the hand on her throat lifted her upwards.

Unable to see clearly and with panic setting in, her first instinct was to scream. She took in a deep breath and instantaneously the hand on her neck tightened. The hand from the back of her head moved rapidly down to the small of her back and grabbed a handful of her uniform. Anna felt herself lifted off her feet, thrown forward, then falling, landing awkwardly on a hard metal floor. She heard the rear doors of the van slam shut, shortly followed by one at the front opening. Now in complete darkness, racked with pain and fear, she was hearing everything. The van jostled sideways as the driver clambered aboard, the door again banged shut and the van lurched into motion. Just as Anna-May attempted to scream for help, the vehicle filled with almost deafeningly loud classical music. Anna began screaming hysterically, kicking out at the back door of the van. She kicked until the soles of her feet felt sore and her legs burned like she'd run a marathon.

As she realised that her screams and cries were useless against the thunderous music, she began to calm down, her eyes started to grow accustomed to the lack of light in the back of the van and she scrabbled around trying desperately to find anything which might allow her to pry open the door or bang on the side to alert passers-by of her distress. Anna-May's frantic search of the floor of the van was fruitless. There was nothing except for what felt like piles of tarpaulin-type bags and sheets at the front end of the van. Each time the vehicle stopped, Anna scurried to the furthest point from the door as if to hide from her attacker.

Half-convinced she was taking part in some twisted nightmare, she tried to wake herself, but to no avail. Her whole face throbbed from the impact of the punch that had grounded her. She wiped the back of her hand across her top lip to disperse the steady trickle of blood that she could feel ebbing from her nose. She felt as if she had been hanged by the neck and was sure she could feel a massive bruise forming across her throat. The van had thrown her this way and that along its journey; any sense of direction she may have had was completely lost. The sides of the van and the roof were lined with rough wood panelling and it splintered as Anna-May grasped at it with her hands in an attempt to steady herself.

Without warning, the music quietened. Anna's anxiety escalated quickly to an unbearable level as the van came to an uneven stop on what sounded like stones or gravel. The engine stopped and the van rocked once more as her assailant disembarked. Again, Anna-May cowered in the corner farthest from the door. She could hear no traffic, no sounds of humanity. All she heard was footsteps alongside the van and around to the rear doors. But the doors didn't open, instead the footsteps began to quieten as they moved away from the vehicle. Her heart was racing – sweat, cold sweat, was soaking her uniform – and thoughts of how to escape coursed through her mind. What would happen when the door finally opened? Would she be released? Could she escape? Or was she miles from anywhere or anyone who could help her? Somehow, amid all the questions that taunted her, her exhaustion won through and sleep washed over her.

Anna-May slept a broken and disturbed sleep. Her forehead rested on her knees as she curled up in the corner of the van like a small child. The occasional noise of a bird or squirrel scampering along the roof disturbed her, and each time she woke, her attention darted to the still-closed door.

A plan had evolved in her mind as she jolted in and out of sleep. The door would open, she would kick the attacker as hard as she could manage, and then she would jump from the van and run for all she was worth. It seemed feasible and it played over and over in her mind. She woke briefly, and in order to execute her plan she moved up close to the door of the large dark cell. She pressed her head and ear against the cold steel door trying to pick out any telltale signs of where she was. All she heard were birds singing. Once again, she drifted into an uncomfortable slumber.

Suddenly she awoke, forced out of sleep by a burst of light. Bright sunlight flooded the inside of the van as the door was flung open, and she could barely see. Her plan to escape failed before it had begun as she felt a net cast over her. She instinctively screamed for help, and once again the gloved fist pummelled into her face – not once this time, but three, four, five times. Anna cried out in agony as her eyes closed tightly in an act of self-preservation. Her nose once more poured blood, and her top lip embedded itself onto her front teeth. Anna-May had never known pain such as this. An excruciating sixth blow caused her to black out, and a blow under her chin sent both top and bottom teeth into her tongue.

Anna-May woke up as a freezing cold ice pack was laid across her forehead and eyelids. She strained to open her eyes to see where she was but could only make out vague shapes due to the swollen state of both her eyes. Her head pulsated from the beating she had sustained, and as she attempted to talk, she found that her tongue was inflamed and useless. It filled the space in her mouth and felt as though someone had driven nails straight through it. She wriggled in vain, making a weak effort to free herself, but she found that her wrists and ankles were shackled to the bed on which she lay.

'Try not to move too much. You've had a tiring day. You need to get some rest.' A calm voice said, sounding as if it was trying to soothe her. Beyond the voice, Anna could hear no sounds to give her a clue as to where she was.

The bed dipped on Anna's right-hand side as her attacker sat down beside her. Anna-May clenched her right fist and punched to the side, her hand making contact with a solid, muscular leg, but only just. Once again her heart rate soared and sweat forced its way from each pore. As she punched out, the shackles snatched at her wrist, sending an acute pain shooting up the length of her arm.

'Now, now, anger won't help. You know that, Nurse Appleby.'

The sound of her name on this monster's lips made her blood run cold.

'I suppose your imagination is running wild, trying to work out what is going to happen – if you're ever going to see Mummy again. Well, young Nurse Appleby, all will be revealed in good time.' The tone was patronising and cold. How did her assailant know about her mother? What was going to be done to her? Anna-May struggled frantically but to no avail. The shackles merely rattled, efficient in their role of keeping her imprisoned.

'Now really, I think you should try to stay calm. I suppose a sedative may help. What do you think? After all, you're the nurse.'

Anna shook her head in a frenzied fashion. Then her arm was clamped to the bed by a large hand.

'Oh good, you have prominent veins. That makes my job so much easier. Now you're just going feel a small prick.'

She felt a small jab in her right arm and a dark blanket of sleep released Anna-May from her agony.

11

The phone lines had gone berserk after the reconstruction of Anna-May's walk to work, but no-one had told Lomas's team anything they didn't already know. The majority of the sightings were of her walking up the main road just before she turned into the park. There were the usual time-wasting hoax callers, claiming they'd seen Anna-May at the other side of town fifteen minutes before she left home. But one caller stood out as maybe being the last person to see Anna-May Appleby. A young paperboy who claimed to have almost run her over on his bike while out doing his rounds and listening to music in his earphones.

Drew interviewed the youngster, along with his mother, who was more concerned that he was making the whole thing up and wasting police time. When asked if he'd noticed anything unusual, young Kevin Daniels told Drew something that piqued her interest.

'On the road where I'd just finished delivering papers, there's an alley leading out of the park. For three days the only thing parked on the road was a big red van, with someone sat behind the wheel.'

'Why is this unusual?' asked Drew.

'I don't suppose it is that weird, only there's

hardly ever anybody out on that road early in a morning. I've never seen that van before either.' The youngster shrugged as if questioning the importance of the information he had shared.

'What about since the day Anna-May disappeared? Have you seen it since then, Kevin? This may be very important. Please try and think.'

Kevin paused for a little while, glanced sideways at his mother, then back at Drew.

'No, I don't think I have.'

'Would you know what kind of van it was, Kevin?'

'Yeah, it was a dark red Transit.'

'Are you sure?'

'Oh he's car and van mad, he'll know what kind of van it is.' His mother interrupted.

'Yep, it was definitely a Transit.' Asserted the youngster.

'OK, thank you Kevin, that's really helpful. Mrs Daniels, he's been a great help.' The teenager's mum looked relieved and smiled weakly at Drew, who nodded her thanks and then showed them to the door. Once they were gone, DC Taylor immediately called Lomas to relay the details of the interview.

They acted without delay, and the registered keepers of all red Transits in the area were soon collated into an alphabetically ordered list. This list was cross-referenced with the police computers against all known offenders, with special emphasis on people with violent or sexual convictions. The list of van owners came up with over three hundred names and addresses, twenty-eight of whom had some form of criminal record. Five, however, matched the last category of violent or sexual offenders. Drew took the lists to Lomas's office. The first three of the five he dismissed almost instantly.

'Collins brothers, Ray and Scott – it's unlikely to be them.'

'How do you know?' Drew asked inquisitively.

'Because I locked them up for armed robbery three years ago, and the third – Adam Roberts – works with the Collins brothers. They set up a plastering company when they got out and they all drive bright red sign-written vans. Our man's van was plain dark red, wasn't it?'

'Yes, that's right, so just two left to check.'

'Who are they?'

'Gordon Dawson and Ian Jackson, both lovely blokes. Dawson has done ten years for rape and battery and Jackson has spent half his thirty-nine years inside. Started as a petty thief and the last stretch he did was for aggravated assault on two women after a row outside a nightclub. A self-confessed woman hater who said under oath that half of them should have been drowned at birth.'

'A real charmer then.'

'Oh yeah, he's an absolute catch. Where do they both live Drew?' Lomas quickly calculated the route based on their addresses and announced.

'We'll start with Dawson, his house is on the

way Jackson's place.'

'Oh, one more thing about Jackson that might be of interest sir – he's a butcher by trade,' Drew added.

'So he is.' Lomas's interest in Ian Jackson heightened with this reminder.

'Yes, he served an apprenticeship as a youngster and works on the markets during breaks from being inside.'

The thought of calling on hardened criminal types, didn't appeal to Drew at all. They were invariably rude and unhelpful. Rapists and women-beaters especially gave her the creeps, but it was all part of the job.

As Lomas and Drew pulled up outside the small mid-terraced house that the Dawson family occupied, a loud argument could be clearly heard coming from inside. Two or more children screamed as a male and female hurled abuse at each other.

Lomas led the way to the door, rolling his eyes at Drew as they stepped onto the path.

'And another thing, when are you gonna get a proppa fuckin' job?' the woman shrieked.

'Aw, shut your fuckin' hole, you bitch,' a male voice boomed back.

'Happy families,' Lomas said, smiling at Drew. Lomas knocked on the pale green door, which had old paint flaking from every panel and a rusty knocker in the shape of a church gargoyle's head.

'Who the fuck can that be?' came a yell from inside.

'I don't know, do I? Open the fuckin' door and find out, you lazy cow,' was the course reply.

The door was thrown open and it banged against the inner wall. A woman, short, greasy and obesely overweight, stood in the doorway clad in black three-quarter-length leggings, that stretched thinly and a burgundy hand-knitted jumper.

'Who are you?' she demanded. 'Whatever you're selling, we ain't buying,' she continued, with hardly a long enough pause to breathe.

'Does Mr Gordon Dawson live here? I'm Detective Inspector—'

'I fuckin' knew it!' She interrupted Lomas and turned her head immediately towards the inside of the house. 'What the fuck have you been up to this time?' she yelled accusingly as a waft of stale cigarette smoke oozed from the house.

'If you've been stickin' it where you shouldn't have again, I'll fuckin' chop it off, you pervert.' Her voice was loud and shrill, the kind of pitch that made you wince. She turned away from Lomas and Drew and stomped into the house. Just before she was out of sight, she turned around. 'Well you'd better come in. Don't want the whole street fuckin' hearing!'

Lomas and Drew entered silently, closing the door behind them. The house was small and damp, it smelled of babies, stale smoke and cat urine. They followed the short woman into a room where sprawled in a stained, dark brown chair was Gordon Dawson. He had curly, almost Afro-style black hair, was unshaven and dressed in a pair of oil-stained corduroy trousers and a checked shirt. He greeted Lomas and Drew with the expected contempt-filled sneer. Lomas had dealt with Dawson before when he'd raped a sixteen-year-old girl and her fifty-eight-year-old grandmother at knifepoint. At the trial he'd claimed there was no knife and that he was paying for the privilege of sex with the two women. Although they'd sounded sincere, the grandmother had a previous conviction for prostitution and soliciting, so Dawson's lawyer had used this to his advantage and negotiated a lesser sentence for Gordon than would have normally been the case. Dawson, due to his lack of co-operation while inside, had served his entire sentence plus three months.

'What have you done, you filthy bastard?' His wife stood in the centre of the room with her fists digging into her thick hips, shrieking at him.

'I 'aven't done fuck all. What do you want, Baxter?' He looked questioningly at Lomas.

'Mr Dawson, do you own a dark red Ford Transit van?' DI Baxter asked, unfazed by Gordon's hostility.

'Yeah, so does half the fuckin' world, what about it?'

'Could we see it please?' Lomas asked insistently.

'If you want.' Dawson scratched his unkempt

head of hair, seeming puzzled by this request. He stood up and led them out through the back door. He opened it and stood to one side, pointing at his van. 'It's there. What's all this about? I haven't done fuck all.'

'That's fine, thank you for your time.' Lomas ignored his question and turned back into the house.

'Goodbye, Gordon, no doubt we'll see you soon. Thank you, Mrs Dawson,' Lomas added as they made their way down the hall to the front door.

A bewildered Gordon Dawson followed them to the front door, still scratching his thick dirty mop of hair. 'Is that it?'

'Yes, thank you, Mr Dawson. We'll be in touch if we need anything else.' Lomas smirked and got into the car. The faded green door slammed shut and the shrieking and hollering began once more.

'The van had windows. The one we want is a panel van,' Lomas said to Drew, in case she was as confused by his actions as the Dawsons had been.

The long track that led down to Jackson's house was about two car widths and covered in loose gravel chippings. The ground was uneven and potholed, and the car jostled Lomas and Drew around until they stopped outside Jackson's house.

'It's quiet around here, isn't it, sir,' Drew observed.

'Yes, and nicely secluded.' Lomas stopped, silent, listening. All they could hear was the sound of birds singing and a gentle breeze nudging the leaves on the trees.

The end cottage of a row of three, Jackson's was painted ivory, with roses growing up a trellis to the right of the door and a tiled porch hung out from the front wall over the doorway. The adjacent two homes were boarded up and appeared derelict. Thick full-length net curtains obscured any view to the inside of the house, and Lomas and Drew got no response from knocking. Drew took a walk around to the side of the cottage looking for some sign of life. As she walked around the outside of the fenced garden, she noticed her feet were in tyre tracks that led round to the rear of the cottage. Her pulse quickened slightly as she stepped along the imprints, not knowing what was going to greet her as she walked past the cottage.

A twig cracked and Drew spun round, heart pounding. Lomas stood directly behind her; she calmed slightly and pointed out the tyre tracks underfoot.

'You were going to go it alone, were you?' Lomas asked disapprovingly.

'Sorry, sir, I just got carried away.'

'You, or your imagination?' Lomas asked, nodding for the young detective to carry on.

They rounded the corner and found a large flat area of dead grass, clearly where Jackson parked his van.

'Nothing here,' Lomas declared.

Drew relaxed slightly as she saw the empty space – saved, this time, from a possible confrontation with Jackson.

12

Anna-May lay motionless, manacles shackling her to the deep soft bed. As the shroud of sleep lifted, Anna recalled the most recent events. A shudder of terror ran through her, and a quick twitch of her wrists and ankles made her aware that she was still captive. Anna-May was groggy from whatever her attacker had sedated her with, but she was alert enough to realise her tongue was still swollen too much to talk, and her face, neck and feet ached a dense, painful ache. As tears welled in Anna's nearly closed eyes, her eyelids still thick with bruising, the door creaked open.

'Are we awake yet?' said a cold, condescending voice.

Anna lay paralysed with fear. Her breathing was shallow but came out in loud hushing noises to due to the small gaps that air could find to flow around her inflamed tongue.

The door eased shut and the catch clicked softly. Anna-May listened intently for any sound of the monster moving towards her or away from the room. Heavy footsteps slowly made their way away from the door until they disappeared from earshot. Relieved, she allowed herself a deep sigh and eased her eyes open the fraction that the bruising would permit. She still couldn't see clearly, but she could now make out shapes and shadows in the light. Then suddenly a succession of heavy, pounding steps raced back towards the room she lay in. Instantly, Anna-May's heart sped up and she felt the rush of adrenalin coursing through her – every muscle tightened and her fists clenched as the door burst open.

'Right, you bitch, time to wake up!'

A heavy solid object smashed into Anna-May's midsection, causing her whole body to convulse as every muscle, every fibre, reacted to the blow. A muted cry ebbed from her lips as she winced with agony. Her wrists and ankles yanked back as her body rose from the bed from the power of a second blow, the pain even worse than the first, shooting outward to the extremes of her fingertips and toes. As her body settled, she lay sobbing, her body racked with hurt.

'That was your wake-up call, Nurse Appleby,' the voice mocked. 'Oh, I'm sorry, did I wake you in the middle of your beauty sleep? Oh, what a shame. Well, never mind, Miss Appleby, you can have all the sleep you want when I've done with you.' The mocking tone was gone, replaced by a malicious one.

Petrified, Anna-May grabbed handfuls of bed sheet, preparing herself for whatever was to come. A hard wooden-sounding object was cast onto a solid, uncarpeted floor. Then a series of other items were moved around on what sounded like a table top. Anna-May opened the slits that she had for eyes, but she was frozen with fear and couldn't turn and see what the noises were or what her assailant was rummaging for. The wait was over far too soon as a huge shadowy figure came into view and loomed over her.

'Let's take a look at these awful bruises.' The voice had once again changed in tone, now caring, soft and compassionate. Anna strained to make out a face on the figure that stood over her, and the single solid shadow began to transform as light caught the face of her attacker. Anna-May's sight improved and the pieces of the mysterious dark puzzle started to become clearer. Then, without warning, a hand was thrust over her face and the most acute sharp sensation dug into Anna-May's forehead, as a razor-sharp blade sliced from just above her temple down towards her right eyebrow. Anna screamed a long, howling, agonising scream. Beads of fresh blood ran down the side of her head into her hair and right ear. The scraping and cutting continued, unabated by the movements of the flesh on her forehead, the blade so deep it caught on her skull. As Anna-May lay helpless, the orchestrator of her pain cupped a gloved hand under her chin, driving her head up and back into the bed. Nurse Appleby prayed for every sob to be her last, but it wasn't to be. She felt every cut, gouge and line being dug into her head. Blood flowed freely down her face. Then, when she thought her torture couldn't get any worse, or any pain more intense, she smelled an only too familiar smell. An antibacterial cleanser she herself had used at the hospital hundreds of times, its pungent and overpowering odour driving terror into her. She had seen the instant but short-lived pain this caused on minor abrasions on patients' faces only too often. She now knew what her aggressor had in store. Once again, every muscle in Anna-May's body grew taut in expectation of the misery she was about to endure.

'Now, Nurse Appleby, we must clean up this nasty cut on your head. We wouldn't want it to get infected now, would we?'

The contemptuous air with which Anna was now being spoken to was lost amid the anguish and terror she felt. The smell of the disinfectant grew stronger and a blindfold was wrapped tightly over Anna-May's swollen eyes. *No, this isn't a blindfold,* she thought, as her head was lifted for it to be wrapped around the back of her skull. The aroma was now stronger than ever. Then the cleanser-saturated bandage was pulled tight across Anna's forehead, and her wrists and ankles rasped against her manacles once more as her entire body went into spasm. Every ounce of torment culminated in one gargantuan moment of pain and the young nurse blacked out, unconscious.

Anna-May drifted in and out of consciousness, always aware, when awake, of the immense agony she was in. She could also feel a bandage from the bridge of her nose to the top of her head. As she tried to distract herself from the pain, her imagination ran wild: thoughts of her mother – would she ever see her again, hear her voice singing around their home? Images of precious, priceless things in life, such as children laughing, fields of wild flowers kissed by the warm sun, walks along the beach with a fresh sea breeze blowing in her hair, filled her head. But these thoughts were fleeting and interrupted by the intensity of her pain and a growing sense of hopelessness.

Reality hit Anna-May with the spine-chilling sound of the catch on the door clicking and the gentle creak as it was eased open once more. Anna had no idea how long she had been there, lying on that bed. The swelling of her tongue had eased and its movement was now possible. She kept her mouth firmly closed, not allowing her torturer to know of the small amount of healing that had taken place.

'Are we awake yet, Nurse?' The malicious tone had returned to the voice, along with a slightly hoarse quality. Anna nodded frantically, hoping to avoid another 'wake-up call'.

'Now let's lift your head and give you something to drink, we can't have you dehydrating now can we?' With that a hand slipped gently under Anna-May's head and lifted it, as a straw touch her bottom lip. She opened her mouth just enough for the straw to go in, keen not to let on that the swelling of her tongue had gone down. She drew thirstily on the straw and a cool blackcurrant flavoured drink filled her mouth, it tasted good. The straw was taken away and the hand eased out from under her skull.

'I have some soup for you, it's not too hot, I do hope you like tomato.' Again the hand slipped under the back of her head and lifted it three or four inches. A wide, flat spoon touched her mouth and a pleasantly warm tomato soup trickled over her bottom lip and into her mouth. This had only happened a handful of times while she had been in captivity and she found herself feeling strangely grateful to her torturer. The soup kept coming until she heard the spoon rattle against an empty bowl, then her head was once more lowered gently down.

'You'll be pleased to know the police are doing everything in their power to find you.' A sarcastic impression of a newsreader accompanied the information.

'Your mummy was on TV as well, crying for her poor dear Anna-May, to let her knows she's safe and well. Well, we're going to give them a hand with that, Nurse Appleby. The least we can do is let them know you're alive. I think it's only fair. Don't you?'

Anna's mind raced once more. What could this mean? How was this monster going to let her mother know she was alive?

'There's a lovely bit in the paper about you – proper little goody-goody, aren't you?'

As her attacker spoke the shackle was slowly undone from her right wrist. Anna moved her hand up to her face; the bandage was thick and applied tightly. Her forearm was grabbed and her hand was moved forcefully away from her face.

'Don't get carried away. You're not going anywhere, or were you checking my bandaging skills?'

The iron was re-attached, only this time around her upper arm. As it was tightened back down to the bed, her elbow and forearm came to rest on a cold metal surface instead of the familiar bed sheet. Anna-May lay perfectly still, terrified as to what would happen next. She heard a low-pitched click as an electrical appliance was plugged into a socket and then a switch clicked.

'Don't worry, you'll not feel a thing – well, not much.'

Suddenly, a high-pitched spinning sound pierced the air and Anna-May's arm was gripped and held down by the wrist. Panic, complete and utter panic, swept over her. She screamed a piercing, deafening scream. The spinning sound stopped instantly.

'Ah, your tongue looks much better, so you can talk now. Well, I didn't bring you here to talk.'

Footsteps hurriedly left the room and returned just as quickly.

'Open wide!'

Anna did as instructed and a large object the size of an orange was forced into her mouth, stretching her jaws until they felt as though they were going to snap.

'Now, back to work.'

Once again, her wrist was restrained and the spinning sound began. Anna-May felt a sharp slicing just above her elbow and bit down hard on the object in her mouth. She bit down harder and harder as the saw that had sliced her skin now ground into the bone in her upper arm. Overcome with pain, she once again slipped into unconsciousness.

13

Mrs Appleby busied herself cleaning and rearranging the various rooms of her home. Every time the phone or the doorbell rang, her heart leapt and a spine-chilling fear coursed through her frail and undernourished body. She sat for hours scanning news reports on TV and in all the papers, hoping for a scrap of news, a sighting, anything.

As promised, Lomas and Drew had kept her informed of every step they were taking to find Anna-May. Ten days had now passed since she had last seen her treasured daughter. Anna's room had remained exactly as she had left it on the last morning she was there, because that was how her mother wanted her to see it when she returned. Since Mrs Appleby's television plea, cards and flowers from well-wishers and people whom she had never even met had poured into their home, some coming via the local TV station, others via the police. Friends and strangers alike offered their support and prayers. The previous morning the postman had knocked as the number of letters were too great to push through the letterbox. She was quite overwhelmed by the fascination people had developed for her daughter's well-being and safe return.

It was nearing 10.30 a.m., just about the time her sister had taken to calling in, on her way back from her morning cleaning job in the old manor house. She had worked there for years and even at the weekend she did a couple of hours for the Lady of the House. Although they talked very little, the company, coupled with the killing of two or so hours, was welcomed by Mrs Appleby. Her sister's disquiet as her niece's absence grew was obvious to see. Margaret, Anna's aunt, had bitten her fingernails down to a painful level and her usual irreverent demeanour was gone. Instead, she was considerate of Mrs Appleby's clear distress and did everything in her power to be reassuring and supportive, in this, her sister's greatest hour of need. The doorbell rang and Mrs Appleby made her way from the kitchen to let her sister in. As she approached the door, she thought nothing of the fact that Margaret's outline wasn't visible through the frosted glass of the front door. She just assumed that, as usual, her sister was fiddling with the hanging baskets of autumn blooms that hung beside the entrance, that she and Margaret kept filled. When she opened the door, Mrs Appleby glanced around and saw no sign of anyone, but there on the welcome mat was a long, plain, cardboard box. Confused, she picked up the box and carried it into the house and onto the kitchen table. In stencilled letters on the top of the box was 'MRS APPLEBY: URGENT, OPEN IMMEDIATELY'.

'More gifts from strangers,' she muttered to

herself, gently shaking her head.

She unpicked the flap at the centre of the long edge that held the box closed and pushed the lid back. Inside, the box was tightly packed with cotton wool, which concealed a black plastic bag. Mrs Appleby emptied the cotton wool onto the table and began to unravel the folded layers of plastic wrapping. Unable to see inside, she gripped the ends of the box and tipped out the plastic bag, as she did the bag dropped it's contents onto the table with a thud, and with it a sight that shocked Mrs Virginia Appleby to her core. Her legs let her down and she crumpled to the kitchen floor, her very soul shattered by the macabre contents of the parcel. She was mesmerised by a very distinctive ring – a sapphire and diamond 18-carat gold ring that she had bought Anna-May as a twenty-first birthday present. The ring was set quite neatly on the finger… on the hand… of the forearm… of her daughter, which had fallen from the box onto the kitchen table.

The arm had been cut above the elbow and displayed a prominent bruise around the wrist. It was, without a doubt, the arm of Virginia Appleby's precious Anna-May. Mrs Appleby wept uncontrollably.

Just then, Margaret came to the door, which sat slightly ajar. From the door she could hear her sister wailing and assumed the worst. As she rushed through and into the kitchen, Margaret was greeted with the most horrific sight she had ever witnessed. The first thing she saw was her sister Virginia, kneeling on the kitchen floor, sobbing and wailing at the top of her voice. Then her gaze was drawn from Virginia, to the table, where, lying as it had landed, she could see the disembodied forearm. Margaret spun quickly back to the sink and disgorged the contents of her stomach into it. She pivoted slowly, not able to believe what she was seeing, taking in every detail of the macabre sight she beheld. Her attention was dragged back to her sister by a wrenching wail. Margaret dropped to the floor, kneeling beside her sister. She extended a soothing arm around her, pulling her in tightly towards her. She held her there as if someone were trying to rip them apart. The two women sat sobbing, shaking, unable to speak, both numb from shock and horror.

When Lomas and Drew arrived, together with a team to study and take the forearm away, the sisters were still crying. They had moved into the living room, unable to stay in the same room as the severed limb. Margaret, who had called, was slightly the more composed of the two. She greeted them at the door and showed them through to the kitchen. The arm lay on the table, the bag and box, now separated, bag on the table and box on the floor where Mrs Appleby had dropped it as she caught sight of Anna-May's removed extremity.

Each item was bagged very carefully by the team

after taking what seemed like a hundred pictures.

They moved to the front room where Drew took a seat next to Mrs Appleby, who looked more frail and vulnerable than ever. She had visibly lost weight from her already slight frame since her daughter had gone missing and looked gaunt.

'Mrs Appleby,' began Lomas gently, 'I know this is a difficult time for you, but Mrs Appleby, wherever Anna-May is, it's highly likely she is still alive, and although this may be difficult to understand, this is the first time this man has done what he did today. It would indicate to me that he's starting to see Anna-May as a person, someone with a family, and that, Mrs Appleby, is because of your television appearance. It means you've had an impact and made him step outside his normal behaviour.'

The soft tone of Lomas's voice seemed to quell Mrs Appleby's tears.

'Without my Anna-May there's nothing… no reason to go on.'

A strange calm came over Mrs Appleby. Her gaze steadied, her tears slowed and her voice was quiet and subdued.

'Will you be all right, Mrs Appleby?' Drew enquired.

'I'll stay with her,' interjected Margaret. 'We'll be fine, won't we, Virginia?'

'Yes, fine.' Her stare never altered. Drew followed Mrs Appleby's eyes. Her gaze led Drew to the polished marble hearth around the fire. Beside the ornate fireplace was a picture of Anna-May, a young, innocent girl standing beside a huge Mickey Mouse at Disney World. Her beaming smile and sparkling eyes were full of happiness, a childhood dream fulfilled. It was strange, Drew thought, how a picture that radiated such joy could fill her heart with such deep sorrow. Drew sat captivated for a moment by the picture, studying every line and shadow on the silver-framed photograph, twisting the ends of her red hair around her finger.

'She was nine years old. I saved for three years to take her there. She loved every second of the whole two weeks. That was all she wanted to do once I'd told her we were going. I want to meet Mickey, Mum. Please can I see Mickey when we get there? On the plane to America that's all she kept saying, over and over. That picture was taken on the very first day we got to Disney World. She saw him from miles away having his photograph taken with some other children. When they'd finished she ran over and threw her arms around him. I'd never seen her so happy. I took five photos just to make sure one came out. On every one she was smiling just the way she is there. The same huge, warm smile she gave everyone. After I'd taken the photo he took her hands and danced around in a circle with her for what felt like an age. I can hear her giggling when I look at that picture. She talked non-stop for the whole two weeks… so excited. Every corner we turned was an adventure, and she remembers it all. To this day she talks about it and the same excited little girl still sings in her voice. Have you been?' Mrs Appleby looked at Drew, totally aware that the young officer had followed her gaze.

'No,' Drew said. 'No, I've, er, never been.'

'You're never too old, you know. How old are you?'

'I'm twenty-four,' Drew answered, slightly puzzled by Mrs Appleby's question.

'Yes, you'd still love it, I'm sure. I was in my thirties when Anna-May and I went, and I loved every second.' Virginia Appleby paused a long thoughtful pause. 'Do you need anything else, Inspector Baxter?'

'No, thank you, we'll get back to you as soon as the test results are confirmed and keep you informed,' Lomas said as he stood to leave.

Mrs Appleby turned to Drew. 'Don't worry, dear, I'll be fine. My sister will stay and keep me company, and I'm sure you'll find my Anna-May soon.' She took Drew's hand. It was as if she felt she had to comfort Drew instead of the other way round. Drew's eyes met the bloodshot, glazed gaze of Virginia Appleby, who nodded slowly, closing her eyes and releasing the young officer's hand.

As Lomas and Drew left, DC Taylor's eyes were full of unused tears, and her heart felt like a lead weight in her chest.

'Are you OK?' asked Lomas. 'Don't worry about getting upset by these things. All that crap about not getting emotionally involved and not taking your work personally is just that. A good copper always cares. It's just that some show it more than others. It's nothing to be ashamed of. Even Marie Carlton would have been moved by that Disney story.' Lomas's words comforted Drew greatly, and she knew that he was aware of how much she looked up to and respected DCI Carlton.

'It does get easier though, right?'

'Oh yeah, it gets easier. You won't always get dragged through an emotional mill every time you investigate a murder. This is the hardest part, talking to the relatives, and especially in this situation, where some poor soul like Mrs Appleby is in limbo, not knowing whether Anna-May is alive or not.'

'What do you think about the arm?'

'I think the arm is this lunatic's way of showing us he's still in charge. There was no postage on the box, so….'

'So that means he took it to the house himself.'

'Yes, or someone else did, which also means he's getting braver. All the others have been dumped in woods or streams, but so far he hasn't tried anything this blasé.'

'So what do we do now?'

'First thing we do is get some surveillance on Mrs Appleby's house. In case he comes calling again with any more gifts. Second, we get the lab reports back on the arm, the box and the plastic bag.'

'And third?'

'Third we try to get hold of our Mr Jackson

again.'

'You still think he's in the frame?' Drew enquired.

'I still think he's the nearest thing we've got to a suspect.'

14

The lab reports confirmed that the limb had been removed in the same fashion as the first two girls had been dismembered, with a surgical saw. It also clarified that the victim was alive at the time of removal, and all indications were that there was no form of anaesthetic. The wrist showed evidence of restraint, both by hand and by a mechanical restraint of some kind.

‘It was a very neat cut carried out with some level of precision.’ Sherlock pointed to the cut on the large picture in the briefing room. ‘There is also evidence in the skin around the wrist that this fellow has quite some grip.’

‘Thank you, Doctor,’ said Lomas respectfully.

The small balding man retreated quickly into the shadows of the briefing room.

Lomas introduced Dr Redman. Once more clad in an oversized brown suit, Dr Redman began his thesis.

‘Your man has developed a whole new aspect to his work. The delivery of a part of her daughter’s body, made directly to the victim’s mother, would indicate a feeling of being untouchable. He is convinced that, having got away with the first three, he can achieve anything. This flagrant disregard for the police, and your attempts to catch him, will, I feel, make him more daring. You can expect him to come out into the open more often, but please don't mistake this as stupidity. He shows a high level of planning and is now starting to believe you can't capture him. Therefore, you can expect Anna-May to be disposed of quickly and another victim will replace her very soon. If he isn't caught, I believe, he now has the drive and arrogance to have an aspiration to become one of the most prolific serial killers of our time.'

Dr Redman turned and moved from the front of the room. Baxter resisted the temptation to pick Redman up on his sensationalist claim, instead making a note to raise it with Marie the next time they spoke.

Sherlock, who was unaccustomed to speaking at briefings, caught Lomas's attention.

'If I may speak on behalf of Grayson Washington who's off today? There was one other thing the scene of crime officers picked up, a foreign fibre was found on Anna-May's arm. We're having it analysed now. I'll let you know as soon as we've identified it.'

'Thank you Dr Paisley.'

Lomas concluded the briefing by handing out various tasks, such as surveillance at Mrs Appleby's and tracking down where and when Ian Jackson signed on, as well as another load of door-to-door enquiries in the area Anna-May Appleby had disappeared.

'Take a good look at these pictures, people. This man has got to be caught quickly. I want any dark red Transits you see indexing and checking out. You may see one that's not on the list, if you do, the same applies. Also, we're having Anna-May's reconstruction aired again this evening, so phone team, be ready. That's all, folks.'

He clapped his hands and the officers filtered away.

Simultaneously, Grayson Washington, a senior scene of crime officer, and a keen young police officer called Nick Swaine entered Lomas's office. Deferentially, Nick stood to one side as Grayson spoke first.

'The fibre, Lomas, it's from a checked shirt. Red and white, made from cotton. Quite old, so the chances of finding where it's from… well…'

'Yeah, I get the picture, thanks Grayson. Any lead is valuable at the moment.'

Lomas shifted his focus to Nick, who was waiting patiently.

'Yes, Nick, what have you got?'

'Sir, Ian Jackson signs on at the Jobcentre in Daisy Street, today, between two and three o'clock.'

'What time is it now?'

'One o'clock,' interjected Washington. Lomas nodded at him.

'Right, Nick, we need pictures of Jackson. And get Drew and Peter.'

Nick stood for a moment seeming quite surprised

at being included in going for Jackson.

'Well, go on then… today!' snapped Lomas.

'Right, sir.' Nick and Grayson left Lomas's office, with Nick in search of filed pictures of Jackson, and to find his two colleagues.

They all met in the car park in front of the station. Nick, keenly handed photos of Jackson to each of the three officers before Lomas spoke.

'OK, Peter, you and Nick park to the north of the Jobcentre, across the road. Drew and I will go just south on the same side as the offices. When we see him, we pick him up on the way out, and we go on my signal, OK?'

'Yes sir, got it.'

Peter, who was a thick-set, dark haired Northerner, and Nick, smaller and more wiry ,went to their car. They sat for a moment while the other pair got into their car, then, with Lomas and Drew leading the way, they set off for Bernard Street.

15

When Anna-May awoke, a numb sensation covered her body from head to toe. There was no obvious pain, which could only mean she had been administered some strong painkillers. Her memory flashed back and replayed the events prior to being unconscious, and she remembered the agony she had endured while her lower arm was removed. Unable to believe her own memory, she tried to pull at the shackle that restrained her right wrist. Instead of the sore twinge from her wrist, the manacle pulled at her upper arm. The stark realisation of the torture she had suffered instantly reduced Anna-May to tears. As she sobbed, she heard a door maybe two or three rooms away from her open and close. Then, heavy, deliberate footsteps became louder and clearer as they approached her door. Anna was now starting to recognise the anxiety that welled up within her every time she heard the clomping footsteps coming near. She craned her head up from her pillow to let her assailant know she was awake, hoping this would help her avoid another beating. Her head and eyes were still tightly bandaged and she was completely reliant on her hearing and smell. One thing Anna was very conscious of was her ability to talk. Her tongue felt

OK and she had decided to attempt to reason with her captor.

The door swung open and she heard the monster who had already subjected Anna-May to so much walk in.

'Nurse Aaapplebeee, are we awake? Yes, well, good morning. I trust you slept well. Anyway in other news, as they say, hasn't your mummy got two perfectly beautiful hanging baskets beside the front door, and my what a wonderfully kept lawn.'

For someone who had done such horrific things to Anna, her attacker's voice was very upbeat and somewhat patronising. Anna-May Appleby was gripped by panic, her imagination running wild with ideas of this animal being at her house. How was her mother? She could contain herself no longer.

'What are you doing going to my house? Is my mother all right? You'd better not have hurt her, you fucking animal.'

'My, my, we are feisty today, and full of bad language too,' the voice mocked.

'If you must know… no, no, I can't tell you.'

Anna-May's temper raged, and at the same time a deep fear for her mother's safety mixed in with her anger. The result was tears of pure frustration and helplessness.

'What have you done? Please tell me you haven't hurt my mum. I don't care what you do to me, but please don't hurt her.'

'Oh come now, I haven't hurt a single hair on your precious mummy's head, although, now you mention it… No, all I did, little miss inquisitive, was to deliver a parcel.'

'A parcel? What kind of parcel?'

'I just thought she might like a souvenir of her lovely daughter, so I wrapped it very neatly and delivered it by hand. There's no *'arm* in that, is there?' A sick bellowing laugh followed, which rang in Anna-May's ears. As she realised what her mother would have unwrapped, her mouth watered and her stomach churned. She turned her head quickly to her right and threw up, repulsed by the thought of what her poor mother must be going through.

The laughter stopped and vomit trickled down the side of her face.

'Oh you fucking dirty bitch! Look at the state of your bed, you filthy cow. I suppose you think I'm gonna clean that up? Well, missy, think again, I'm not!' Her captor raged. Then, in an instant change to a calmer tone, they continued. 'Right, well, what shall we send Mummy next? Fingers, toes, maybe a whole leg? What do you think? Any preference, Nurse Appleby?' The voice escalated in both tone and speed.

'No, please, no more, don't hurt me any more. Why are you doing this?' Anna-May sobbed and pleaded.

'You have no idea, do you? No idea why, miss goody two shoes. Well, it's because I can. You're not the first and you won't be the last. Because there's more like you on my list… oh yes, so many more… just like you… all so perfect, all so pretty, all so preened and wholesome.’

Anna-May felt the warm breath of her captor as each word was spoken quietly and viciously through gritted teeth. Her jailer was almost on top of her now, and she felt the heat from the monster leaning close to her chest.

‘What do you mean “like me”?’ asked Anna-May, terrified and shaking beneath her captor.

‘You and all those like you, slim, pretty and too high and mighty to talk to normal people. People maybe not so aesthetically gifted as you. All those people who you and your little petite giggly friends snub, when they manage to build up enough courage to talk to you in a bar or a club. I am all those fat ugly people you sneer at, you and your little size eight and ten friends. Well, you’re all there on my list, and we’ll see who’s laughing at the end of it all. We’ll see. You and your fucking haughty bitch friends.’ A quiet rage dripped from each of the words as they encircled Anna-May’s head like whispered fury.

The weight lifted from Anna-May’s chest and from the bed, and footsteps hurried across the room and the door was slammed shut. As the steps moved away from the room, Anna-May relaxed, and then she heard another distant door bang shut, the engine she recognised as being from the van fired into life and it sped off. Anna breathed a huge sigh and then thoughts of her poor lonely mother filled her head.

Minutes seemed like hours as Anna-May lay on

the bed. The painkillers were wearing off and an intense throbbing sensation was coming from her severed arm. Her face and head ached with a dull continuous ache and her torso felt as if she'd been trampled by a herd of elephants. During the time she'd been lying shackled to the bed, Anna-May had convinced herself that the next time her attacker returned she was going to die. At first, the thought of death had sent cold shivers of fear through her body, but the more she contemplated it, the more accustomed to it she became. After a while, she saw dying as the only true way to be free from the torturous animal who was keeping her hostage, it seemed, purely for amusement and some sick, mass revenge.

Suddenly, the noise of the van returning broke Anna-May's thoughts. She heard it stop, and as one door shut, another creaked open. She recognised the noise as the one she'd heard when the back door of the van had been opened for her.

'Shut the fuck up!' commanded the familiar voice.

A high-pitched whimper came from the same direction.

Is someone else here? Anna-May panicked. Was it her mother, or one of her friends that the sick bastard had intimated were on the list? Beads of sweat lined her top lip and a cold chill swept over her. A sharp slap snapped through the air and a distant door was flung open.

'Come on, you bitch. Come and meet your room-mate.'

Anna-May Appleby's door opened, and to her surprise she only heard two footsteps, the same two as always. But then there was a dull thud as something dropped to the floor, followed by a guttural moan and soft crying.

'Nurse Appleby, meet Christina Marley. I thought you might be getting lonely so I went and picked up Christina here. Now, I know you can't see her, so… she's about five foot three, size eight, is very pretty and has long auburn hair. She's a junior school teacher and lives near your mummy. Christina struggled quite a bit when I invited her to come and see you, so she can't talk right now… and, oh, she can't see you either.' The customary mocking tone was now starting to frighten Anna-May, as she knew only too well the kind of agony that followed.

Anna heard more shackles rattling, she assumed, being attached to Christina. She lay silently listening, counting the shackles. When the fourth one clamped shut, the only noise that Anna-May could hear was Christina's muted cry.

'Oh, how rude of me. Christina, as you can't see Anna-May – or should I say Nurse Appleby – I'd better be the gracious host and describe her to you. OK, she's five foot six, with a bandaged head and face, which was prettier than it is now. She has one arm, although that's a recent change to her appearance, oh yes, a bruised midsection and a shattered right kneecap.'

Anna-May flexed her right knee as much as the shackle would allow. It was fine. Instantly, with her left hand, she grabbed a handful of bed sheet and clenched her teeth. Both her legs shot out straight and rigid as she waited for the preannounced battering. She didn't have to wait long.

A moment later, a solid, heavy object, crashed down with huge amount of force onto Anna-May's right knee. Her leg jerked backwards down into the bed, crushed by the weight of the impact. But Anna didn't scream. In fact, not a single sound came from her. As she writhed in agony once more, it was Christina who screamed a strangled scream.

'What's wrong with you, you stupid screaming bitch? I didn't do anything to you, but as you're so fucking vocal, maybe you'd like to see how it felt?'

'No!' screamed Anna-May.

'Shut it, you, or maybe we can take out your other knee, or send your other arm to Mummy maybe?'

Anna-May fell silent, terrified of what the maniac might do next.

'Now, Christina, just lie nice and still and we'll give you two girls matching knees.'

Once more the girl's captor swung a huge sledgehammer high overhead, plunging it into one of Christina's kneecaps. This time, Christina screamed and cried for herself, as she thrashed around in pain on the bed.

'Well, righty, righty, right, ladies. Bye for now.'

The door closed quietly and the footsteps retreated from the door until they faded from earshot.

16

As Lomas left the gym and got into his car to drive home, he had a distinct air of agitation about him. Ian Jackson hadn't shown at the Jobcentre to sign on. It later turned out that the girl who Nick had spoken to had got her days confused and Jackson wasn't due to appear for two more days. He'd put in a terrible performance at the gym, which always annoyed him, and to top it all off, another woman had disappeared.

She'd been snatched in the afternoon, but all the witnesses had reported seeing was a large figure and a dark red Transit van.

Lomas was furious. He and Drew were one and a half miles from the place where Christina Marley had been thrown in the back of the van and no one else had anything more to offer by way of information. It's as if the van had just vanished.

As Lomas drove, a familiar figure appeared walking beside the road. The man was staggering along dressed in a pale beige suit. He had blonde wispy hair and his hands were thrust deep into his trouser pockets. Lomas stopped and rolled down the window.

'Mr Matthews?' he enquired.

Louis Matthews turned to face the car. His left

eye was swollen, almost closed. Blood was dripping from his nose and he had a swollen bottom lip.

'Who are you?' asked Louis as he leaned towards the window.

'It's DI Baxter.' Lomas leapt from the car. 'What happened to you?'

'Sorry? Oh, the blood. Well, let me see, how best to phrase this. Ben happened to me, Inspector.'

'What? Ben Carter, your brother-in-law?'

'Yes, the very same. I knew it was just a matter of time before Ben found out.'

'So what happened?' Lomas persisted.

'Funnily enough Inspector, Coline had a sudden attack of conscience and confessed all to Ben. He forgave her and punched me. Quite simple really.'

Louis was very drunk, and his swollen lip made his speech even worse.

Lomas persuaded him to be driven to hospital to have his injuries checked out, and on the way Louis started recalling and comparing the differences between his deceased wife and her sister.

'Titia was such a bitch by the time she left, it was almost a relief. All the time she was working and busy, she was lovely. As soon as she swapped law for shopping… uh, awful. She was a different woman. But Coline, she was how Titia used to be, full of fun and life.' He hiccupped and laughed a drunken laugh. 'That's what drew us together. She was full of everything Titia had lost. Ben was never there for her, so…' His words trailed off as he out his hand across his mouth and drifted into a drunken slumber, the smell of alcohol filling the inside of Lomas Baxter's car. He glanced across at the sleeping, drunk widower, feeling a sense of pity for someone who it seemed had once had everything and now had nothing.

They arrived at the hospital and Lomas walked Matthews into the Accident and Emergency reception. Lomas rattled off Louis's basic details and turned to leave.

'You will find him, won't you, Inspector? The bastard that took her away.'

'Yes, Mr Matthews, I'll find him.' Lomas smiled.

Prisoner

17

Anna-May and Christina jumped in unison as the latch on their prison door clicked open.

'Good evening ladies, we have all kinds of fun in store for you, but first things first.'

Anna felt the glow of close body heat as her assailant drew near. A cloth gag was placed in her mouth and tied behind her neck, and then slowly the lower part of her bandages were removed, only to be replaced quickly with a blindfold. Then the rest of the bandage was taken away and the engraving on her forehead was inspected. Her blindfold was then removed, only for her to discover that she couldn't open her eyes. Anna-May's eyelids were sore and blistered from crying into the tight bandages and were too painful to open.

'OK, just a small anaesthetic for you to start with Nurse Appleby. Hold your head still please.'

The easily recognisable touch of a gloved hand clamped her head in place, the feel of which made Anna-May tremble uncontrollably.

'Oh, Nurse Appleby, surely you're not afraid of a little needle, or maybe that's not it? Don't worry, there's nothing for you to be worried about.' Mock sincerity rang in the words.

A long needle was inserted into her neck and the

contents injected into Anna-May.

Christina shook with fear. During the day, Anna-May had talked her through everything that had happened to her, at Christina's request, so she might at least be prepared for some of what could befall her. However, no amount of preparation could have been enough for the pain she felt as a sharp blade dug into her forehead a few minutes later. Christina screamed and banged her fists, pounding them in an attempt to alleviate the pain somehow. The blade scraped and dragged along her head, tearing her skin, just as her battered room-mate had described. As blood mixed with tears, she could only wait for what was sure to follow. The enormity of the torment that followed was incomprehensible, but as the disinfectant-soaked bandage was applied to Christina's head, she managed to stay conscious, fully intent on knowing what her captor was doing to her.

Four steps away at the other side of the room, Anna-May was now heavily sedated.

'Are we ready, Nurse Appleby? Good, then let us begin.'

To Anna-May, the spinning of the surgical saw sounded faint and distant, as if in another room, and as it ground and cut a perfect gouge into her hip, Anna-May was relatively oblivious to the horrendous mutilation that was taking place.

The surgical saw stopped and was exchanged for

a large meat cleaver. Anna-May's legs and remaining arm were quickly and efficiently removed.

The noises of dismemberment were loud and clear enough for Christina to hear every cut and slice. She lay biting on her bottom lip so not to scream or cry too loud, and in her head she prayed for Anna-May over and over, all the while a pungent smell hung in the air, thick and heavy.

'Christina, oh Christina, are you listening? Say goodbye to Anna-May, for on this bed she'll die today.' The cleaver fell swiftly, exactly onto Anna-May's throat, with such force that she was released instantly from her torture.

Christina, on the other hand, was anything but released. As she heard a dull sound from the other side of the room, she was unaware that it was made by the cleaver removing Anna-May's head from what was left of her body. Christina's body trembled with fear. She wept quietly, sobbing into the bandage, not for Anna-May Appleby, but for herself and for what she would have to endure between now and whenever the same fate befell her.

Now the voice, which had made the hairs on the back of Anna-May's neck stand on end, drove fear into the heart of her successor.

'So, Christina, we're alone at last. How's the knee? Painful, is it? Well, why don't we remove that pain for you while I've still got the saw plugged in?'

Christina shook her head frantically.

'No? Oh well, maybe later then.' A pause, a hushed, motionless pause, followed by the closing of the door that Nurse Appleby had become so accustomed to. Then silence fell on the room. The carnage of Anna-May littered the bed across the room and Christina lay alone, head bandaged and knee shattered, left to contemplate her pain.

18

Lomas continued his drive home, leaving Louis Matthews in the capable hands of the hospital staff. As he waited to pull away from the hospital main entrance, a dark red Transit passed him, he immediately slotted in to the flow of traffic and followed at a safe distance, with three cars between him and the van. He followed for a couple of miles in a direction that was taking him back towards the gym. Lomas's heart quickened, and as he pursued the van he called the station for a check on the registration number. When the identity of the owner came back, his heart sank.

'Hi, Lomas, it's registered to a Miss Monica Silverman.' That was as much as Lomas needed. He peeled off the main road and turned his car around at the next available junction, heading for home. Monica was a member of the same gym as Lomas. A big woman who threw the shot and hammer for the local athletics club. She was a strong woman with short dark hair and was extremely good at both events due to an unusual mix of size and speed, that made her able to lift more than many of the guys in the gym. But she wasn't Ian Jackson, and the next piece of information that came over the radio Lomas already knew.

'Registered address Silverman House, Old Barn Walk.'

'OK, thanks, goodnight Jim,' said Lomas, cutting the connection without waiting for a response.

By the time he made it home, all the lights except for the one in the porch were off. He pulled his car slowly onto the driveway and parked behind Heidi's fiesta. As he approached the darkened house something caught his eye. A plain box the size of a kettle sat neatly pushed up against the wall of his home. He could see that there was writing on the lid of the box, but it was difficult to make out, so Lomas crouched to read it. In stencilled letters on the top of the box, it said, 'DI BAXTER: URGENT. OPEN IMMEDIATELY'.

The writing looked identical to that of Mrs Appleby's package. A rare moment of panic hit Lomas hard. He stood up and rushed into his house, fearing for the safety of his family. He burst through the door, which flew open, banging on the wall inside. He ran upstairs, clearing multiple steps, shouting as he bounded.

'Heidi, Eve, Ant!' he yelled as he raced into Heidi and his bedroom.

Suddenly all three were awake and wondering what was wrong with Lomas. Heidi sat bolt upright in bed.

'Lomas, what it is?'

'Oh, thank God. Where are the kids?'

Eve and Ant came hurtling into their parent's bedroom.

'What's wrong Dad?' they asked worriedly.

'You're all fine.' Lomas sighed a huge sigh of relief and hugged each member of his family, then turned, towards the door.

'You're all OK, that's the most important thing.'

'Lomas, what is it?' Heidi insisted, unsteadied by her husband's uncharacteristic outburst.

'Has anyone heard anything tonight? Anyone come to the house? Any cars or vans pull up and stop outside?'

'No,' they answered together, shaking their heads.

'Why, Lomas?' Heidi's insistence heightened.

'A package has been delivered here tonight. It's outside and it's similar to another one in the case I'm working on.'

'What, the murdered girls?' Eve clung to Heidi.

'Yes, but please try to not get too worked up, it might be nothing,' Lomas said reassuringly. He hugged them all again and went downstairs, asking them to stay inside.

Lomas called the station, and within minutes a team arrived, headed by Sherlock.

As they stood outside Lomas's house, lighting the driveway and garden with temporary floodlights, Sherlock donned white hooded overalls and handed Lomas a set.

'Heidi, keep the kids inside please?' Lomas shouted the request again into the hallway. He then closed the door behind him, keen to protect his family from seeing whatever the team were to find inside the box.

As he stepped outside, lights along the quiet street started to be switched on, as neighbours, disturbed by the noise and arrival of the police and their floodlights, strained from bedroom windows to catch a glimpse of events unfolding in their street. With his whole garden and driveway cordoned off, Lomas watched as the package was checked by a member of the local bomb squad. Once they were cleared to undo the box, Sherlock and Lomas stepped forward and crouched in front of the brown package.

Lomas eased the lid of the box open, and as he did, nothing could have prepared him for the contents. Staring directly back at him was the scarred and battered, once beautiful face of Anna-May Appleby.

Her hair was matted with blood, her eyelids swollen and sore, her nose disjointed and bloodied, and now, as had become customary, there were the almost trademark etchings in the forehead of the girl who featured in almost every photograph in Virginia Appleby's house.

Lomas closed his eyes and turned away, feelings of rage and sorrow boiling within him, and pictures of the broken Mrs Appleby appeared in his mind's eye.

He looked at Sherlock.

'We're too late, Sherlock. He's done it again. We're too fucking late!'

Lomas stood and retreated to his house.

19

'Everything appears to be normal, Mr Matthews, your lip and eye are fine, and the swelling will go down in a few days. The X-ray of your face shows a small break in your nose but nothing too serious. If it's any consolation, the door you walked into will probably have bruised knuckles.' The doctor smiled and handed Louis's notes to a waiting nurse.

Louis had actually offered no explanation as to how his injuries had occurred, but the doctor had obviously heard many excuses and reasons for facial damage in his time.

'Is there anyone at home you want me to call to collect you?' the nurse enquired.

'No, nobody at all.'

Louis hesitated. Then he asked, 'Is that missing nurse from here… you know, Anna-May, is it?'

'Yes, she works down in paediatrics. They reckon it's the same man who killed the other three, don't they? I tell you, it scares me to death the thought of someone watching you and then – uhh!' She shivered. 'Well, that last poor woman was found in bits in the woods, wasn't she – it makes my stomach turn.'

The nurse stopped abruptly as Louis Matthews' swollen face erupted into floods of tears.

'I know just how that poor girl's mother feels,' Louis said, weeping.

'What's wrong? Are you all right, Mr Matthews?' The nurse's concern grew as Louis started to shake uncontrollably.

'Now please try to calm down. What's wrong, Mr Matthews?'

'That woman, the woman they found in the woods hacked into pieces…'

'Yes.'

'That was my wife!'

'Oh, oh my God. I'm so sorry, Mr Matthews. Here, lie back, make yourself comfortable. I am really sorry. I had no idea.' A wave of guilt swept over the mortified nurse and her face flushed crimson.

'Don't worry please. How could you? It's not the kind of thing I announce on being admitted to hospital, is it? Hello, I'm Louis Matthews, and my wife was butchered by the murdering bastard who's now got one of your nurses.'

'Mr Matthews, would you like me to get you anything?' said the nurse, racked with guilt and close to tears herself.

'A cup of tea and five minutes on my own would be good, thank you,' said Louis, beginning to compose himself.

'Yes, of course. Er, I'll just be a couple of minutes.' She covered Louis with a blanket and pulled the curtain around his bed.

Louis lay quietly gathering himself, but he could

find no way to stop the tears that were in free-fall down his bruised face. The immense weight of his loss hung round him like a huge stone. And guilt. Guilt for the affair with Coline that had driven his wife away to meet her fate.

As he lay sobbing quietly, a face appeared through the curtain from the adjacent bed. A scruffy soiled face, with untidy hair and an unkempt beard. Two small, bloodshot eyes stared at Louis.

'Oi, did I just hear you right? Are you the bloke whose wife was killed and found in bits?'

His breath, even from across the hospital bay, reeked of alcohol. Louis tried to ignore him, instead fixing his attention on the end of his bed.

'Ere, I'm talking to you. Are you the bloke?'

'Yes, yes I am. Why? What can I do for you?' Louis said abruptly. As the man swayed, Louis recognised him as the drunk from the police station, the day he had gone in to be interviewed by Lomas and Drew. Louis had always possessed an excellent memory for faces. He was clearly inebriated again, as he staggered, clutching a handful of the curtain for support.

'You must really miss her. Fuckin' shame what he did to her… you know, chopping her up like that. Mind you, I bet he had some fun first though.'

'What?' Louis scowled, incapable of ignoring the drunk's last remark.

'Well, she was a gorgeous bird, weren't she. I bet he gave her one… You know, before 'he chopped her up.'

Louis could take no more. The black and yellow teeth of the drunk leered as he conveyed his lurid opinion, his bloodshot eyes bulging with perverted glee. Louis leapt from his bed and grabbed the drunk by his throat, forcing him backwards to the floor. As the man fell to the cold surface, he struggled lamely, placing both his cigarette-stained hands around Louis's wrist. Matthews gripped his throat, pinning his head to the floor, he punched him repeatedly in the face. All Louis's pent-up rage and aggression was being hammered out with every blow slamming into the drunk's face. Six, seven, eight times, and then the drunk stopped struggling and went limp, his tired hands falling from Louis's wrist.

The widower was restrained by two security guards as they yanked him backwards off the beaten man. He looked down at his right hand, his knuckles covered in blood. The guards sat Louis down on his bed as a doctor and nurse ran to the aid of the immobile man on the floor.

'Is he all right?' Louis asked, panicked and shocked by his own outburst of rage.

The curtain was pulled shut and Louis heard the commotion as they manoeuvred the drunken man, motionless, from the floor.

Louis's nurse returned with his tea. 'What happened?' she asked, as she looked at the blood on his fist coupled with the noise from the next bay.

'He insulted Titia and I flipped. I should have known better. He was drunk and…'

‘I’m sure he’ll be fine, let’s take a look at your hand.’

Louis sat staring at his fist, appalled by his lack of self-control. As he sat being cleaned up by the nurse, the activity in the adjacent bay grew. A huge trolley thundered past with all kinds of leads and gadgets attached to it. Louis listened intently as all manner of medical jargon was bandied hurriedly back and forth between the nursing staff. The look on his nurse’s face said it all.

‘He’s dying, isn’t he? I’ve killed him. Tell me the truth,’ he pleaded.

‘They’re trying to revive him now. I’m sure he’ll be fine. Try and stay calm, Mr Matthews.’

A strange unnerving quiet fell on the bay next to Louis, and after what felt like an eternity, the quiet was broken by a solitary voice, and four words that would stay with Louis Matthews for the rest of his days.

‘We’ve got a pulse…… Thank you, everyone. Now let’s get him stabilised, quickly and moved to intensive care.’

Louis sank back into his pillow, hands clutched to his face.

‘What have I done? Why is this happening to me?’

A man in his late forties with receding grey hair approached Louis’s bed as the nurse left.

‘Hello, sorry to disturb you, but I saw the whole thing and I really don’t think you have anything to worry about.’

'And you are?' Louis questioned.

'Sorry, Trevor, Trevor Desman.' He held his hand out towards Louis.

'I've left my details, name and address at reception so you can contact me if the police need a witness. I only caught the last part of the conversation, when he clearly provoked you. Was that your wife or girlfriend he was talking about? Whoever she was, it sounded as though he deserved a slap.'

'She was my wife, Titia. She was murdered and found in the woods.' Louis was calmer now and much more able to talk to Trevor than he had been to the drunk.

'Oh, I'm so sorry. I had… well, you don't think, do you.' Trevor stumbled over his words.

'No, really, it's fine,' replied Louis.

'I'm sorry to pry, was she the third one?'

'Yes, and I believe he's got a fourth now, a young nurse from the hospital.'

'I'm terribly sorry. I don't know what to say. Well, if you need to contact me, my details are at the desk.'

They shook hands once more and Trevor left.

Louis sat alone for a moment, the pictures of Titia's motionless body in the morgue now mixed with images of the drunk lying limp on the hospital floor.

Suddenly Louis was jerked back into reality, the curtain to his bay flung open. Standing before him was a police officer, tall and imposing, with a neat grey and black beard.

'Mr Louis Matthews?'

Louis nodded.

'I'm arresting you on suspicion of assault. You do not have to say anything…' The caution droned on as Louis disappeared into a world of his own.

20

'Lomas, is everything all right?' Heidi asked as he closed the door.

'The package, it was to do with those girls, wasn't it? What was in it?' she continued.

'Where are the kids?' Lomas asked avoiding her question.

'They've gone back to bed. What was it? Lomas, it's ok you can tell me.' The anxiety in Heidi's voice was understandable.

'Try and stay calm and I'll explain in a minute.' Lomas walked upstairs, and just as he reached the top a voice came from Eve's room.

'Dad, what's going on?'

'Ant, are you awake as well?'

'Yes.'

'Come on then, downstairs both of you. I want to talk to you all.'

Lomas descended the staircase and joined Heidi in the living room. The family congregated, all waiting with bated breath.

'The package outside was linked to the investigation.'

'What was in it, Dad?' interrupted Ant.

'It serves no purpose to tell you that.' He looked at Heidi. 'Now, what I want you to do is go to your mum's for a few days until I get this thing sorted out.' Lomas's gaze moved from Heidi to each of the children and then back again to rest on his wife.

'But we don't want to go,' Ant and Eve said almost in unison.

'I know you don't want to, but it's for the best. What you have to understand is that this man is no ordinary man. Not only has he killed four times but he also knows who I am and where I live, and, whether we like that or not, that places you three in immediate danger. It won't be for long, but it's the best way for me to keep you safe while we're trying to catch him. I'll wrap this up a lot quicker knowing you three are safe and out of harm's way.'

The children walked across the room, hugged Lomas and made their way upstairs to pack, both of them knowing there was no negotiation to be done.

Heidi joined Lomas for a moment. Sitting on his lap with her arm across his shoulders, she asked, 'Is this the only way?'

'It's the only way I can think of. I have to know you're all safe. He's too close and he's sick, very sick.'

'What was in the package?' Heidi looked deep into Lomas's eyes. Sometimes, when she looked at him that way, he was sure she could see right into his soul. Her warm jade green eyes were searching, needing to know what he was thinking and feeling.

He knew she could take it if he told her the contents of the box. She was strong and not at all squeamish.

'It was Anna-May's head. Don't let the kids know. I don't want them freaking out or saying anything to anyone else.'

Heidi drew in a deep breath, turned her head slightly and closed her eyes tightly, as if trying to block out the picture of a boxed head, which must have formed almost immediately in her mind.

'Oh, Lomas, why, why would he deliver that here, to you?' the disgust in her voice echoed the sentiment felt by everyone who had seen the grim package so far.

'It's a power thing. He delivers it to me to show that he can get to anyone, no matter who or what they are.'

'What about her mother? Does she—'

'No, not yet, the press haven't been informed, so it gives me at least until the morning to tell her. That poor woman, she has had the most tragic life you can imagine, and to top everything this happens. I can't figure it out sometimes – why some people suffer and some walk around as if they're in a bubble, like nothing can get to them or nothing bad ever happens. Do you know, from Mrs Appleby's whole family the only ones left are her and her sister. Parents, partners, kids, all gone…' His words trailed off and a sombre silence fell between them.

'When do you want us to go?' said Heidi softly, breaking the peace.

'First thing tomorrow will do. We could all do with trying to get a good night's sleep first.'

Night had come and gone with a succession of brief catnaps and the following morning arrived all too quickly for Lomas. He had lain by Heidi, watching her sleep restlessly, stroking her hair intermittently in an attempt to ease her rest. Ant and Eve could be heard padding from bedroom to toilet and back, killing time, also unable to sleep. As Lomas watched Heidi's face, her hair slipping through his fingers, he played over the day's events to follow: Mrs Appleby and her sister; Drew and the team. All of them would need an explanation and all would look to him to provide it. He knew the officers that surrounded him daily were all starting to feel the strain. Short tense arguments and conflicting opinions regarding possible evidence, had spiked the air over the past few days. Every single man and woman on the team wanted to snare this monster before anyone else had to die. They were working long hours on few leads, trying desperately to eradicate unnecessary information from the mounds of paperwork and files they were painstakingly working through. Information on known sex offenders, stalkers, anyone and everyone who knew or were associated with the victims. Now, as if to add insult to injury, Anna-May had been added to their list of murder victims.

'They probably already know,' he mumbled to himself, thinking of how quickly word of things like this spread round the station.

He rested his head back against the headboard, and rubbing his fingers over the short bristle on his neck, he mentally planned the briefing, so at least that would go smoothly. The matter of Mrs Appleby was one which couldn't be easily planned. If only they could have caught this rampaging murderer before Anna-May had been killed. He would have much preferred the job of returning the young nurse to her mother and seeing them reunited, rather than the alternative.

Heidi and the kids were up and packed by 6.30 a.m. A car arrived outside to escort them and they said their goodbyes. Quickly, and without ceremony, the family got into Heidi's car, and with tears welling in her eyes, Heidi blew Lomas a kiss, waved and they were gone.

Hard as it was to watch them leave, Lomas knew he had made the right decision. While ever his wife and children remained, they would have been under scrutiny from all angles and, more importantly, the killer knew where to find them. He watched as the car disappeared from view, glancing at the spot on his driveway where the grim package had sat the night before, now only covered by a thin coating of dew. Lomas took a deep breath of the cool morning air and went to get some breakfast.

He called Drew and arranged for her to come to the house so they could head straight for Virginia Appleby's home as it was on the same side of town.

He dressed slowly, thinking all the while of the tasks ahead. He picked out a dark blue single-breasted suit with a pale venetian stripe. He carefully removed the dry cleaner's plastic wrapping and donned the trousers. A crisp white shirt with razor-sharp creases went on next, and then, thinking of the task at hand, he selected a silk tie with a muted dark blue mixed pattern. He finished the outfit off with his immaculately polished black shoes and the jacket.

As Lomas descended the stairs a shadow appeared at the front door. As he approached he recognised Drew through the frosted glass, her arm outstretched to press the doorbell. He reached forward and opened the door as the bell rang. Instantly, upon looking at Drew, he knew that word had already made its way to her about his atrocious package.

'She's dead, isn't she?' asked Drew immediately as the door swung open.

'Come in,' he replied, standing back and holding the door open. 'Take a seat, Drew. Yes, Anna-May is dead. How did you hear?'

'I got a call late last night.'

'No one was supposed to know until today… well, anyway, are you OK?'

'Yes, I'm pissed off that we didn't manage to stop him before he killed Anna-May, but yeah I'll be fine. What on earth are we going to say to Mrs Appleby boss?'

'There's only one thing to tell her – Anna-May is dead. Nothing else really matters. Unless she asks for specifics, let's keep the detail to a minimum. Come on, we'll take my car, you can drive.'

He threw the keys to Drew as he closed the door

of his vacated house, knowing it was better for her to concentrate on driving on the way to break the news, as the young officer had already made a connection with the frail Mrs Appleby.

On the way to Mrs Appleby's they sat in virtual silence, each consumed by their own thoughts. As they rounded the top of Glasshouse Close and slowly made their way into the quiet cul-de-sac, DC Taylor was struck by the calm and tranquillity of the close.

'How can someone like Mrs Appleby deserve this? How can she lose everything? What makes this sick bastard think he has the right to take her daughter away?' Drew seethed.

'Drew, I need you to keep control. The last thing Mrs Appleby needs is to see you wound up. Now, I know we're all affected by this, but that's the job, it's what we do. We choose to deal with the scum of society and we have to learn to deal with it. You going to be OK?' She nodded. 'Right come on then, let's go and break the news to Mrs Appleby.'

Drew nodded again and got out of the car.

The well-ordered hanging baskets either side of the door bloomed gloriously with yellow and purple winter pansies. As Lomas pushed the doorbell, he noticed the door was open slightly, as if held by a sticky catch or a swollen frame. He pushed it softly, the door opening freely with no sign of obstruction.

'Mrs Appleby? Hello, it's Detective Inspector Baxter and DC Taylor, Mrs Appleby.' He called but received no answer.

'Do you think she's all right, sir?' Drew's concern was clear.

'I don't know, I hope so. Mrs Appleby?' Lomas shouted louder this time. 'It's Detective Inspector Baxter, are you home?'

'Drew, check the living room. I'll check the kitchen. She's probably asleep in the chair,' said Lomas. Seconds later, Drew joined Lomas in the kitchen.

'She's not in the living room, sir.'

'No? Upstairs then.'

Lomas led as they turned and walked out of the kitchen. As they started up the stairs, they found a picture of Anna-May on the third step. The glass was smashed and the side of the dark wooden frame was hanging off. Lomas stepped over it and cautiously climbed the stairs.

'Mrs Appleby, are you all right?'

He turned at the top of the stairs and pushed the white panelled door to the first bedroom open. Drew followed closely behind. As they walked through the open door, Lomas gasped.

'Oh Jesus Christ.'

Drew looked around the door and the sight took her breath away. Mrs Appleby was hanging limp and lifeless, suspended by a leather belt fastened around her neck and then around the black iron curtain rail. Her eyes were bulging from their sockets, her skin visibly grey and cold.

Drew turned and ran downstairs to get some

water to ease the feelings of nausea. Suddenly her gaze was captured by something in the garden.

'Sir, sir!' she shrieked.

Lomas ran downstairs.

'What is it?'

Drew motioned with an outstretched finger towards the garden. On the tree in the centre of the garden was a picture of the face of Anna-May. The picture was the one used on the front page of all the papers from the press release. Beneath it were four boxes. They were arranged in the shape of a body and suspended from the tree by two thin ropes. One of them had a black glove wedged on the end of it. On the centre of the main package was a white sheet of paper, and on it were the words 'Hi Mum, I'm home.'

'What in God's name are we dealing with? Is there anything this man won't do?'

Drew cupped her face in her hands and shook her head slowly.

'As if killing Anna-May wasn't enough, he does this. This is the sickest thing I have ever seen!' Drew's copper hair fell forward over her hands as she shook her head, trying in vain to clear the image.

Drew followed Lomas through to the living room.

'Come on, sit down, take a minute. It's OK to feel like this. I've never seen anything quite like it either.' His words were quiet and calming. Drew sat, slowly processing a whole new level of depravity. She had never come across anything that had shocked her so deeply and with such and immediate impact. All her life Drew had wanted to be a detective. Now, all her beliefs, all her faith in human nature and decent behaviour were being challenged. Even criminals and their often warped behaviour seldom stooped to these levels of debauchery.

In Lomas's eyes, the horrific discovery that awaited Mrs Appleby on opening her kitchen curtains served to take the killer to a whole new level. He now posed an even greater threat, as he was not only torturing his victims, but was also making a play for their families. As was apparent from Mrs Appleby's suicide, mental and physical torture could reach the same ultimate conclusion. While he sat in a thoughtful silence with Drew, Lomas was aware that the sight of Anna-May, boxed up and propped against the tree, was also having an effect on him. On seeing the display he had felt his stomach churn and mouth instantly salivate. He'd grabbed for a glass of water in order to quell the inevitable. Luckily, that was sufficient, and Drew's shock had diverted his attention from his own feelings to his younger, less experienced aide.

He made the necessary calls, and very soon the home of the Appleby's was taped, and cordoned off, swarming with police officers of all kinds. The garden was being meticulously analysed by the forensic team. Attired in their familiar white hooded overalls, they combed each and every centimetre of the garden, trying to uncover just one clue or shred of evidence that would lead Lomas and his team to the murderer they so desperately wanted to capture. A police photographer worked his way skilfully around the tree, stepping around his colleagues without so much as a glance down to check where they were. He seemed to glide around them like a ballroom dancer with precise, well-placed steps. Lomas watched for a while from the edge of the immaculately kept garden, where seasonal blooms decorated ornate borders and a carpet of grass that unusually, for the time of year, was neatly trimmed and stretched from the rear of the house, broken only by the thick towering trunk that rose from the centre of the lawn. Baxter was mesmerised by the activity of the officers around the tree from which the bizarre range of boxes hung in a scarecrow-like shape. He pondered how the mind of someone who would do such a thing worked, what warped sense of pleasure could be gleaned from such an act, but no answers came.

He glanced over his shoulder as Drew came to join him.

'We need to find Mrs Appleby's sister Drew. I know she said she was going to stay with her, but I'm guessing she doesn't know about any of this yet and we need to find her before word of this spreads. Let's get Pete and Nick over to her house and work, but tell them when they find her they're to take her to the station. We can’t have them bringing her here, there’s no need for her to see this.’ The young detective nodded and pulled her phone out of her pocket to call her colleagues.

21

‘Good morning, class, Miss Marley won’t be in today, so I shall begin with the register and your day’s lessons will be planned afterwards.’

Twenty-six enquiring eight-year-olds looked questioningly at the short, dumpy, bald man who stood before them wearing grey flannels with light grey loafers and a cream short-sleeved shirt. He was the headmaster, Mr Irons, an awkward, blunt-speaking man who exercised the full extent of his power within the walls of his school. He strutted the corridors, halting youngsters who ran energetically along the shiny passageways with a glare or a booming ‘Stop!’ followed by an instructional ‘Carry on, but walk!’ Often, these small victories were accompanied by a sharp tug on the lapels of his stereotypical tweed jacket.

Christina Marley’s non-attendance was of great inconvenience to the ill-tempered little man, and having to step into her classroom to call register did not amuse him.

‘No phone call. She’d better have a good explanation for this when she reappears,’ he muttered to his secretary as he left his office.

‘Why isn’t Miss Marley here today, Mr Irons?’ The question came, predictably enough.

'She's not very well, Steven,' Irons replied rather frostily.

'What's wrong with her, Mr Irons?' the youngster persisted.

'Steven, I don't know. Now, can you all take your books out and turn to page seven? Steven, as you're in fine voice today, you can begin reading aloud please, from the top of the page.'

At Christina's flat the phone rang, as it had done all through the night and morning. After three short, shrill tones the answering machine clicked obediently into action.

'*Hi, this is Christina, sorry, but I can't get to the phone right now, so leave a message and if you're lucky I'll call you back.*' Christina's recorded voice was upbeat and jovial, as was her nature. The message left was anything but.

'Christina, this is Mr Irons. Could you give me a call at your earliest convenience? An explanation for your absence from school would be much appreciated.'

A monotone beep signalled the end of his message, a sound that chased itself around the silent flat. An iron and ironing board stood in the centre of a lived-in sitting room from which Christina had made a mad dash to get to work the previous day. Her breakfast dish was half-full of uneaten cereal beside an untouched cup of tea in the kitchen. In her bedroom, underwear and other items of clothing were strewn about after a wild night of passion with her boyfriend Tom Anderson. Tom had left early and neglected to wake Christina as he had an early lecture to prepare for at the university and he had to head home first to take his dog, Max, for a quick walk, as his house-mate would definitely not do it. His was amongst many other messages also left on Christina's answering machine. Her mother had called several times, as had two friends whom she was supposed to meet for a drink and dinner after work. They had left a couple of messages, hinting that she and Tom were cuddled up in bed listening to them speaking and that Tom was detaining her longer than he should. Then they had both giggled at their remarks and hung up. It was one of these friends who first got concerned about Christina's absence.

Rebecca Eddison, who, as well as being Christina's friend, worked with her at the school, became worried by her friend's non-attendance and, from Mr Irons' mood, she realised that he'd received no word from her either.

'Mr Irons, have you heard from Christina Marley yet?' She said when she stopped the short, offensive man in the corridor.

'No, I have not, and, if you see her before I do, please convey to her the fact that she is in very hot water indeed. Good day, Miss Eddison.'

Rebecca hurried to the staffroom and retrieved her mobile phone from her handbag.

'I wonder if Tom's seen her today?' she muttered to herself as she searched the phone for his number.

After four rings an automated voice took over.

'*The person you are calling is not available. Please hold while your call is diverted.*' Rebecca was transferred to Tom Anderson's voicemail.

'Hi, Tom, it's Rebecca. I'm just calling to see if you've seen Chrissie today, only she's not at school and Irons is hopping.'

Next she tried Chrissie's mum. No delay in getting connected this time.

'Hello, Mrs Marley, it's Rebecca, how are you?'

'Fine, thank you, dear. Have you seen Christina today, only I've been trying to get hold of her since yesterday?'

Mrs Marley's greeting answered Rebecca's question but did nothing to allay her concerns for her friend's whereabouts. Deciding not to worry Christina's mother unduly, Rebecca quickly made an excuse for calling.

'No, I haven't seen her. I think she has a day off. The reason I called is Chrissie's birthday next week. I wondered if you had any ideas what she might like?'

'You probably have more of a clue than I do, dear, to be honest. She does like that perfume though – Orchid, is it?'

'Oh yes, so she does. Thanks, Mrs Marley, that's really helpful. I've got to go, but if I see Chrissie I'll get her to give you a call, bye.'

Convinced she'd managed to bluff her way

through the conversation convincingly, Rebecca gave a huge sigh of relief.

The bell rang for the class to start again and Rebecca put her phone back into her bag and returned to her pupils, resolving to go to Christina's flat at lunchtime in an attempt to track down her wayward friend.

22

Christina wrenched at her wrist shackles as the door to her room opened with a loud bang. Pain shot up both forearms as her wrists were yanked back into place by the large metal manacles.

'Good morning, Miss Marley. How will your good little pupils be getting on today without the enlightened guidance of Miss? Are you a good teacher, Miss Marley, or are you a complete bitch, like all the skinny whores I used to be patronised by?' The faceless voice changed quite dramatically from airy and jolly to vicious and thunderous with effortless ease.

Christina remembered the warnings that Anna-May had given her prior to her death, and she tensed, readying herself for the predicted onslaught. Her mind raced through the list of horrific injuries her predecessor had endured before she met her ultimate fate. Christina's fists clenched tightly, her nails digging into the palms of her hands. A cold sweat perspired from every pore on her petrified body. Her head was still bandaged, so she relied completely on her ears and sense of smell to alert her of impending danger. Panic ran through her at the thought of losing a limb, a terror more extreme, more intense, than anything she had endured thus far. She listened carefully, latching onto any sound, building on her own anxiety. She heard a metal on metal sound and her mind set off at hare's pace once more, her heart beating so quickly she thought it was going to explode from her chest. How she longed for the quiet tones of Tom's voice, the safety of his arms. There it was again, a noise unlike any tool she could identify. Her father was a carpenter, so the sound of chisels was familiar, but this was lighter. The not knowing drove terror to her core. Then, a footstep… closer, louder. They quickened and then stopped. Silence, complete silence. The only sounds she could hear were the birds outside chirping constantly. The silence spiralled her deeper into her own pit of terror. Chrissie's mind was alive with vivid images of a leg or an arm being severed as she screamed in agony.

'Who are you? What are you going to do?' she whimpered. No reply was forthcoming. Still silence, a long, penetrating silence. It permeated the air in the room, steeped in malice and intent, driving her to the edge of hysteria.

A footstep, heavy and deliberate. Chrissie could hear breathing. Close and heavy, an intense odour of deep musk filled the air and the breathing became louder.

Christina held her breath, afraid to make a sound. Once more, every muscle and fibre in her body braced for impact. Her heart rate accelerated.

Then…

A new sound, faint, but there nonetheless. Gravel

crunched outside, as if a car had just stopped, but too far away to hear the engine. Suddenly the silence inside the room broke.

'Oh fuck, who the fuck can that be?'

For the first time Christina sensed panic in her abductor's voice.

'Don't scream, you slag, or I'll take your fuckin' head off.'

A piece of cloth was jammed into Christina's mouth and tied around the back of her head to gag her. Then she heard her attacker flee across the room. The light switch clicked and the door closed, quickly but quietly. A lock turned and she heard hurried footsteps leaving the other side of the building. The next thing Chrissie heard was an engine being cranked into action. Then more unfamiliar sounds. Voices shouting outside, from somewhere nearby. They were loud, urgent shouts. 'Quick, there's a vehicle starting round the back.'

'Drew, get to the car and radio through for backup. This is the only way out. Pete, Nick, block the exit with your car. Now!'

Christina's heart leapt. *They're here! They've found me*, she thought. A huge wave of relief flooded over her.

There were footsteps in the gravel, running past the room where she lay, shackled and gagged. Her attention was shifted momentarily by the sound of a vehicle being revved hard and spinning wheels in loose gravel. But it didn't move as the voice outside had predicted, towards them only to be blocked in, but instead it was moving away from the same side as it was parked. Quickly, the noise from the vehicle diminished, it was gone. Her captor had made their escape. Then more voices outside the house – first from the side where the van was parked.

'Bollocks!' A deep booming shout.

This one word made Chrissie's heart sink. Her interpretation of the noises had been right, the driver had escaped.

'What is it, sir?' said a much lighter voice,

'There's a track leading off into the woods. Why didn't we know there was a bloody track? He's got away. We had him and he's got away,' the booming voice retorted.

'Where does it lead sir?'

'I don't know. We didn't even know it existed, did we. It could go anywhere. Pete, Nick, get down here. Seal this off. I don't want anyone in or out, even through the woods. Anyone appears, I want to know. Drew, we're going to get a warrant to search this place. If he's been here, maybe there's some clue as to where he's gone. We're going to rip this place apart. You two be all right? Good, we'll crack on then. Come on, Drew.'

Chrissie cried, she cried with joy. *If they're going for a warrant I'll be saved*, she thought. Her mind returned once more to the pain emanating from her head and knee.

As the four people she could hear drifted away, there was just the gentle echo of birdsong left behind and solitude returned once more to Christina

Marley's world.

23

Fuelled by their grotesque discovery at the Appleby's, Lomas and Drew, together with two supporting officers, headed for Ian Jackson's cottage. The two cars pulled onto the top of the path that led to the small terrace of cottages. Drew felt the uneven terrain and the sound of gravel crackling under the tyres like early morning cereal being poured into a bowl. They stopped short of the end property. Lomas led the way with Drew, Pete and Nick following closely behind.

Suddenly, a metal door banged shut and an engine sparked into life. Guided by Lomas, the other three officers sprang into action.

Drew ran back to radio for backup, while Pete and Nick hurriedly reversed their car up the narrow path. With a quick flick of the brakes and a twist of the wheel, the car skidded backwards and sideways to block the exit.

Lomas ran to the rear of the cottage, adrenalin pumping through his veins. His footing was made more difficult by the uneven ground, but he moved swiftly. With feelings of almost overpowering excitement at having Jackson trapped with nowhere to go, he turned the corner only to see the side of a dark red Transit making off at speed down a very narrow track and disappearing into the woods behind the cottage.

His pace faded as excitement turned into bitter disappointment, and then anger.

'Bollocks!' His shout boomed out into the woods as he kicked at a mound of stones disturbed by the escaping van. Incensed by the split-second luck of his escapee, he turned to see Drew running around the cottage.

Pete Savage and Nick Swaine ran towards the cottage as summoned by Lomas. He instructed them to cordon off the area and then he and Drew left.

For a few short moments, the bleak, undisturbed wood was full of shouting and people running. Then, as quickly as it had erupted, it was calm once more.

24

At the station Lomas gave Marie Carlton a full briefing of what had occurred at the cottage, as well as his rationale for needing an immediate search warrant. Marie could see the disdain her colleague had cultivated for Jackson, which she put down to the fact that he had been evaded, something that she knew from previous experience would be grating on Baxter. His determination was apparent and rationale sound, so she asked him to leave it with her for a while in order that she could work on his request.

Lomas paced his office waiting for the confirmation call from DCI Carlton. His normal level-headed calm and patience was eluding him. Instead, he was being driven by a passion and conviction so strong that it obscured anything that was going on elsewhere in the busy station. He was sure that once inside the secluded dwelling, all manner of vital clues would be uncovered.

While waiting for Marie to call through, Grayson Washington knocked and entered Lomas's office, his athletic frame filling the doorway. He was a good looking black man in his mid-thirties, with a shaved head and thin beard, who in his ten years or so with the force had generated a massive amount of respect from the police officers and detectives he worked alongside.

'What is it?' Lomas asked abruptly.

'The Appleby's garden – we found a couple of footprints in the grass behind the tree, and another clothing thread, which on first inspection looks like the same pattern as was found on the thread of fibre from Anna-May's arm.'

'And the footprints, have you cast them yet?'

'Yes, size nine running shoe. I'm just waiting for an exact type for you.'

'Good… oh, Grayson, I'm going to need your team when I get into this house. I want every nook and cranny inspected and turned over – can you arrange that?'

'Yeah, sure, no problem. Give me a shout when you're going.'

'OK, thanks.'

The phone rang once, a long single tone. Grayson nodded and left. Lomas quickly grabbed the handset.

'Baxter…' There was a pause before Marie confirmed the status of the warrant.

'Good, right, thank you, ma'am. I won't let you down.'

'Just one thing Lomas. How did he get into Virginia Appleby's garden? Didn't we have a team watching the house?'

'We think he came in through the back of the garden ma'am, the team were in a unit on the road at the front, watching the house,' said Loams apologetically.

'Sneaky bastard! OK, keep me in the loop will you?'

The handset went down.

'Drew!' Lomas shouted.

'Yes, boss?' Her head popped round the door.

'Have you set up the team?'

'All sorted.'

'Good, let's go. Give forensics a quick call and let them know we're leaving now.'

They returned to the cottage along with an entire search team. Lomas wanted the search to be one hundred per cent thorough. As the officers all gathered outside the door of the cottage, Lomas went over his instructions once more, just to make sure that no potential evidence was compromised by anyone cutting corners.

'I want this place turning upside down from top to bottom. I want nothing missed. If you find anything, and I mean anything, you come and find me immediately. Do I make myself clear? I want no mistakes, people. OK, let's do it.'

With three strikes of a battering ram the door swung open to reveal an empty hallway. Completely empty. The small space was totally devoid of furniture, carpets, even wallpaper. The stone floor was cold and unwelcoming and the walls were scraped of any remains of décor. Pale pink-grey plaster was riddled with cracks and patches of damp. Lomas led as they walked into the cottage. The brief hallway came to an end with dark and gloomy corridors running both left and right. He separated the team into two groups and led his team down the left passage. There were floorboards underfoot, unlike the stone floor of the main entrance, which were old and creaky with gaps of varying size between each of the boards, and there were four heavy-looking wooden doors set into the walls of the corridor, the first of these they reached quickly.

The sound of the front door crashing open woke Christina with a start. The horrors she'd endured so far made it impossible for her to stay calm. The slightest noise sent her reeling into fits of panic, and triggered a burst of adrenalin, which together with the racing of her pulse triggered a now customary train of thought. What would her attacker do to her next? How would the torture be escalated one more stage? The catalogue of Anna-May's injuries spread through her panic-stricken mind as she lay awaiting her fate.

Lomas opened the stiff wooden door to reveal a largely empty room. Unlike the hallway the room had an old covering of wallpaper, the floor was bare and Lomas's footsteps echoed as he cautiously entered to check that all was as it appeared. A pair of dark brown curtains, with a floral pattern of beige and orange flowers, blocked out most of the light from a window surrounded by a rotten white frame. There was a musty smell, as if the room had stood empty for a long time with nothing but tiny shafts of light that leaked through the sides of the curtains illuminating the gloom.

Drew pushed her finger down on the light switch just inside the room. Light filled the area and revealed tiny white daisies painted across the ceiling, that had been hidden from sight by the dark. A bare bulb hung in the centre of a ceiling rose that had yellowed with age.

'Well at least the lights work,' commented Lomas, satisfied that there was nothing of interest in the first room. 'Come on, let's see what's behind door number two.'

Lomas gripped the cold, black handle on the second door. It had a bulky feel to it, and was decorated with leaves carved into the back-plate that was screwed to the door. The dark solid wood refused to move at first, sticking stubbornly within its frame as if guarding the interior from intruders. Lomas pushed down on the handle and placed his bulky frame against the door. It gave way but didn't open freely – the hinges, stiff and uncooperative, only allowed it to open slowly.

Christina's panic had eased slightly after she heard an unfamiliar noise. Not one set of footsteps but several, all moving some way away from her but nonetheless in the same building. Her thoughts skipped back to the conversation she'd heard outside between a woman called Drew and a man whom she'd called sir. Chrissie's fear was now mixed with a smattering of excitement. The thought of finally being free was almost too much to bear. She tried to shout but the gag was too tight. Instead, she rattled the manacles around her wrists, making a sharp metallic rattling noise that she hoped would be loud enough to attract attention and help whoever was in the building find her.

Drew flicked the light switch in the second room only to find that it wasn't working. As the rest of the group scrambled for a torch, Lomas shone a solitary beam around the room with his mobile phone. The same old, yellowing wallpaper as room one clung to the walls and a ceiling of painted daisies met the light from Lomas's torch once more . Along the back wall weighty, dark-brown velvet curtains hung from a wooden curtain pole. Once more the room stood completely empty, except for a small but solidly built wooden stool, which had been left isolated in the centre of the room, directly beneath the inoperative light fitting. Just then, Lomas heard something.

'Shh, be quiet everyone,' he insisted. They all listened intently.

'Do you hear that?'

'Yes,' replied Drew. 'Yes, I do.'

Lomas barged past the second team, who were waiting, gathered in the doorway of the darkened room, and dashed down the corridor. He pinpointed the noise and burst through another door. A horrifying sight awaited him as he flicked a switch and flooded the room with light, that took his breath away. In the centre of the room was a large wooden table, on top of which were four large silver trays, each one containing a myriad of surgical tools. Some were sparkling clean, others were stained with blood. In the far right-hand corner of the white room was a bed covered with a heavily bloodstained green sheet. On the wall next to the bed were countless lines and splashes of deep red blood.

The loud rattling sound that had brought him to the room caught Lomas's attention. He spun to his left. There, lying in the far left of the room, was a woman shackled to another bed. She wore a gag made from thick dark blue cloth and her head was bandaged heavily all the way down to the top of her nostrils.

Lomas rushed to remove her restraints.

'Don't worry, I'm a police officer. You're all right. Everything's going to be all right,' he reassured her as he sat beside her on the bed.

'Someone call an ambulance – now!' Lomas shouted at the top of his voice.

He removed the gag carefully, lowering it around the woman's neck.

'You're all right,' he said again, comforting her. 'What's your name?'

'Chris… Christina Marley,' she stammered between her tears.

Thank God for that, thought Lomas, relieved that

he had at least managed to stop Christina being victim number five.

'We're going to get an ambulance and get you off to hospital really soon. Now, tell me, are you in any pain?'

'Yes, m-my… knee… left knee… and m-my head is so sore.'

'OK, just lie nice and still until the ambulance arrives.'

Lomas motioned to Drew.

'This is Detective Constable Taylor. She'll sit with you until they arrive.'

He moved away, placing Christina's quivering hand in Drew's, and left the room.

'Hello, Christina, they shouldn't be long now,' Drew said quietly.

'You're Drew, aren't you?' said Chrissie.

'Yes, yes, I am,' said Drew, confused by the recognition.

'I heard you outside earlier. The officer who was just here, he was with you, wasn't he, when the van got away?'

'Yes, DI Baxter, he's the one who found you. Tell me, Christina, do you know who the man is, the man who abducted you? Have you any idea?' Drew asked cautiously.

'No, I-I don't know.' Christina broke down once more into floods of tears.

'Anna-May didn't know him either,' Chrissie added.

'Anna-May?' said Drew hesitantly.

'Yes, she was here on the other side of the room when I got here.' Christina paused, sobbing hard, heart-wrenching sobs.

'We talked all night and then... then he...' Unable to continue, she sank back onto the bed, her cries shaking her whole body.

'It's OK now. It's all over. We're here to take you home. He can't hurt you any more.' Drew smoothed the back of her hand over Christina's cheek and squeezed her hand reassuringly.

Lomas returned with some more of the search party. He stood looking at the array of tools on the table while a photographer took a series of photos of the room, labelling up as he went, for future identification of shots. A tray of scalpels and scissors lay before Lomas on the edge of the table. With a gloved hand he picked up a long-bladed scalpel. Dried blood ran from the tip of the blade all the way down to the end of the handle. A hideously sharp-looking saw blade lay half-cleaned in the centre of the table. Beside it was a blood-soaked stencil kit. He turned to the empty bed, unable for a moment to comprehend the scale of the horror he was seeing. The grey steel-framed bed against the wall was splattered in blood. Restraints identical to those still being worn by Christina hung from a small raised handle welded halfway along the side of the frame. A headboard and footboard made from grey steel bars capped the ends of the bed, the bottom of which had two more empty restraints chained to it. Standing against the wall at the head of the bed was a large wooden-handled sledgehammer. A strange addition, Lomas thought, to an otherwise surgical environment. A pillow on the bed had a very definite shape of a head left imprinted on it, highlighted by the blood which surrounded it. Then there was a green sheet, most of which was stained in random patterns from the blood of Anna-May Appleby he assumed. Lomas shook his head in disgust at the obvious disregard this monster held for human life. Just under the pillow, in another small patch of dried blood, Lomas noticed something glinting. He called the photographer over.

'Quick, take a picture of this please.'

Once the image was captured, Lomas plucked the object from its repugnant resting place. As he did so, a thin necklace came away from the blood-soaked bed. Lomas lowered it carefully into a plastic bag, and as he did, he recognised the small cross on it as one worn by Anna-May Appleby in the picture on the stairs in her mother's house. This served only to make him even more resolute in his bid to track and imprison the animal who had so blatantly slain four young women for no apparent reason.

25

Louis Matthews woke with a start as the flap on his cell door was banged shut. The door opened and a young fresh-faced officer stood in the doorway.

'Morning, Mr Matthews, would you come with me please?'

Louis stood and walked towards the door. The officer, number 358, waited as Louis made his way wearily across the cell. Taking him by the arm, 358 led Louis along the corridor towards an interview room. As they passed the desk sergeant, Louis caught sight of a newspaper on the edge of the desk. The headline hit him like a speeding train.

MURDER VICTIM'S HUSBAND BEATS MAN UNCONSCIOUS IN HOSPITAL

Powerless to stop himself, Louis sank to his knees, images of the limp drunk flooding his imagination.

Officer 358 tightened his grip on Louis's arm and raised him back to a standing position.

'Come on now, Mr Matthews, take it easy. We'll sit you down in the interview room and get you a cup of tea.'

Louis nodded his appreciation.

As he sat alone in the uncomfortable stark room, his vivid imagination spewed images into his mind's eye. The one that had haunted him the whole of the previous night was an image of Titia. Her mutilated body lay on the slab in the morgue. Suddenly she sat up, her eyes opened, and she stared mockingly at him.

'I always said you were a loser,' she taunted. 'You can't even grieve without fucking it up, can you, poor little Louis.'

The door opened and Louis jumped out of his nightmare and back into the interview room.

In front of him stood a short, spindly man with thin wiry brown hair and round wire-framed glasses. His face looked weathered, showing the stresses of a life spent in the police force. He wore a white shirt with a wide dark blue stripe running down it and sleeves rolled to the elbow. A mismatched tie and tan trousers rounded off the appearance of this stereotypically scruffy copper.

'Mr Matthews, I am DI Plant. This is PC Chapel.' He motioned towards number 358, who had been with Louis all morning. Detective Plant sat down across the table from Louis, checked the recording equipment and started the interview officially. He went through the formalities of people present and then said, 'So, Mr Matthews, in your own time, can you tell me exactly what happened at the hospital.'

Louis felt the intensity of Plant's stare, which was aimed directly into his eyes,. Louis could see that Plant was waiting for him to begin, a tense silence building in the room.

Louis paused a long deep pause. Then he took a breath and began. He started from the fight with Ben and continued through meeting Lomas and the events at the hospital. As he spoke, Plant listened intently, not interrupting him and hanging on every word and phrase that Louis uttered. During the recounting of events, Matthew's eyes welled up on a few occasions, still deeply disturbed by the fact that in a momentary loss of control he had beaten a helpless drunk, nearly to death. It was eating at Louis. During his waking and sleeping moments there was no escape, as he replayed the battered face of the helpless drunk, fear filling his eyes as Matthews rained blows down on him.

The tears had no effect whatsoever on Plant. He had seen too many criminals feign emotions of one kind or another to win over police and juries alike. In twenty-five years on the force, he had grown to despise criminals of all types, from petty thieves to rapists and murderers. He wasn't sure yet where on this scale Louis Matthews sat, but he knew that Louis had severely beaten a man in a hospital of all places, and at the moment he could feel nothing but disdain.

Thirty-five minutes passed and Plant hadn't interrupted Matthews once. Instead, he was building a new picture of the man seated before him, a victim in more ways than one. He was a man who was caught in a world, partly of his own creation and partly out of his control. A victim firstly of his own lust and self-pity, which had led him into the arms of his wife's sister, and secondly a victim of the killer who had taken his wife. Estranged or not, Plant could see that this had obviously taken a huge toll on Louis Matthews' mental state. Maybe the mumblings of the drunk were the last straw in a long line of vicious incidents that had befallen the tragic man, to whom Plant was listening pouring out his soul. It was unfortunate for the drunken man that Louis had snapped with him and unleashed weeks of pent-up frustration and aggression. Plant thumbed through a file which lay on the desk. A file created about Louis Matthews. In it were pictures of Louis and also of the drunken man, his face cut and battered from the beating he'd received. Also in the dossier were pictures of Titia's body. As Plant believed she was the reason Louis had beaten the sorry figure in the hospital, he wanted to see what Louis had witnessed when identifying her. It was these photos that helped Plant build his picture of Louis into a more rounded one.

Louis was finishing recounting the long chain of events as Plant closed the file.

'… and then I heard the doctor say they'd got a pulse. I couldn't believe it, I was so relieved. I mean, I've never really even hit anyone before, let alone punched them nearly to death. I am so, so sorry. I just snapped. I know he was drunk and I know he probably didn't even know what he was saying, but it got to me, it really got to me. I couldn't listen to him go on about Titia any more. You've got to believe me. I didn't mean to hurt him. I just wanted him to stop, to stop talking about her. I never wanted him to get hurt so badly, let alone nearly end up dead.'

Louis sat, fists clenched to his forehead, face flushed and eyes filled with tears, waiting to fall down his reddened cheeks.

Plant didn't need to know any more. Louis had told him everything in fine detail and all the questions Plant had intended to pose, should there have been gaps, were answered. Silently he waved the young officer over from the doorway.

'Take Mr Matthews back to his cell please. I have nothing more to ask him.'

'What happens now?' asked Louis frantically.

'I'll let you know soon, Mr Matthews. Thank you for being so open and helpful,' said Plant peering over his glasses at Louis. Officer 358 led a teary Louis back to his cell and the door slammed shut.

26

The nurse burst through the door as a shrill scream pierced the air. Christina Marley sat bolt upright in bed, her face covered in sweat. She was shaking visibly as she dabbed her hands around her cut and bruised wrists.

'It's all right, Christina. You're in hospital. Tom's just gone downstairs to get a coffee. He'll be back in a minute. Come on, lie back, relax. No one's going to hurt you.' She smoothed her hand softly over Christina's hair as she lay back against her stack of soft white pillows.

Her head was unbandaged showing some of the visible signs of her ordeal. The blisters on her eyelids were beginning to ease as a result of the consistent medical attention she was receiving. A large white plaster covered the inscription on her forehead, her broken cheekbone and jaw were swollen and dappled with shades of black and purple and the doctor had reassured her that the break was aligned well and would heal without causing disfigurement. The constant supply of painkillers was only able to dull the excruciating pain from her knee and head. Her leg was in traction so that her knee wouldn't be too deformed and she had already been told that corrective surgery would be required in order that she might avoid longer term problems. However, none of the catalogue of injuries she had sustained mattered to Chrissie – she was just happy to be alive.

The door clicked open and Christina jumped as Tom entered the room.

'It's only me. Are you OK?' he asked.

'Yeah, fine, I just had another dream.'

'Oh, babe, you'll be OK. I won't let anything else happen to you.' He placed his coffee on her bed tray and held her. It was a warm, strong hug that Chrissie wished could last forever. She only ever wanted to be around people who wouldn't hurt her from now on. That was what she'd told her friend Rebecca earlier that day.

'With Tom I feel safe, and that's most important thing of all,' she had stated as her friend and colleague sat and wept joyfully at Chrissie's safe return.

Christina's room was an array of blooms. Bunches of flowers and plants from friends, relatives and well-wishers filled the small cubicle. Cards were on every conceivable shelf and table, with more were pinned to the wall. People Christina didn't even know that well, if at all, had sent the most beautiful cards and floral gifts.

'The papers are full of it, you know. You're a celebrity,' he said, smiling warmly, aware of Christina's dislike for modern celebrity culture.

'Hmmm, maybe, but they haven't got him yet,

have they? He can still do this to somebody else,' Chrissie retorted hastily.

'It won't be long now. They've got his house and they know what his van looks like. They'll get him, you'll see,' Tom added, trying to reassure her.

He had left the newspapers he'd read outside, fearing that the headlines alone might cause Christina too much upset.

'VICTIM NUMBER 5, RESCUED FROM THE JAWS OF DEATH' read one.

'THE NET IS CLOSING' read another of the more eye-catching front pages. *Where on earth do these people get their information? Or is it not information but just wild speculation?* He wondered to himself while reading one of the articles. It had Christina described as vulnerable and easy prey for the murderer, amongst other dubious descriptions.

He was relieved to have her back, but also frightened by the changes that would doubtless occur within Christina, due to the ordeal she had suffered. Would she become a recluse, scared to go out, or would she stare the world straight in the eye and carry on with life? He had no way of knowing, and as yet he couldn't tell from Chrissie's behaviour so far how she would handle even the most basic aspects of everyday life.

By the time he released her from his arms she was, once more, asleep. Tom had taken extended leave from his lectures to be with Chrissie while she was convalescing. He wanted desperately to be close by whenever she needed him. He held onto her hand and watched her sleep. His vigil carried on far into the night, until he too drifted into a semi-slumber, sitting up in the chair beside her bed.

Early the next morning a huge bouquet of flowers set in a pink woven basket was delivered to the hospital ward reception. Tucked into the front edge of the basket was an envelope with Christina's name on it. The nurse carried the bouquet through, passing the police officer stationed outside the door and put it on the bed beside Chrissie.

'More flowers,' she said cheerily.

'Where on earth are we going to put them all?'

Tom and the nurse smiled.

'Oh, we'll find somewhere I'm sure,' the nurse said.

'Shall we see who they're from?' said Tom, passing Christina the envelope.

Christina peeled open the top edge of the envelope. With her thumb and forefinger she removed not a card, but a folded sheet of white paper. She unfolded it, looking slightly puzzled. Immediately on seeing the note her hands began to shake and her eyes filled with tears. As her pupils dilated with fear and the tears flowed, she passed the sheet of paper to Tom.

'What is it, what's wrong?' Tom asked, concern filling his voice.

The reason for Chrissie's shock became instantly clear, for on the paper in stencilled letters were the words …

Christina Marley lying there
Scars on your face
And bloodstained hair
You cannot rest
You cannot sleep
Your precious life
You cannot keep.

Christina wailed and she saw the officer run into the room in an instant response to her cry. She looked straight at Tom with pleading, desperate eyes.

'He's found me! He knows where I am. He-he's going to kill me. Please, Tom, don't let him kill me!' The fear in her eyes grew with every word she uttered. Sobbing heavily, she threw her arms around Tom's neck, clinging onto him with every ounce of strength she possessed.

Tom, overwhelmed by the depravity of the note, was unable to console her. He held her silently, rocking her gently, incapable of comprehending the agony that Chrissie had endured at the hands of the twisted animal responsible for the poetic death threat.

27

Lomas and Drew arrived at the hospital within minutes of receiving the call from the officer stationed there. On entering the room they found a near hysterical Christina with a shell-shocked and dumbfounded Tom.

'Nurse, could you take Mr Anderson and get him a cup of tea please?' Lomas requested. He nodded to Drew to accompany them, then turned his attention to Chrissie. Holding both of her hands in his, he looked into her eyes.

'Christina, listen to me. We need to move you from this hospital. Don't worry, you'll still be under police guard and the officers won't let you out of their sight. They'll stay with you around the clock.'

Christina began to calm down. At last someone was taking control. The way Lomas handled things made her feel more at ease, almost safe. After all, he was the one responsible for finding her, alive.

'Where's Tom?' asked Christina, oblivious to the previous conversations in the room.

'He's with my detective constable,'

'Is that Drew?'

'Yes, he's with Drew. You need to understand, this is hard for Tom to get his head around. He hasn't been through the trauma that you have. It'll take time for him to know what you need and how to make you feel protected. He'll get there, though. Trust me, he will get there.'

Lomas's analysis of Tom's perspective made her feel awkward, ashamed even, as when the flower delivery containing the note had first arrived, for a moment she'd blamed Tom for letting her be exposed to it, and although she knew Tom meant well, he had seemed so weak when the note arrived, so weak when she needed him to be the exact opposite. Chrissie wished, just for a moment, that Tom was more like Lomas, strong and sure, knowing precisely what to do even in the most extreme circumstances. She needed to feel safe, protected.

Into the underground car park of the hospital rolled a small convoy of police vehicles, driving at close quarters, perfectly synchronised, and in the middle of the police vehicles was an ambulance.

Lomas headed the party out to meet the convoy. Drew, Christina and Tom, along with two nurses, accompanied him. Chrissie lay secured to a rolling stretcher, a feeling she was not particularly comfortable with. She had protested about her ability to walk but had been overridden by almost everyone, including Tom, which infuriated the petite, but fiercely independent teacher. They all stood in the lift, huddled around the stretcher. The elevator bumped to a halt and the doors slid open.

'Where are we going?' asked Christina.

'Somewhere safe – don't worry, you'll be fine,' Drew reassured her.

They were met at the ambulance and Christina's stretcher was secured inside. Lomas and Drew jumped into an unmarked car at the rear of the convoy. Two more headed it up in front, while inside the ambulance Tom held Chrissie's hand tightly, reassuring her all the while that everything would be all right. Christina's thoughts were still awash with the fear and anxiety that had begun with the opening of the envelope and been escalated by the message. Words which would stay with her and haunt her for the rest of her days. Images raced through her mind of the torture she had endured, mostly made up of colours and shadows cast by her captor as she was beaten, tainted by the changes in light that she had seen through her swollen eyelids. Then the complete darkness that had enveloped her, as her head was bandaged, returned to haunt her. She could hear once more the noise of her own blood coursing through her head, a noise that had seemed amplified, almost deafening, by the tight bindings that had been around her skull. This recollection linked into a vivid memory of the incredible pain Christina had experienced as her forehead was being scarred: the blade digging and scraping along her brow, furrowing lines deep and long.

She was ripped from her thoughts by a loud bang, and the ambulance veered sharply to the left. Christina screamed a high, shrill scream. Panic shook her to her core and in her mind she was instantly transported back to her prison. The safety harnesses on the stretcher suddenly felt as restrictive and binding as the shackles of the bed on which she was imprisoned. The explosion was in fact a tyre on the ambulance blowing out, but it mutated in Chrissie's mind into the sound of the sledgehammer that had shattered Anna-May's knee being hurled onto the wooden floor. Christina thrashed violently on the stretcher as her vivid revisiting of her ordeal continued, the voice of her abuser booming as if it were being spoken up close and in they were in the ambulance with her.

'What's wrong with you, you stupid screaming bitch? I didn't do anything to you, but seeing as you're so fucking vocal, maybe you'd like to see how it felt?'

Chrissie heard Anna's piercing scream *'No!'* in an attempt to save her from the same fate, every second of the scene playing out in full detail.

Both nurses and Tom tried desperately to pull her back to reality, but despite their best efforts, Chrissie writhed on the bed, with the phrases, sounds and smells filling her head, spilling into her reality, invading the safety of the ambulance.

The voice shrieked at Anna to shut it and threatened her with mailing an arm to her mother. Then attention switched back to Chrissie.

'Now, Christina, just lie nice and still and we'll give you two girls matching knees.'

Christina stayed anything but still. Instead, she

jerked and thrashed, bouncing her head and shoulders up from the stretcher, her whole body writhing in an attempt to stop the sledgehammer falling onto her knee.

Her memory recalled the pain in crystal-clear, excruciating detail, as her protective hands failed to stop the imaginary re-occurrence of the crushing pain that drove her knee downwards.

Tom clasped his hands tightly over his ears as Christina screamed once more, an unbearable animalistic shriek, that he couldn't bear to listen to.

As he saw her body momentarily relaxed, the older of the two nurses forced a syringe into Chrissie's arm. Within a few seconds, a restful tranquillity overcame her. As she lay quiet and calm, the nurses turned their attention to settling Tom.

'What was that?' he asked, a look of anxiety drawn across his face.

'A flashback, I think. It's very common in people who've been through a highly traumatic experience. Some blank it completely, as if to erase it from their memory. Others react, as Christina just did. It's called post-traumatic stress, and everything she goes through, in her mind, is a hundred per cent real. She can see, feel and even smell everything just as if it were happening all over again,' the nurse who'd sedated Christina explained.

'So how long does it last? What do we do? Can she get over it?' Tom's questions flowed quickly.

'It's difficult to say. What I can tell you is that Chrissie will need help. There are people who specialise in this sort of thing, but the best thing you can do for her is to be there. She needs you now, more than ever, and as she goes through her transition period you need to be patient. She may not want to go out, or to be alone for quite some time, or alternatively she may want leaving alone. Also, certain rooms, sights, smells or situations could cause her to become agitated. Christina will need your help to get over each hurdle in her own time and as hard as it is, you'll need to be patient with her. That doesn't mean you're on your own, because there are help groups for you too, and there is a huge support team within the community.' She smiled reassuringly and put her hand on his shoulder.

'Now, I'm going to see what's happening with this ambulance.'

She walked to the front to talk to the driver.

Tom picked up Chrissie's hand in his. As he sat beside her, he smoothed his fingers through her hair and watched her sleeping peacefully, musing over how immeasurably their seemingly perfect lives would be changed by the events that had befallen Christina.

'I'm not going anywhere. We're in this together. I love you,' he whispered gently. Then he bent over her and kissed her softly on her cheek. He smiled and, with a tear in his eye, continued his bedside vigil.

The ambulance jerked back into motion and their journey continued. Some forty-five minutes later they came to a standstill and the rear doors were pulled open.

As Tom clambered out of the rear of the ambulance, he stretched his aching legs and back. His natural curiosity was driving him insane wondering where they were.

The move had been carried out so surreptitiously that it had even bypassed the normal chain of command. The only person Lomas had trusted to arrange everything was Marie Carlton. She'd arranged for Christina to stay at a private country hospital. There was to be a twenty-four-hour guard at her door, with only security-cleared personnel to be allowed in or out. Marie had assured Lomas that Chrissie would be guarded like the crown jewels.

Tom turned to follow Chrissie's stretcher in through the doors of the hospital, closely followed by the rest of the entourage.

A nurse led the way to a private room and Tom listened as she introduced the now awake Christina to her nursing staff.

'Everyone who is allowed in to see you will be wearing one of these,' she said, lifting a coded plastic tag from her uniform. 'On it, as well as our name and photo, is a barcode. Outside your door is a code scanner, and only when this tag has been scanned and accepted will we be allowed through the auto-locked door.' She paused and smiled reassuringly at Chrissie.

'So, the only thing you have to worry about is getting better. If the rest of you will come with me, we'll get tags made up for you. Christina, all I want you to do is relax and get some rest. If you want us there's a buzzer beside your head, just press it and one of us will come and see you.' Christina nodded and the nurse turned and walked towards the door.

'I'll be back in a minute.' Tom smiled and let go of Christina's hand.

Tom, Lomas and Drew all went out to the nurse's station as instructed. On top of a PC was a small grey lens that looked like a large eyeball.

'Tom, if you could look directly into our little eye here so that I can take a picture of you for your tag… that's lovely.' Nurse Gail Parker typed Tom's details into the computer next to the image of his face that had appeared there. Within seconds, a barcoded tag had emerged and was clipped to Tom's jacket.

'To get in, all you have to do is stand in front of the scanner. This will read the code and unlock Christina's door.'

'How do we know that only authorised personnel can get in or out?' asked Lomas.

'Well, Inspector, I've entered all your details into the computer under Christina's door file. The scanner checks your code with the computer before it unlocks the door, this is the only bedroom door you will be authorised to access in the building.' Nurse Parker replied.

'Good enough, can I have a list of names of everyone who is allowed in when you've finished please?' Lomas requested. The nurse smiled and nodded.

Once they'd all got their tags, Lomas and Drew bid Tom goodnight and left the hospital.

28

'Will she be OK now?' Drew asked Lomas as they walked towards the car.

'Yes, you heard the nurse, only authorised people on this list are allowed in or out,' Lomas said, tapping the list with the back of his hand.

They arrived back at the station, both exhausted from the day's events. Lomas looked at Drew, studying her face. The stress of the investigation was taking its toll on everyone. It was affecting Drew especially, as she was right in the forefront with Lomas.

'You're meant to be off aren't you? Make sure you take the day off. It's been a hell of a week and we could all do with a breather,' he said as they walked inside.

She looked at him, slightly confused.

'Sir?'

'Take tomorrow off Drew, you can't keep going without recharging and you'll feel much better for it. If you feel half as exhausted as I do, then you definitely need it. Go shopping. Go to the gym, do whatever. Just take a day out and unwind.'

'But I'm fine, sir,' she said in a feeble attempt at defiance.

'Drew, it's not a crime to be tired, and I'm not

telling you to take the day off because I don't think you can handle the pace. I'm telling you because I need you to be alert and on the ball. You can't be alert if you're drained, so take tomorrow off.'

Reluctantly she agreed. In the back of her mind she was grateful for the rest, and if she was to be honest with herself she desperately needed a small break. The investigation was now in its ninth week and the rollercoaster Drew had ridden for that nine weeks had her emotions in turmoil. Still relatively inexperienced, the things she had witnessed and been involved in had brought back to her the reasons that had made her want to become a police officer. The victims, their families, even the other officers on the investigation, were all filling Drew's mind with fresh insight and life experience that would be impossible to get from any other job.

'Goodnight, boss.' She waved to Lomas as she left the office and headed home.

Lomas glanced up, waved his pen in the air and started working on the notes he wanted to make, pulling together everything they'd found out so far by getting it all out of his head and onto paper. It was a practice he'd employed for years. He needed to empty his head, and as he did he started joining up ideas. The visual prompts gained from the picture growing in front of him helped Lomas to form new ideas, new perspectives, which he invariably bounced off other members of his team to see if they had legs. He worked long into the night. With Heidi and the kids at her mother's, there was nothing pulling him towards home. He'd called and spoken to them, made sure they were OK and that they hadn't experienced anything out of the ordinary. They hadn't and they were fine. It helped Baxter to focus, knowing his family were out of harm's way.

DI Lomas Baxter woke early, as daylight streamed into his office. His head lay in the middle of a pile of paperwork strewn over his desk, scribbled notes with lines and circles drawn around prominent findings. His neck and back were aching from the unfamiliar position he'd slept in. He stretched his arms out in front of him and cracked his neck from one side to the other.

He cast an eye over the final sheet he'd read before drifting off to sleep. It was an additional list of red Transit van owners, all of whom had been checked and cleared. As he read, becoming more convinced that Jackson was their man, Nick Swaine burst through the office door.

'Sorry, sir, should have knocked, but have you heard about Louis Matthews? Everyone in the station is talking about him,' Nick blurted out.

'What do you mean everyone is talking? Why? What's happened to him?' Lomas asked.

'It's not what's happened to him, it's what he's done, sir. He's beaten a drunk up in the General Hospital.'

'What?' Lomas's shock was clear having not seen any local news or spoken to anyone since arriving at the station the previous night.

'Where is he? Who's in charge of the case?' He probed Nick for the answers.

'DI Plant, I think, sir. One of the other lads said he was down in the holding cells, so I checked and he is – he's here.'

'Right, come on, Nick, let's go and see Plant.'

Lomas headed for the holding cells and asked the desk sergeant if Louis was being detained. Lomas didn't want to believe that Louis Matthews was in the cells being detained for battering someone, after all he'd been through, but the sergeant confirmed it to be true. As Lomas chatted to Sergeant Collins, DI Plant rounded the corner.

'Lomas, how are you?' he said with a forced warmth in his voice.

'Fine, thanks, Derek, you?' Lomas didn't wait for a reply but continued, 'What's happening to Louis Matthews?'

'Yesss… interesting one that.' Plant dragged the statement out, stroking his chin and feigning a thoughtful look.

Lomas waited, not wanting to give Plant any more reason to draw out an explanation, or a chance for a dramatic re-enactment of the interview, as was often the case with the scruffy detective.

After a lengthy pause, Derek started.

'I don't really think there is much chance of getting a conviction to stick. Of course, CPS may disagree, Lomas, but I think, and it is only my oh so humble opinion, but I think any move to prosecute would easily be rebutted with a claim of diminished responsibility, or even a long testimony that would have jury feeling nothing but sympathy for Mr Matthews. There's no doubt that he punched the drunken man repeatedly, but, and here's the sting in the tail. There are witnesses to say he was provoked. The victim is known to police and the courts. He has a lengthy record of drunken disorderly behaviour, which would all go in Mr Matthews' favour. As I have no doubt he would employ the very best of solicitors, I just don't think it's a good use of public money. That said, I will be referring his case to the CPS and see what they make of it.' Plant drawled.

'So you think you're going to release him then?' Lomas asked.

'Well that's up to the powers that be, as you know I have little influence over that Lomas. But, I think under the circumstances it would be a drain on our valuable resources to detain Mr Matthews any longer than is absolutely necessary, and looking at the outcome realistically, my guess would be that he will probably be bailed.' As Derek's voice droned monotonously, Collins and Baxter exchanged knowing, weary glances.

'Thanks Derek, you've been enlightening,' Lomas said, trying not to sound too sarcastic.

'You're welcome, Lomas, any time.'

Lomas and Nick turned and left the detaining

area.

'Is he always that boring, boss?' Nick asked.

'Ah, watch yourself, young Swaine, that's one of your senior officers and as such he's to be respected and revered by the likes of you.' Lomas smiled, as he wagged a mock cautionary finger at Nick. 'Anyway, I'm sure I don't know what you mean, DI Plant, boring? Never.' He continued sarcastically. 'Now, do we have any more information on the whereabouts of our Mr Jackson?' He said, changing the subject.

'Not really, sir. The address his giro letters get posted to is an empty house on the outskirts of town. The benefit office said as soon as the next one is due to be issued they would let us know, or if he makes contact for any reason.'

'Another empty house in Jackson's name Nick, what's going on? Has this guy amassed a small property portfolio we don't know anything about?'

'Not exactly boss, I asked around and it looks like he has a brother who's a builder that develops property. My guess would be that he buys houses in his families' names.'

'OK, good work Nick.'

'Oh, sir, DC Savage and I have been driving past the house at regular intervals, on the off-chance we might see some sign of life.'

'Knock that idea on the head for a while, until you hear from the benefit office, or we get another lead. If Jackson thinks we're watching him, he won't show, and then all your hard work will be wasted,' Lomas said.

29

Drew stirred from a deep peaceful sleep, snug and warm in her bed. A thin shaft of bright sunlight pierced a gap at the top edge of her bedroom curtains. She turned slowly to see the clock on her pine bedside chest and screwed her eyes up to focus on the black roman numerals.

'Half past seven,' she groaned to herself. *'I wanted to sleep until at least ten.'* Drew mused in a half-awake self-pitying whinge. *'Oh well, no point going back to sleep now, you'll only wake up with a headache.'* She stayed in bed, wrapped in her duvet, comfortably drifting in and out of a light sleep until after eight thirty. Eventually she sat up and dropped her feet over the side of the bed in a vain attempt to get up.

She walked into her living room and flicked on breakfast tv, then wandered through to the kitchen to make a drink. As the kettle came to the boil her phone rang.

It was her mum, they chatted for a while and arranged to meet for lunch, something they hadn't done for a little while. Drew enjoyed the odd girly lunch with her mum. They invariably ended up shopping, and her mother always quizzed her about when she was going to find a nice man and settle down. It was a part of their ritual that Drew tried her very best to avoid. It wasn't that she didn't want to meet someone, it was just that the men she met either couldn't work round her shifts and unpredictable hours, at which point things fizzled out, or they were wary of dating a police officer for some unknown reason. Except for one weirdo, who seemed lovely for the first hour or so and then all he wanted to know about was her uniform and where she kept her handcuffs, and not in a funny way either. Drew chuckled at the memory of that one, shaking her head at the sad predictability of men's questions. She remembered her mum once being very shocked when, one day, during a bit of her matchmaking, the man that her mum had just proudly told that Drew was a police officer, replied with a smile, 'So, do you like to have a big truncheon in your hands then?' Mother gasped and he left quite soon afterwards. That was the last time she'd tried to pair Drew up. Lunch with her mother became much safer for Drew after that.

With nothing planned until she had to go and meet her mum, Drew took the opportunity to catch up on some trashy tv, grabbing her remote, she surfed through a seemingly endless list of channels. She cycled through twice and stopped on This Morning. The familiar, friendly faces of Phillip Schofield and Holly Willoughby popped onto the screen and Drew was lost in an unchallenging feast of celebrity cooks and short interviews.

Drew showered late after getting engrossed in a

piece about a woman that was about to marry a man serving life for murder, with whom she had started a relationship by writing to him in prison, after seeing him on the news.

She picked out black skinny jeans, a fitted grey-and-white long-sleeved top and short light grey boots. With the smallest amount of make-up around her eyes and her copper hair left to fall straight and to her shoulders, Drew was ready to go.

Of course, her mother would never approve of her not doing her hair and make-up as if she were going to the Oscars, but she was as far past trying to change her daughter as Drew was listening to the back-handed compliments and criticism her mum dished out. Their relationship was however, a strongly bonded one, and they shared some of their most intimate thoughts.

As usual, her mother had arrived early at the wine bar and ordered two glasses of white wine. Drew's mother, Lauren, was in her late forties. She was an attractive woman, with the same petite figure and copper hair as her daughter, which she wore at a slightly shorter length and bobbed. Today, she was dressed immaculately in a dark skirt and polo-necked top. A modicum of stylish jewellery and new high-heeled suede shoes with a matching bag finished off her accessories.

She stood to greet Drew, who arrived on time almost to the second. Drew kissed her mother on the cheek, hugged her, then sat down and took a quick sip of her wine. Lauren's usual line of questioning started with a couple of quick fire queries, 'How are you? Are you eating properly, working all those hours? I hope you're getting enough sleep?' She paused briefly for breath.

Drew had learned over the years to use these breaks to interrupt, as it was the only way to avoid another barrage of questions.

'Yes, Mum, I'm fine. I'm sleeping and eating well and work is going fine. Now, what are we having for lunch?' A question to divert her mother's attention, at least temporarily.

The waiter came over and they ordered lunch. Much to Drew's amazement, the conversation moved on to matters more trivial than she'd expected and they sat chatting about nothing of any great importance until their food arrived and beyond.

As they gossiped, Drew noticed something out of the corner of her eye. Her focus moved from her mother and the conversation stopped. Over Lauren's shoulder, some seventy or eighty yards away, Drew saw a dark red Transit, and as she watched she saw the vague pattern of a red-and-white checked shirt being worn by what looked like a stocky man with short hair.

Without a word to her mother, Drew sprang to her feet. Pushing her chair backwards, she cast a chair which was in front of her aside and broke into a sprint. Exiting the wine bar, Drew ran as fast as she could towards the van, which by now was moving away from her in the flow of traffic. It turned right off the high street and headed away from her between two imposing large grey office blocks. Undaunted, she ran down the centre of the road, every muscle and sinew stretching and pumping, propelling Drew at her absolute maximum speed along the white line in pursuit of the van.

It slowed and Drew gained to within fifteen to twenty feet. She felt as if she could almost reach out and touch it, she was so close. Again it pulled away, and without signalling, it turned left down a narrow one-way street. Drew cut the corner, gaining her precious distance, and she was now within ten feet. Then, without warning, the dark red van accelerated and gradually pulled farther away. Drew reach out in a vain effort to stop it but could only watch as the gap between them grew wider. She eased her pace and stopped running, moving off the road, sinking to a crouch against a wall, deflated, completely exhausted and overcome by her gargantuan effort. As she sat down, frustration boiled within her, and she punched her clenched fists down onto the floor either side of her, pushed her head back against the wall and screamed out loud at her failure to catch the van, which could so easily have been the break they needed.

30

‘Me and the kids are fine, how are you?’ Heidi’s voice was like an oasis of calm amongst the desert of chaos that surrounded Lomas.

‘Yeah, I’m fine,’ he replied.

‘We’ve been out with Mum and Dad, the kids are moaning that they’re bored and there’s nothing to do here, but as long as they’ve got Wi-Fi I think they’ll be fine.’

‘Yeah, glad you’re all OK,’ Lomas replied vacantly, distracted by a growing hum of activity behind him.

‘Lomas, are you OK?’

‘Sorry? Yeah, er, things are a bit hectic around here at the moment. I’ll call you back later.’

‘OK, no problem darling. I love you.’

‘Love you too, bye.’ Lomas dropped the receiver back into its groove.

He spun around in his chair and barked, ‘What the hell is going on in here? I can’t hear myself think!’

The noise abated instantly and he used the pause to find out what was happening.

‘Would someone please tell me why we’re all in such a flap?’ he asked in a calmer tone.

Nick Swaine piped up. ‘Drew just called, boss.

She just chased a man in a dark red transit van, on foot, and came within an arm's length of catching it.'

Instantly, Baxter became concerned for his young protégé's safety.

'Is she OK?' Lomas asked.

'She sounds fine boss, pissed off, but fine. She says she's on her way in.'

A flustered Drew arrived a little while later to give a blow-by-blow of the chase to the DI.

Lomas ushered her into his office and got her a glass of water.

'Thanks for heading in so quickly Drew. Take your time and from the beginning, in as much detail as you can remember, tell me what happened.' He waved Nick in to listen and take notes of DC Taylor's account of her chase. Nick perched on a chair next to Drew, notepad on his lap, pen poised.

'I was sitting with Mum at a wine bar in town and ordered lunch…'

As Drew gave Lomas a step-by-step account of the incident and Nick began to take notes, Baxter sensed two characteristics that, like him, she possessed. Not only did she have an unwavering determination to catch the killer, irrespective of how much personal effort was needed, but she also suffered huge personal frustration and disappointment when her efforts didn't give the results she wanted. Although there was absolutely nothing she could have done to prevent the van from accelerating away from her, Drew still felt there must have been something she could have done better: seen the van earlier, set off a little sooner, quicker than she did. Her annoyance was clear, as she ground her hands together while she spoke. Lomas knew that Drew's emotions always shone through; part of her she couldn't disguise no matter how hard she tried.

'I'm really sorry I didn't catch it, sir. I was so very nearly there.'

Disappointment now replaced anger in Drew's eyes and her voice ebbed away.

'There's absolutely no need to beat yourself up. You just chased a van down, on foot, through town. There aren't many who would have set off after it. Most would have called it in and watched it disappear,' said Lomas reassuringly.

'Look at Tommo over there…' He motioned to a balding, portly man walking past his office. 'Do you think he could have come within feet of this moving Transit of yours? I don't think so. He has trouble getting from his house to the car without being out of breath.'

Drew smiled a humble, slightly embarrassed smile. 'Thank you, boss.'

'No, thank you. With the information you've provided about the van you saw, we're hopefully another step closer to catching this lunatic. Now, off you go and enjoy the rest of your day off.'

'OK, will do.' She smiled again, this time a different, more confidant smile that lit up her whole face. She turned to leave the office and Nick opened the door for her.

'Well done today, Drew, that was really impressive,' he said, with an awkwardness that was uncharacteristic. Drew held his gaze for moment.

'Thanks, Nick.' Drew smiled and stepped through the open doorway.

'Oh, Drew, there are better ways to do cardio than chasing vans through town. Try a run in the park, I've heard the air's better,' Lomas said, laughing.

'Thanks, boss, I'll give it a try. See you tomorrow. See you tomorrow, Nick.'

The day was drawing to an end as the internal phone on DI Baxter's desk rang.

'Lomas?' asked a gruff caller immediately.

'Yes, Rob, what can I do for you?' Rob was one of the desk sergeants who worked downstairs.

'There's a couple in reception I think maybe you should see.'

'Why, Rob, what have they done?' Lomas enquired.

'They've done nothing. Well, except reported their twenty-four-year-old daughter missing.'

Lomas dropped the receiver quickly back on the hook and dashed downstairs.

'So where are they, Rob?'

'Over there....Mr and Mrs Kemp. She's been missing for two days now. Needless to say they're a bit concerned.' Rob's brow creased in the centre above his nose and a concerned look filled his slightly tanned, round face. He didn't need to say any more. Lomas knew what the normally jovial sergeant was thinking.

'OK, I'll take it from here, thanks, Rob.'

Mr and Mrs Kemp were sat holding hands on the wooden bench seat which ran along the bland grey wall in reception.

Mr Kemp wore dark blue trainers, jeans and a navy blue fleecy sweatshirt, his hair reddish brown, swept back in a neat, short style. Mrs Kemp was dressed not dissimilar to her partner except in slightly more feminine colouring. Her eyes were tinged red, from what looked to Lomas like hours of crying.

'Mr and Mrs Kemp?'

They looked up at Lomas like rabbits caught in car headlights, eyes fixed and wide.

'Yes,' Mr Kemp answered.

'I'm DI Baxter. My colleague Sergeant Wordsworth asked me to come and have a chat with you about your daughter. Would you like to step this way?'

He guided them into an interview room just beyond reception. As they sat in front of the table in the sparse room, Lomas asked if they'd like tea or coffee. After requesting their drinks from a passing officer, he sat and began to gather information which he hoped would point anywhere other than towards this couple's daughter being victim number six.

'OK, first things first, let's get your daughter

registered as a missing person. That way, all police forces will be given a description of her and alerted regarding her disappearance.'

Tina Kemp erupted into floods of tears. The emotions that she had clearly being struggling to keep in check were instantly apparent. Lomas had seen this many times – a parent broken by a lack of knowledge as to the whereabouts of their child. As a parent himself, he identified only too readily with the panic this couple must have been feeling. The helplessness of not knowing where to look, who to call. Scenes such as these hammered home to Lomas just how little he himself knew about his own children's friends and associates. He had asked Heidi once if they would know where to start if plunged into the same powerless position. There were few things Lomas could say to console Mrs Kemp. Her daughter was missing. The papers were splashed daily with updates and sordid stories of the last five victims. How could these two innocent people think anything other than the same fate had befallen their cherished daughter?

As they spoke, Tina and Richard Kemp painted a picture of a beautiful, vibrant, twenty-four-year-old advertising executive who had various sporting interests and nothing known in the way of enemies. Tina spoke through a stuttered cry, while Richard remained relatively composed throughout, comforting his traumatised wife every step of the way. They had come armed with an array of highly useful contacts and up-to-date photos of their daughter, Victoria.

At twenty-four years old, five feet six inches tall, pretty with long dark straight hair, and well established and successful in her chosen profession, Victoria Kemp fitted exactly into the mould for a possible number six.

After reassuring Mr and Mrs Kemp that he would do everything in his power to track down their daughter in his usual calm and caring manner, then seeing them out to reception, Lomas called an immediate meeting of the team working the investigation. The hum of separate conversations ceased abruptly as Baxter walked into the briefing room. Everyone's attention focussed immediately on the front of the room.

'All right, people, listen up. This is Victoria Kemp, a twenty-four-year-old advertising exec,' Lomas announced, holding up a blown-up photo of the Kemps' daughter.

'She's been missing for two days and fits the description we now have to associate with this investigation. We have pictures, contacts, names and addresses.' His speech was precise and brusque, with no pause or room for contradiction or questioning.

'Now, what I need from you people is for you to explore each and every one of the usual avenues of enquiry. In order that Miss Kemp doesn't become victim number six, we have to move with the utmost speed and urgency. There's no room for mistakes or missed opportunities. Now, I know each and every one of you is giving a hundred per cent to this investigation. What I need and what Victoria Kemp and her parents need is just that little bit more. We need to find this girl before anything terrible happens.'

31

An old vicarage stood dark and unoccupied in the extensive grounds of a huge church. Shadows loomed large across the surroundings, broken by white pools of moonlight. The house was imposing, cold and decaying, ringed by overgrown grass and weeds, which swayed in the chill breeze. It grew tall, tall enough to lap over deep stone windowsills that ran along the bottom of large bay windows, some of which were obscured by huge wooden boards nailed to the frames, others still clung to their original glass panes.

The garden was edged by a crumbling red brick wall, on top of which were rusty iron railings, long neglected and flaky with age. A gap in the wall made way for a concrete path that wound through the centre of the garden, now overgrown and indistinguishable from its surroundings. It had once guided the way to a huge oak door with an arched top and black rusty hinges running from the right side of the frame halfway across the wooden panels.

A soft squeak of brakes shattered the silence around the eerie house, followed by an engine shuddering to a halt. A van door opened and footsteps could be heard. Another door opened, creaking briefly, a dry, metallic creak. A leather-gloved hand grabbed at a limp figure slumped in the darkness of the back of the van and dragged the body, dumping it unceremoniously onto the ground. The door was slammed shut, and silence fell once more on the church grounds. The hand then snatched a handful of clothing behind the neck of the figure and dragged the body towards the huge oak door.

A decrepit hinge groaned under the weight of the oak door as it swung open. There was no light from within – the huge hallway stood derelict and looked as if it had been unused for years. The gloved hand grappled awkwardly in a pocket for a torch and seconds later a single beam cut through the darkness revealing an old blue carpet, curled up at the edges, with a large hole in the centre that revealed wooden floorboards that were green with age and exposure to the damp, cold air. The still, slumped figure was dragged over the threshold and into the vicarage, feet trailing behind, bumping over the step, heels knocking ever so quietly as they moved from the carpet to floorboards. A doorway to the left was highlighted by the solitary shaft of light from the torch, beyond which was a huge room where the smell of mildew and rotting carpets filled the air. A single drop of water fell from a crack in the ceiling and splashed onto a baroque hearth. It dissipated across the marble, above which was an elaborate black fireplace that was edged with marble and finished with twists of black iron.

'Huh, fuckin' dump.' The weight of silence was

such that the short phrase seemed to fill the room. The beam of the torch flicked across the flaking wall and out of the room. Next it illuminated not one, but two open doorways. The first off to the left, the second directly in front and down two steps. Through the second room a corridor led off to both the left and right and at the end of the hallway stood a wide staircase. The glow from the torch danced over steps that seemed to go on indefinitely, reaching upwards. Suddenly, the light was reflected back by two staring eyes – a cat sat staring directly back into the torchlight. The hand tightened its grip on the body.

'You aren't half getting heavy, you bitch. Still, off up to bed you go.'

The sound of the voice, cutting through the silence, made the cat turn and flee, disappearing into the darkness at the top of the stairs.

Steadily, one step at a time, the sound of the two heavy feet echoed up the bare wooden stairs. Being dragged behind the figure was the slumped body, its shins and feet beating their way one step at a time towards the top. Still no murmur came from the corpse-like figure as it was hauled over each stair. At the top of the staircase the corridor went off to the left. Directly in front was a closed door. The torchlight was reflected by gloss paint. The figure stood motionless for a moment at the top of the stairs and then the solitary torch beam was guided along a threadbare rug, which was partially covering dusty floorboards. A brief flash up the walls showed long deep watermarks from years of leaks through the fractured roof tiles above. There was another closed door at the end of the hallway. The figure manoeuvred the body around a post that stood at the top of the stairs, dragged it down the uninviting corridor to the room at the end and opened the door.

Moonlight flooded through an uncovered window, painting the shape of the window onto a bare floor. The room was empty except for a large hand-built wooden chest and a wooden slatted bed. The bed was made from rough timber and was pushed into a shadowy corner. At the head of the bed, secured to the wall, were two shackles made from dull metal. Bolted to the bottom edge of the bed frame was another set of restraints.

The body was dropped on the floor beside the bed.

'Wait there bitch.' The torch was switched off, and shadows cast by the moonlight danced on the walls as a tree outside the window swayed in the breeze. There was a sharp rattle from the opening of the manacles and the bundled figure was lifted from the floor and then dropped, face up, onto the coarse wooden platform. A muffled groan was the first sign of life from the woman now lying on the bed. The response from the captor to this low moan was a sharp, well-directed punch, full in the face, the dark fist splitting the woman's top lip, which was already bloody and swollen from previous blows. Both of her hands were grabbed and shackled to the wall.

Her ankles were secured to the foot of the bed and a gloved hand checked that all four restraints were secure and tight enough to be digging ever so slightly into the skin on each of the woman's limbs.

'Now, you lie nice and still. You've already caused more trouble than you're worth. Dragging you up all those fucking stairs was a complete pain in the arse. Still, you'll be lighter on the way down.' The voice was malicious and mocking, and it boomed through the empty house. Somewhere on a wooden floor in another room the cat scrabbled away, scared by the reverberating voice that broke the silence of the old house once more.

The huge figure moved slowly through the shadows, reaching for the wooden chest and pulling open the lid of the rough, splintered box. The torch was switched back on and its light filled the chest. Inside was an array of surgical tools, some looking more modern than others. The shiny implements were swept aside to reveal a long strap made from a woven material, not dissimilar to a car seat belt. This was pulled from the bottom of the chest, flicking instruments of torture around the chest as it snaked its way out. On one end of the strap was a buckle, on the other a series of holes with shiny brass eyelets. It was carried over to the bed and then the long belt was passed across the unconscious woman's hips and fed down between the wall and the far side of the bed. The bulky assailant crouched under the bed, feeling in the dark for the end of the strap. The metal buckle tapped on the wall as fingertips caught hold of the belt. It was passed through the buckle and pulled tight, pinning the woman's hips down onto the splintered bed.

'Right, nightie night. See you bright and early in the morning. Sleep tight. Don't let the wood mites bite.' The voice was cold and devoid of any emotion.

Once again the torch beam pointed to the door leading out of the room. The figure paced out through the doorway and down the stairs, leaving the room still and dark, except for the shadows of a tree dancing menacingly in the moonlight.

32

Lomas and Drew sat in a car at the far end of Dickens Road, silently watching number 12, a red-brick terraced house. A bit further down, facing them on the opposite side, were Pete and Nick, also focussed totally on the house. Nick had been tipped off by an informant that Ian Jackson was staying at 12 Dickens Road, and that he was working on and off with his old gang on various small-time jobs. Lomas hadn't needed much persuasion to set up a surveillance operation at the house. Marie Carlton had also given her full support, giving Lomas carte blanche over any of the officers at the station he needed, uniform or not. In his usual self-assured manner, Lomas had only taken the minimum number of competent officers that he thought would get the job done. As Pete and Nick had been an integral part of tracking Jackson, it was only right they should be there at what Lomas hoped would be the closing of the net and the prevention of any more deaths.

They'd been watching the house for nearly four hours when a dark red Transit van drove into Dickens Road. It pulled up across the road from number 12 and out of the passenger side jumped a stocky, well-built man with dark scruffy hair, wearing a red and blue lumberjack shirt.

Lomas radioed through to the pair in the other car.

'Nick, what kind of view have you got?'

'A good one, sir. That's our man.'

'The one on the passenger side?' Lomas asked.

'Yes, sir. I'm not sure who the driver is but he's just about to get out as well.'

'OK, we wait until they're through the gate and in the house. Is that understood?'

'Yes, sir, up the path and in the house,' Nick replied.

'We go on my signal. You and Pete take the back door, and we'll take the front.'

'Understood, sir.'

The two men made their way across the road, over the grass verge and up to the wooden gate, either side of which stood a red brick wall. A paved path ran in a straight line from the gate towards the front door, which was at the top of some concrete steps. Either side of the path was an untidy, slightly overgrown garden, with half a dozen grey concrete breeze blocks scattered near the wall at the bottom of the garden.

Jackson reached over the gate and clicked the latch open. With a brief glance to their left and right, the two men entered the garden. They left the gate half-open, almost inviting Lomas and his team in to do what they had waited four hours to do.

Lomas watched silently until the men reached the door, put the key in the lock and stepped into the house. As the door banged shut behind them, Lomas broke the tense silence.

'Right, let's get in position, quickly and quietly.'

Simultaneously, all four leapt from their respective cars.

Nick and Pete made their way briskly up a side passageway of the neighbouring house to gain access to number 12's back door.

Lomas's radio crackled into action.

'OK, boss, we're in place and ready.' Loams glanced at Drew and nodded, she nodded back indicating her readiness.

'Well done. Right, I'm going in. Repeat, I'm going in.'

Lomas and Drew bounded up the steps to the front door of the house. Lomas banged on the door.

'Ian Jackson, open up, this is the police!'

Inside the house, Jackson spun on his heels to face Joe, his side-kick, who had been driving the van, both of them displaying the look of startled animals.

'Fuck, it's the old bill!' exclaimed Jackson.

'What the fuck do they want?' Joe retorted.

'Let's get the fuck out of here. Quick, the back door. Go now!'

Joe stood, frozen for a second.

'Well, fuckin' move it, you prick!' Jackson shrieked, already running towards the back door. He grabbed the handle and yanked the door open. Blocking his way stood Nick Swaine. Jackson launched himself at Nick before he had a chance to speak. His forehead crushed Nick's nose and instantly covered his face in blood. Nick buckled from the blow clutching his face, and as he fell backwards. Pete stepped forward and grabbed Jackson, spinning him around. As he struggled, Pete put him swiftly into a headlock. Jackson dug his heel into Pete's shin, slid his head down into the headlock and sunk his teeth into Pete's forearm. He bit down hard, like a wild dog tearing at its prey, breaking through the skin on the officer's arm, making him instinctively release the headlock. Pete made no sound, but with his teeth clenched tightly, he curled his right hand into a fist, and with blood pouring from his arm he dug his elbow into Jackson's eye socket. Nick stood up at this point and reapplied a stranglehold on Jackson from behind while wrenching his left arm up behind his back.

As this was all going on, Lomas and Drew had forced their way into the house and effortlessly apprehended Joe, still frozen to the spot in the living room.

'Ian Jackson, I am arresting you on suspicion of murder, and for assaulting a police officer…'

Nick shouted Jackson's rights at him over the screaming of his prisoner. Handcuffed and bleeding, Jackson was forced through the house and into a waiting police van.

Pete and Nick clambered into a waiting

ambulance, spattered in blood, while Lomas and Drew put a shell-shocked Joe into the back of their car and set off for the station.

33

Ian Jackson took off his checked shirt and dropped it on the floor by his feet. The white t-shirt he had on underneath was damp under the arms. It stretched across his stocky frame and was tucked into black combat trousers. He ran a hand through his messy, dark brown hair and set a steely gaze on the cell door, through cold blue eyes. He sat on the hard bed in his cell, listening to the quiet, the bare, cold walls, empty and pale blue in colour, surrounding him on all sides. The heavy metal door stood between him and the rest of the police station.

These were not unfamiliar surroundings to Jackson, as he'd spent half of his life in one institution or another. His first brush with the law had come at the tender age of twelve, when he'd been caught no less than eighteen times in seven months stealing from various shops, one of which was a shop within his school. This had earned him not only expulsion, but also a month in borstal. Although he wasn't a very successful thief when he went in, during his month inside he had learned very quickly from his peers and hooked up with the people who would help form the early part of his criminal career. By the time he reached eighteen he had grown in more than just build and stature. He'd matured into an accomplished thief, stealing from houses, shops, post offices, and by this time his acts invariably contained a violent element. Jackson had made a name for himself as a hard, up-and-coming youngster on the local criminal gang scene. He completed his apprenticeship as a butcher working for a nearby family business, where at twenty-two he stole a whole truck full of meat from their deep freeze and sold it, truck and all, to a competitor and rival family across town. When the father of the family, his boss, confronted Jackson and questioned him about the missing truck full of meat, Ian flipped, and during a frenzied attack he punched the man, who was in his fifties, until he couldn't see out of either of his eyes. That got him four years for actual bodily harm and theft. When sentenced, Jackson said, 'Serves the stupid old fucker right. He shouldn't ask dumb questions.'

A string of sentences followed over the next twenty years of Jackson's life, everything from armed robbery to GBH and assault with a deadly weapon. Ian Jackson wasn't a stupid criminal though. As soon as he was inside, a model prisoner emerged. He did his own time and got paroled early for good behaviour.

He now sat accused of murder, the most serious of any charge levelled at him to date.

He sat emotionless, no fear or anguish showing on his face. Jackson's attitude was to show the police nothing. Whether guilty or innocent he wouldn't give them the satisfaction of 'getting a rise', as he called it. He once told a young crook who was working with him, 'The only thing you've gotta remember if you get caught, don't show 'em nothing, don't tell 'em nothing, don't give 'em nothing, especially not the satisfaction of getting a rise out of ya.'

The lad Jackson had bestowed these words of wisdom on was shot by armed police two years later on a bungled armed post office robbery with Ian. He escaped without a scratch, and in all the confusion of the shooting he actually managed to get away with the money.

Again, Jackson looked around the holding cell, his strong hands gripping the edge of the bed. The heavy lock clanked and the cell door swung open to reveal not one, but two huge police officers.

'Come on, Mr Jackson,' said the front one, 'time for you to see the DI.'

Jackson's face remained unchanged. He stood slowly and made his way over to the door. The officers took him by each arm and walked him along the corridor and through a door labelled 'Interview Room Four'. Inside he was greeted by a familiar face. A tanned, grey-haired gent in a pinstriped dark grey suit held out his hand to Ian. Brian Gordon-Thomas, Jackson's solicitor, was a well-known defence lawyer. He defended everyone in the circles in which Jackson worked and lived. His nickname amongst the villainy he represented was 'G and T', not only because of his double-barrelled surname, but also because, coincidentally, it was his favourite tipple.

A smarmy self-assured grin emanated from Gordon-Thomas's furrowed face, wrinkled from the effects of endless hours in the sun.

'Ian, how are you? Hope they're treating you well.' He nodded towards the two officers who had accompanied Jackson.

'Yeah, fine, except for these bullshit charges they've thrown at me.'

Jackson was gruff and blunt, with a well rehearsed ambivalence towards the police. His demeanour was more one of a man who was unhappy about being stopped for speeding, than one accused of murder.

'Yes,' pondered Gordon-Thomas, 'they do seem farfetched. Let's see what the good officers have to say, shall we?' He spoke in a drawl that sounded deliberately patronising, and he dragged his sentences out, stretching each word to the full.

As the two men sat side by side, the door to interview room four opened and in walked a solemn DI Baxter followed closely by DC Taylor.

Lomas nodded to Jackson's representative.

'Mr Gordon-Thomas, how are you?'

'Fine, Lomas, how's the lovely family? And who might this beautiful young lady be?' he said, as he looked Drew up and down, ignoring the unimpressed look on the young officer's face.

'DC Taylor,' Lomas replied coldly. 'Shall we get started?' continued Lomas, as he and Drew sat across the table from Jackson and his counsel.

Lomas quickly dispensed with the trivia, stating the names of those present and beginning the interview for the benefit of the recording.

'You've been a busy boy since you got out, haven't you, Ian?' Lomas threw the question bluntly, staring directly into Jackson's cold eyes. A brief silence followed, but there was no response from the prisoner, just a blank, unchanging expression.

'It would seem that your hatred for women has intensified this past couple of years.'

'What hatred?' Jackson retorted.

'Oh come-on, Ian. We all know what your opinion of the weaker sex is, after your rather eloquent speech on the subject at your last trial.'

'What fuckin' speech? What the fuck are you talkin' about?' Jackson's face began to redden at DI Baxter's remarks.

'DI Baxter, I do hope you are not attempting to antagonise my client by suggesting that he possesses a dislike for females?' interrupted Gordon-Thomas.

'Certainly not, Mr Gordon-Thomas, but any man who states, under oath, that half of all woman should have been drowned at birth, does have a demonstrable loathing of women. Wouldn't you say?' Lomas grinned inwardly at the satisfaction of rebuffing G & T with such a watertight argument.

'That's as maybe, but what does that statement have to do with my client's current situation? He was reformed and is now attempting to rebuild his life as an honest and upright member of society.' This was a standard line Gordon-Thomas used and he'd used it so many times that half the senior officers in the station could recite it for him.

'OK,' Lomas restarted, 'let's assume that's all true. Maybe you, Mr Jackson, can help us clear up a few things up regarding a current investigation. If everything checks out, you could be on your way home before you know it. Let's start with a few pictures.'

Drew passed Lomas a picture of the first victim, a twenty-three-year-old vet called Sarah Rosewood. The picture, taken four weeks before she was found dismembered, showed a stunningly attractive girl with wavy long blonde hair and huge chestnut eyes. She was standing next to her horse, just outside a stable at her family's farm. Lomas pushed the picture across the cold grey table and with his fingers on the corner of the photo, Lomas began to speak quietly.

'A lovely girl by all accounts. Her name was Sarah. She'd wanted to be a vet all the time she was growing up as a young girl on her parent's farm. She had three sisters – one twin and two older than her.'

'What the fuck has that got to do with me?' Jackson interrupted.

'Do you recognise her?' Lomas continued, his voice low, with his tone and pace of speech deliberate.

'Never seen her before in my life, why?' asked Ian bluntly.

Lomas glared into Jackson's eyes, almost as if trying to see into his soul.

'She's dead. She was found cut up into six pieces that were dumped all over the woods on the edge of town near your old house. Are you sure you don't recognise her, Ian, or did she look a bit different the last time you saw her?' The severity of Lomas's voice intensified as he reached the end of his sentence.

Jackson's eyes narrowed into a steely glower.

'I told you. I've never seen her before and I certainly didn't fuckin' kill her.' His voice was almost a whisper as he leaned over the table towards Lomas, his words and tone wilful, in an attempt to convince the detective.

'Try this one.' DI Baxter slid another photo across the smooth pale surface.

'Lindsey Demitri, a twenty-six-year-old junior doctor, glowing reports from university, was determined to do great things, had an eight-year-old brother who cries himself to sleep at night since his mum and dad had to tell him his big sister's never coming home again. She was found, again in six pieces, floating in the stream in the woods near your old house.'

Jackson put his left hand up to cradle his forehead. Staring at the picture, he shook his head. He closed his eyes slowly, and then, very steadily, said, 'Will you listen to what I say?' He released his head, his eyes flicked open, and he glared directly at Lomas as he shouted, 'I haven't seen these girls and I haven't killed anybody. Have you got that, you stupid fucker, and stop showing me these fuckin' pictures, you sick bastard!' His fists were clenched tightly on the table and his eyes didn't move from Lomas's.

Lomas didn't flinch. Instead, he continued looking Ian Jackson straight in the eye, searching for a reaction that would give him away.

'Tell me, Mr Jackson, what's your trade? What did you serve your apprenticeship as?'

'A butcher, why?' His eyes narrowed once more, but this time a confused look came across his face, his brow furrowed vertically in two lines from the bridge of his nose as a frown formed, a perplexed frown. Bewildered by the officer's question, he awaited a response to his answer.

Then it hit him, as Lomas responded to his question, 'So you're used to, and probably very skilled at, chopping up carcasses. You know joints, where to cut, what tools to use, all that kind of stuff. Yes?'

Jackson's face erupted in anger, flushing a deep red, eyes almost protruding from his skull. He leapt from his chair over the desk towards Lomas.

'You cunt. You're fuckin' fittin' me up!' Jackson shrieked.

Lomas stood back quickly, sending his chair flying across the interview room floor. Jackson then pushed the table aside, still screaming obscenities.

In self-defence, Lomas grabbed a handful of Jackson's collar, pushing him face first to the floor. Then he dropped his knee into the top of Jackson's spine and the two officers and Drew all hurried to assist him. The two officers dragged a handcuffed Ian Jackson out of the interview room as he almost foamed at the mouth with rage.

Lomas turned to Drew, and with a smile said, 'I guess he didn't like being a butcher.'

34

'So what do you think of our Mr Jackson's little outburst?' Lomas asked Drew as he held the door of interview room four ajar.

'He certainly got offended, didn't he?'

As they walked side by side along the corridor, walls covered in the latest police crime prevention posters, Lomas outlined the next conversation they would have with Jackson. Then a voice broke into their conversation, a familiar monotone voice. Drew and Lomas turned to see DI Plant walking down the corridor.

'Good day, DI Baxter, DC Taylor. There's someone in reception I think you'll be quite keen to speak to,' Derek drawled.

'And who might that be, Derek?' queried Lomas.

Derek smiled, turned and walked back towards the front of the station.

Lomas shrugged and motioned to Drew to follow. With no idea as to who may be in reception, they followed Derek through the heavy double doors that led into the public waiting area.

They both stopped dead in their tracks. Lomas and Drew looked at their visitor, then at each other. For a moment there was a heavy silence, then a very nervous-looking Victoria Kemp said, 'Mum sent me in to see you. She says you've had everyone looking for me. I-I didn't mean to cause any trouble. I just needed to get away for a few days. I had no idea Mum and Dad would react like this.'

Her speech was hurried and pressured, and she stood looking from Lomas to Drew and back again, a nervous tension clear across her face.

'Am I in trouble? I've never been in trouble with the police before. I'm really, really sorry.'

Victoria's face began to redden as she chewed the nail on her left index finger.

'Victoria… no, you're not in any trouble. Please, take a seat.' Lomas nodded towards the vinyl-covered padded seats in reception.

'As long as you're OK, that's all we're concerned about,' he continued.

Victoria stopped biting her nails.

'Yes, I'm fine. Me and a couple of friends just drove up to the coast. We haven't watched any TV or listened to the radio for days, otherwise I would have called.'

'We'll need a brief statement, just so that we can close your file. Is now good?' asked Drew.

'Yes, yes, fine, I really am sorry.'

They went through to an interview room where Victoria continued to explain that she and two friends had all decided on the spur of the moment to go away for a few days. They had each phoned their employers and faked illness, then jumped in a car and, despite the fact that it was freezing cold, headed for the coast. They had rented a room in a small B & B and spent the following days relaxing, never thinking to phone home. On their return, they'd been greeted with the news that Victoria was the subject of a massive hunt as a missing person. Tina Kemp had apparently blown up at Victoria and ordered her to come down and clear everything up with Lomas and Drew. Once again, Miss Kemp apologised profusely. Then she left the station to go home and patch things up with her parents, whom twenty-four hours earlier had been fearing their daughter missing or dead.

35

Louis Matthews sat alone by a roaring fire. Above the fire on the stone-built chimney breast were brass horseshoes of various sizes. He was sitting on a hard wooden chair, his arms resting on a round oak table, gazing at the bubbles which rose upwards from the bottom of his beer glass, up until they became one with the frothy head.

Images of Titia haunted his every moment. Sleep was something he snatched in ten-or fifteen-minute dozes. The pictures his mind conjured up were a mixture of her disjointed corpse laid bare on the mortuary table and that of the living, breathing Titia, neither one any more bearable than the other. Occasional snippets of the drunk from the hospital interrupted or weaved around his thoughts of Titia. The changes in the man's features as he pounded his fist indiscriminately into the drunk's face. Even the putrid smells accompanied the images sometimes. The rancid drunk, the disinfectant from the morgue, all the odours, pungent and clear, as if he was still there, witnessing each moment again and again. Titia's perfume seemed linked to the visions of her alive. Sometimes in the night, exhausted from lack of sleep, Louis had looked around the house, just to check he wasn't in some awful nightmare, hoping to walk into a room and find his wife sitting there waiting for him.

A regular in the pub asked Mo, the barmaid, 'Isn't that the bloke who beat that tramp up in hospital?'

'Yeah, he's been in here every day for the past week. Just sits by that fire, doesn't talk, except to order a beer, and walks out at closing. Well, more like falls out into a taxi,' Mo replied.

'Shame though.'

'What is?' the regular asked inquisitively.

'Well, he lost his wife, didn't he? She was the third one they found chopped up.'

'Really?'

'Yeah, poor bugger. Gives me the shivers just thinking about it. They found her in bits in the stream, you know, the one that runs through the woods.'

The regular, Jed, looked over towards Louis.

'What's he drink? I think I'll buy the poor bugger a beer.'

Louis finished his drink. As he placed it carefully onto a red beer mat, another pint was plonked heavily onto the table.

'There you go, you look like you could use another one.' A man was patting Louis on the back in a friendly manner and placing the beer in front of him.

'Mo just told me about your wife. Sorry to hear

about that. Sick bastards, they want bloody hanging. Anyway, that one's on me. Jed's the name, and if you ever want to talk… well, I'm usually in here.' Jed finished quickly, looking uncomfortable, and stepped back half a pace.

'Thanks for the beer,' said Louis, grasping the glass in his right hand. His gaze moved from the old glass to this new full pint, and once more he became transfixed by the bubbles floating up the inside of his golden drink. His sea of thoughts quickly returned to his gallery of haunting images.

'If only this was TV,' Louis said quietly in his slurred, half-drunken tones. 'At least then I could turn the fucking thing off. Why don't you leave me alone?' His voice increased slightly in volume.

'Go on, fuck off, leave me alone. You and the drunk.' His speech became even louder and the words he was stringing together were slurred and elongated.

'Hey, Mo, how many has he had?' enquired Jed, feeling quite sorry for Louis since hearing his story.

'With that one you just got him, about twelve or so.'

'Jesus, no wonder he's slurring his words,' replied Jed. He continued, 'Right, call us a taxi, Mo. I'll get the poor bugger home before he drinks himself to death right there next to your fire.'

'Aren't we the good Samaritan. Since when did you give a toss about the other pissheads in this place?' Mo said, mocking him.

'Look, just book the taxi will you, and I'll get him to finish his beer.'

'Alright, keep your hair on.'

Jed sat down beside Louis and tapped the table. Louis's eyes rolled in his head as he looked up from his pint glass and attempted to focus on Jed.

'Come on, drink up, we've just ordered you a taxi to take you home.' Jed spoke slowly and quite loud, as if talking to someone hard of hearing.

'Who are you?' Louis demanded.

'My name is Jed. I bought you the beer.'

'Thanks for the beer.' Louis raised his hand, then dropped it heavily back onto the table.

'Come on, drink up,' Jed urged.

Jed grabbed Louis's left arm and hoisted him to his feet.

'Wait, wait, wait, I've got to finish my beer,' Louis insisted, once again raising his hand. Jed watched Louis as he sat back down, he began swirling his beer around in the pint glass, first one way, then the other, he did this for a few minutes and seemed to Jed to be struggling to control his hand as it turned. Then he tipped what was left of the golden liquid down his throat.

'Now you've finished,' Jed said with a chuckle, amused by Louis's antics.

'Jed, the taxi is here,' Mo shouted.

'Perfect timing, come on, the taxi's this way.'

Jed, a slightly built man, struggled, but just managed to get Louis into the taxi.

'Where to?' asked the driver.

'Where do you live?' enquired Jed.

'On the hill.'

'Which hill?'

'The hill,' retorted Louis bluntly. Jed stared, shocked, as the taxi took them both away from the pub. The hill was a place outside town where, to the best of Jed's knowledge, a handful of extremely wealthy people lived, surrounded by woods and beautiful scenery for as far as they cared to look, but this drunken, slurring mess surely didn't live up there, thought Jed, hoping he wasn't heading into trouble.

The houses on the hill were named, and all the taxi drivers knew which was located where.

'Which one are you?' asked the driver sarcastically.

'Five Acres,' replied Louis, half-asleep. The driver nodded, and as the taxi pulled up outside two huge black gates, Louis fumbled in his pocket. He pointed a very neat, small remote control at the gates and pressed. The gates swung open slowly, graciously.

'Flash git,' mumbled the driver.

Jed sat silent, looking out through his window at the palatial residence of the drunken man sprawled beside him. Four massive floodlights sat on the ground facing up at the huge home, bathing it in a flattering glow.

'How much?' asked Louis.

The driver looked round, glaring at Jed with

frustrated eyes.

'Twenty-two quid thanks,' he muttered.

'Twenty-two.' Louis fumbled with the money he'd drawn from his pocket. 'Oh, here, have twenty-five. Are you gonna have a beer with me?' Louis asked Jed as he paid the cabbie.

'Yes, why not?' replied an awestruck Jed.

They got out of the taxi and Jed closed the car door and as the cab turned around and disappeared down the driveway, Louis muttered, 'I'm sure they normally charge thirty-five for that trip… oh well.' He shrugged and staggered to the front door.

As they walked into the huge house Jed's amazement grew. It was immaculately clean and decorated in the most exquisite patterns and colours he had ever seen.

'Are these paintings—?'

'Originals… yes, mostly,' interrupted a very drunk Louis, waving a disinterested hand towards the large pieces of artwork that hung precisely on the high walls.

Louis staggered, right arm outstretched, feeling the wall for security as he made his way to the living room.

Jed watched as Louis made his way across the room, noticing the vast expanse of pale timber which covered the floor. He stopped momentarily to kiss a baby held by a carved woman, which stood at the side of a long leather sofa.

'Grab a couple of beers and come in,' said Louis warmly.

Jed did as instructed. A young man in his mid-twenties, Jed was overwhelmed and slightly intimidated by the vastness of Louis's home. He found his way to the kitchen and removed two bottles of beer from a wide, well-stocked silver fridge. As he walked from the kitchen he caught a glimpse of his reflection in the door of a glass display cabinet. He paused, turned and looked at his handsome dark-haired reflection, then cast his gaze around the more than impressive kitchen in which he stood. He tried to imagine owning and living in a house like this, with its vast rooms and gorgeous furniture.

'This room alone must have cost a fortune,' he whispered to himself.

At the far end of the room stood a solid oak table surrounded by eight heavily carved, decorative chairs. On the wall to his left were several heavy-looking cupboards, all with polished silver handles, and in each available space sat an appliance that matched its setting. Everything was in its place and everything was spotlessly clean.

Jed turned and made his way back to the lounge, where a half-asleep Louis was lying on a long ivory sofa, one leg along the back of the seat, the other with his foot on the floor. His eyes flickered open as Jed approached with his bottle of beer.

'Ah, marvellous, the only thing in this world you can rely on, cold beer.' Louis raised his bottle and downed half of its contents in one go.

'So, young Jed,' he slurred, 'why did you bring

me home?'

'I thought you'd had enough,' replied Jed hesitantly.

'Ah, ah, ah, naughty boy, telling such lies.' Louis waved a finger, attempting to focus on Jed. 'The real reason.'

'I'm sorry, I don't follow.'

'I saw the way you looked at me in that pub.' Louis's drunken speech was slow but still coherent.

'I-I…' Jed flushed and took a gulp from his bottle,

'Shh, don't say any more. Just come and sit down, here,' Louis drawled as he patted the sofa.

Jed did as instructed. He sat as close to Louis as he dared, his heart racing. The sweat from his palms was making it difficult to hold on to his bottle.

'Closer,' said Louis, attempting to drag Jed along the seat towards him.

'Now, put that bottle down, and take advantage of a drunken man,' Louis commanded.

Jed drank the last drop of his beer, leaned across towards Louis and kissed him, a full, passionate kiss, and within moments Louis's trousers were open. As both of Matthews' hands ran erratically through Jed's hair and the younger man tugged at Louis's clothes, he pushed Jed's head down, down past his unfastened shirt. Once more, Jed did as commanded, taking Louis in his mouth as the older of the two escaped his world of mental torture temporarily, completely lost in the ecstasy of the moment and the warmth of the younger man.

36

The mail arrived promptly on the cold winter morning, dumped in a disorderly pile on Marie Carlton's desk. She flicked randomly through the envelopes, most of which were embossed with stamps from various police forces around the country. There was one in particular that stood out. It had no postmark and the font blazoned across the front of the envelope was stencilled in block capitals and said:

FOR THE PRIVATE AND EXCLUSIVE ATTENTION OF
DI LOMAS BAXTER AND
DC DREW TAYLOR

Marie reached out a slender finger and punched Lomas's extension number into her telephone. As she sat waiting for an answer, she flipped the envelope, looking first at the back, then the front, then she placed it in the centre of her desk.

Lomas strolled to his desk in quite a relaxed mood. Victoria Kemp was safe and well, Jackson was in the cells, everything was going well, at last. DCI Carlton's name displayed on his phone as he lifted the handset.

'Morning, ma'am, how are you?' he asked cheerily.

'I'll tell you in about five minutes. Could you come up please, Lomas?'

'Yeah, sure, I'll be right there.'

A mild curiosity crept over him as he climbed the familiar stairs to Marie's office. Her tone had been tense and clipped, not her usual style. He knocked politely and then entered.

'What can I do for you?' he enquired with a quizzical look.

'This arrived in the post,' replied Marie, pointing to the envelope.

Lomas's gaze followed her indication.

'I thought we could open it and see why there was a need for privacy,' said Marie.

Lomas's look changed immediately from cheery and curious to deadly serious and intense.

'Lomas… Lomas, are you all right?' Marie asked, noticing his change of expression.

'No, I don't think I am,' he replied, running his left hand through his hair. 'It's him. It's the same stencilling we've had on every note.'

'But Jackson's in the cells,' Marie retorted.

'I know. We'd better see what he has to say.'

Lomas picked up Marie's phone and called down to the incident room for someone to bring a pair of gloves, some tweezers and some evidence bags to DCI Carlton's office.

A breathless young officer, who, from the

flushed look on his face, had clearly run through the station, knocked at Carlton's door. Lomas opened the door, took the items from the officer, thanked him, and closed the door. He put the gloves on. Next, he carefully picked up the envelope as if it were made of the finest china. Baxter picked along the gummed edge of the envelope with the tweezers, gently teasing the white paper pouch open. Then slowly he removed two sheets of plain white paper, stapled together with a single staple through the top left corner. He placed the envelope in a clear evidence bag and then carefully laid the letter down on top of another clear plastic bag. Both sheets carried stencilled blue lettering.

To get a better view, Marie moved around the desk and stood beside Lomas who started to read aloud.

'DI Baxter and DC Taylor,
You'd better go and tell the jailor,
To release poor Jackson, poor, poor man,
He's not your killer 'cause I am.
You thought you caught me, found my lair,
But were too slow to catch me there.
I've moved around and now I'm back,
To carry on and spring my traps.
The girls so far were only toys,
There'll be more girls, no time for boys.
My precious van you'll never find,
I've changed the plates time after time,
I lie in wait and watch my prey.

You catch me? no how, no way.
Christina Marley got away,
But I'll be back for her some day.
You see, I choose who, when and how,
And so I'll tell you who I've got now.
She's five foot one, with curly brown hair,
All strapped down and really scared.
I like to leave her in cold and dark,
Her name is, Elinor, Mary, Clarke.
Oh damn, oh well, oh I don't care,
I've told you now, no time to spare,
Go tell her folks, so they can mourn,
That soon will die, what once was born.
Their little girl with curly locks,
I'll chop her up, into a box,
I'll mail her back, though bit by bit,
You put them together, make them fit.
I've got to go now, Lomas and Drew,
No time to stop and talk to you.
No nearer now, than when commenced,
The gap between us grows immense.
No hint, or clue, to light your day,
For I don't play the game that way.
I'll see you soon, you won't know where,
I'll stand and look, or sit and stare.'

A shiver ran down Marie Carlton's back as Lomas reached the end of the twisted verse. Her steely blue eyes had been fixed on Lomas from the outset. She had watched the disappointment and rage well up in his face as he read. The narrowing of his eyes at each reference to the victims, and the look of horror that passed over his countenance as he narrated the identity of a victim who until that moment had been unknown. Marie watched in silence as Lomas slid the sheets containing the poem into the larger bag, being careful not to let it come into contact with anything else.

'Bollocks!' he exclaimed loudly. 'All this time, Jackson's been the key focus and he's the wrong man.'

As Lomas uncharacteristically paced her office, Marie grew concerned.

'Lomas, are you going to be OK?'

'I've got to catch him, Marie. I've got to get him before he kills another one. I can't rest, won't rest, until he's banged up!' he raged.

'Lomas, calm down. First, let's get Drew up here. Then we'd better assemble the troops,' she said calmly.

'I thought I'd got him Marie. I so thought Jackson was the one. How could I be so blinded by one suspect?' Lomas continued, apparently oblivious to Marie's attempt at guidance.

'We all thought Jackson was the one. Let's check this out before we make any hasty moves, we don't know that it wasn't sent by someone who knows Jackson.' Marie said.

'No Marie, it's him, the one we've been hunting, and it's not Jackson. I was wrong and now he's got another one.'

Once again, Marie reached for her phone. This

time it was Drew's number she dialled.

'Drew, DCI Carlton, could you come up immediately please?'

Without waiting for confirmation, Marie cut the call short. Turning back to Lomas, who was still pacing in a rage, she spoke quietly, but firmly, taking control of the situation. 'Lomas, please sit. Drew's on her way up and I need you to put this to her your way. She's a committed girl and will be just as disappointed as you by all this, so I need you at your best.'

Baxter nodded, rubbing his hands together and taking a deep breath. 'Sorry for ranting at you Marie.'

'No need to apologise. It's been an emotional investigation and I know how much you've got invested in this, and with Heidi and the kids being away, it can't be easy.'

He smiled, seeming slightly embarrassed by his outburst, and then took another deep breath.

Drew bounded up the stairs, knocked and entered. She was immediately hit by the sombre atmosphere that seemed to consume the room.

'Take a seat please, Drew.' Marie motioned to a leather chair next to Lomas.

'We received this in the post this morning, addressed to you and I,' said Lomas, handing the bagged letter to Drew.

Drew's eyes widened as she carefully read the printed verse. She eased forward onto the edge of her seat and a look of anguish crossed her face.

'No, this is not… I mean, it can't be… The stencilled lettering is the same as on the other poems… It is, isn't it?' Her speech was fast, yet disjointed, and her eyes filled with dread.

'Who's Elinor Clarke?' she continued.

'We don't know yet,' replied Lomas.

'That's the first thing we need you to do, Drew,' Marie interrupted.

'Yes, of course. I'll get on it straight away, ma'am.'

Drew stood and went to leave, feeling deflated and aware of a growing concern for whoever Elinor Mary Clarke was.

'Are you all right?' Lomas asked as Drew reached the door.

'Yes, I'll be fine. Back to square one I suppose sir,' she replied, her voice weighed down with disappointment.

'Call me the minute you find out who she is and where she's from, yes?'

'Yes, boss.'

'And Drew.'

'Yes boss?'

'Keep this to yourself for now. I don't want to wind everyone up until we know what we're dealing with.'

'Got it.'

Drew closed the door behind her and walked to the nearest toilet. Once inside she locked the door, turned her back to it, clenched her fists and beat them on the side of the cubicle in utter frustration.

37

Lomas placed the bag containing the letter carefully on Marie's desk and looked towards her for help with a solution to the next problem.

'Jackson.' Marie sighed heavily, crossing her fingers under her chin.

'We need to sit on this for a few hours. At least until we can confirm that it's for real,' Lomas said, pointing at the letter.

'Yes, you're right, but be quick. If this is the real thing, not only do we have a fresh victim, but also an apology to make to our Mr Jackson.'

'Gordon-Thomas will have a field day with this. I gave Jackson a proper going over in questioning.'

'We'll cross that bridge if and when we come to it. For now, Elinor Mary Clarke is the priority. If this is for real we need to find her and find her quick.'

The urgency in Marie Carlton's voice spoke volumes. The embarrassment she would endure if the letter wasn't a hoax would be huge. First another woman was at risk of suffering who-knew what atrocities, then the press, then Gordon-Thomas, and not to mention the hierarchy to whom she would have to explain their actions. All these were reasons Lomas had never craved the role

Marie held, never envied her position in the slightest. As a DI he got to more or less run his investigations as he liked, which meant being involved at ground level. All the politics he quite happily left to Marie.

After leaving DCI Carlton's office, Lomas headed off to drop the note into forensics for analysis. Once he'd handed it over and made the team suitably aware of the urgency in processing it, he went across the station in search of Drew. He had no time to sit around and wait for her to bring him information on Elinor Clarke. He walked into the office where Drew was, just as she put down the phone.

'Well, what have we got?' he asked her.

'Elinor's mum, who is now panicking, says that Elinor and two friends flew to Spain a few days ago on holiday and are due back in four hours time.'

'So we get someone to meet her flight at the airport. Did you get a description?'

'Yes, twenty-five years old, five foot one, with long, curly brown hair.'

'OK,' Lomas said, 'so she matches the description in the letter. I still want someone at the airport waiting for her, and hopefully her friends, fresh back from a break in the sun.'

'I'll see to it now boss.' Drew turned away and picked up the phone again.

38

Elinor Mary Clarke was woken abruptly by a savage punch to her right eye. Too shocked to scream, a quiet moan was all she could muster. This too was met with a vicious blow, this time to her jaw.

'Shut the fuck up, you moaning bitch,' said a harsh voice.

A gloved hand, which smelled of leather, was pushed hard onto her eyes, forcing her eyeballs back in their sockets, the glove seams digging into cuts on her cheekbones. She writhed in agony.

'First, I think a gag, because the last thing I want to do is listen to your whingeing.' The voice became more sarcastic.

Elinor's mouth was forced open and a soft cotton rag was jammed inside. She drew in a sharp breath through her nose and tried in vain to shake her head free, but the grip over her eyes tightened, fingertips digging into her left temple. The pain enflamed a panic within her and she attempted once more to struggle free, violently kicking and punching, trying desperately to liberate herself from her manacles, but all to no avail. Her struggle merely caused her more pain as her sore wrists and ankles rubbed against their bindings.

'My, we are a feisty little devil, aren't we? Just think, all that energy and having to lie on this bed all day. Oh well, what a pity.' Elinor's jailer laughed, a loud, booming laugh that seemed to hang in the air.

Elinor trembled. She felt alone and afraid, and she had a nagging fear that no one was going to find her, no one was going to come and save her. As her overwhelming sense of dread grew, a strong smell like bleach or disinfectant filled air. Then Elinor felt a wet cloth of some kind placed on her midsection. Her assailant moved it around as if unfolding it.

The smell grew more intense, and then, with no warning, the hand, which until now had been pinning her head down, was wrenched away and the cold bleach-covered cloth was dropped onto Elinor's face. At first it felt like ice, and then she screamed a muffled scream through her gag as the bleach burned into each open wound on her battered face. The pain was more severe than anything she had ever experienced, and before long, Elinor's head fell loosely to the side as she slipped into unconsciousness.

'Well, you're no fuckin fun, are you? If you're going to pass out every time you feel a little bit of pain, this won't be any fun at all.' The voice was jovial and spoken as if in dialogue with a friend. A couple of light slaps broke the momentary silence in the room. Elinor's cheek contorted at the impact, but she didn't regain consciousness. A harder smack struck the left side of the young woman's face and her head flopped dramatically to the right, but still no reaction came.

'Fuckin' wake up, you bitch!' Still nothing.

'Oh fuck it, stay asleep then. There'll be plenty of time to play later.'

With that, Elinor Mary Clarke's assailant turned and left her alone and battered in the darkness.

39

Flight 215 from Mallorca had touched down fifteen minutes after Nick Swaine had got to Southampton airport arrivals. A steady stream of travellers returning from foreign holidays and business-suited executives who looked like they spent their lives in terminals trooped through the airport. They took a well-trodden path towards waiting taxi drivers and smiling family members, squealing with open arms for their homecoming clan.

In the short time he'd been there, Nick had managed to find out from the flight records that Elinor Clarke hadn't boarded just days earlier. He only needed what he expected to be verbal confirmation from her two friends that she hadn't been on holiday with them.

This confirmation came in the form of two tanned women in their mid-twenties, confused at their friend's failure to get to the airport, but joking that Elinor had probably met a bloke the night before they were due to leave and spent a weekend in bed.

'Elinor hasn't been seen since the day you flew to Mallorca,' Nick told them. 'Did she have any regular boyfriends that maybe her mum didn't know about?'

The girls were looking increasingly concerned. They shook their heads.

'No, no one I can think of,' they said, almost as one.

'What kind of trouble is she in?' asked Gabrielle, the taller of the two.

'We don't know if she is yet. We just need to find her as soon as possible. If you could tell me about anyone who Elinor may have been with over the last few days, it would be very helpful.'

The girls both scanned their mobile phones, giving Nick a list of people to contact.

'Thank you for your help. I'd better let you get home, please get in touch if you think of anywhere else she may have gone, or anyone else Elinor may have stayed with.' Said Nick, passing the girls his card.

'You'll let us know if you find her, won't you?' said Gabrielle in a rather shaky voice.

'Try not to worry,' he reassured her. Nick smiled, turned, and walked quickly out of earshot of the girls.

He called Lomas on his mobile phone.

'Hello boss, it's Nick. No joy at the airport. She didn't fly out, and her friends haven't seen or heard from her since the day before they flew.'

'OK, Nick, well done. Get yourself back here as quick as you can.'

'Will do boss.'

Lomas ran up the narrow grey staircase to Marie Carlton's office. He knocked and opened the door.

'All right, Lomas, we treat the letter as the real thing. Get every available person on this. We need a result yesterday.' Her instructions were both calm and direct, capturing the full gravity of the situation, aware of both the pressure from above to find the killer and the media storm that was being whipped up around the victims and their families.

The briefing room was buzzing with thirty or more separate conversations as Lomas opened the door and entered. Unusually, the room didn't come to an immediate hush as Baxter walked through the door. Instead, many of Lomas's colleagues and junior officers commented quietly on how tired he was looking.

He was. The strain of the last few weeks were taking their toll. Lomas felt jaded. The investigation was draining him of his energy, sapping his inspiration and depriving him of sleep. The uncompromising way with which he handled these large cases meant that every waking hour was concentrated on reaching his objective. This in turn led to his waking hours getting longer as the hunt went on. Like a lion hunting its prey, Lomas's focus never wavered.

'Right, people!' he barked as he approached the front of the room. 'We have a situation. As I'm sure you are aware, we have another missing woman. A picture is being circulated. Please take a copy and commit her face to memory. Now, in addition to this we also have a letter from our killer claiming to have this woman. Her name is Elinor Mary Clarke, and he claims to be holding her. Not only has he told us he's holding her, but also that he intends to kill her and dispose of her in pieces.' Lomas paused, drew in a deep breath, his head tipped back slightly and his eyes closed for a second. He continued, his voice rising to a near shout.

'This is not acceptable. *We will not lose this girl.*' Each word was heavily emphasised, driving his point home. The anger that had built within Lomas during the course of this investigation bubbled at the surface for all to see.

'I don't care if we have to knock on every door in this city, we will find Elinor Clarke before it's too late. Do I make myself clear?' His piercing eyes scanned the room and was met with nods of acknowledgement. His instructions were crystal clear.

'He will not claim a sixth trophy,'

'Don't you mean fifth?' a young officer in the middle of the room said.

'And how do you make it five?' Lomas replied, the intensity still audible.

'Well, er, only that, er, we got Christina Marley out, sir.'

'So you think that just because he didn't kill Miss Marley that she isn't a victim? That she has no psychological scars to carry? Because she's not dead, she doesn't count? Is that where your thinking is taking you?'

'Er, no, of course not, sorry, sir.' The officer quickly apologised, probably hoping it would be enough for Lomas's focus to shift from him. DI Baxter glared at the officer but said no more on the matter, confident that his point had been made. He moved on.

'You will take your individual briefs from DC Taylor and I want everyone's best efforts. Ladies, gentlemen,' his tone softened, 'I know how hard you're all working and that we all want the same result, so good luck.' He walked quickly from the briefing room, and as the door closed behind him, the buzz started once more.

40

Jed smoothed his hand through Louis Matthews' fine wispy blonde hair. The sun streamed in through thin cream bedroom curtains, and a solitary shaft of sunlight gently kissed the forehead of the sleeping Louis.

Jed cast his gaze around the beautifully furnished room. Freestanding finely crafted oak chests stood at each side of an equally elegant triple wardrobe with ornate black hinges and handles. A highly polished wooden floor ran the length and breadth of the room, the centrepiece of which was a monstrously large four poster bed, complete with fine ivory-coloured lace drapes. This is where Jed lay alongside Louis in a dreamy make-believe state.

Louis reached up with his left hand and brushed Jed's hand from his hair, and still sleeping, he rolled towards the centre of the bed. He stopped and woke as his hip made contact with Jed's knee.

'Morning,' greeted Jed cheerily.

'Who the hell are you?' came the impromptu reply.

Jed looked confused and shocked. He paused for a moment. This was a moment too long for the impatient and hungover Louis.

'Didn't you hear me? Who the fuck are you?

Why are you?' He stopped and rubbed his forehead. Leaning back on one elbow, he continued.

'No wait, I remember now. The pub. You're the one who bought me a beer.'

'Then I called you a taxi and brought you home.'

'And you invited yourself in.'

'No, no, it wasn't like that. You asked me in,' Jed insisted.

'Hmm, so let's suppose I invited you in, and then what, we ended up in bed together? OK, well now it's morning and I'm not pissed any more, so be a good chap, get dressed, call yourself a taxi and go, would you?' His manner was curt and patronising.

Jed's confusion turned to a mixture of anger and embarrassment. He was miles from home in a stranger's bed, being treated like a cheap whore. Quickly, he got out of bed and gathered up his clothes.

'Do you mind if I stay long enough to get washed and dressed?' he asked sarcastically.

'If you really must, there's a bathroom down the hall to your right, but do be quick,' replied Louis condescendingly.

Jed hurried from the room naked, clutching his clothes in a bundle in front of him. He made his way into the sumptuous bathroom to which Louis had directed him and found himself standing on a marble floor flanked by a white bathroom suite with rose gold fittings, copper-tinted mirrors and the most sophisticated lighting he'd ever seen. He turned two large taps protruding from the wall and a ceiling shower sprang into action.

'You fucking idiot, Jed,' he mumbled to himself. 'How the fuck could you land yourself in this position?'

By the time he'd showered and dressed, Louis was downstairs. As he made his way down, Jed marvelled at the huge paintings that hung on the walls. He saw Louis walking through into the living room. Once again he stopped and kissed the baby's head on the statue beside his sofa, just as he had done the previous night.

'Bloody fruitcake,' Jed muttered under his breath, utterly disenamoured with his begrudging host.

Louis glanced round but didn't make the effort to turn fully, instead calling over his shoulder. 'I've called you a taxi. It'll be here any minute. You'll have to meet it at the end of the driveway. Oh, there's some money on the table beside the front door for your fare.'

Without a word, Jed turned on his heels and headed to the door. He looked at the money on the table. *Fifty pounds, more than double the taxi fare,* he thought.

Jed opened the door and closed it gently behind him as he left.

Louis waited a few moments and then walked through the house towards the front door. The money still lay on the table, untouched.

'Unappreciative prick,' said Louis in mock

disgust. He turned and walked back to the living room, taking a swig of his first beer of the day.

Jed's taxi ride back home was one which left him feeling used and embarrassed. He was dreading showing his face in the pub for fear of ridicule and the ribbing he knew he would get from Mo if she got wind of how his night and subsequent morning had unravelled.

41

As Elinor regained a more lasting consciousness, she became aware of a tight binding that was covering the bridge of her nose, extending up to the top of her forehead. This, together with an intense throbbing coming from her brow, triggered tiny explosions of pain, a scraping, scratching pain that she felt she had endured yet couldn't clearly remember. She tried in vain to open her eyes but her blindfold was far too tight to allow it. The same bleach-like smell as the day before lingered, and as she lay there, she became more aware of different pains around her face and jaw. Still gagged, but now with tape, Elinor breathed heavily through her nose, drawing in every breath as if it were her last.

She heard a click from what sounded like across the room: a light switch. Elinor tensed with fear, and although her eyes were closed, she tightened them shut even more. Clenching both fists, she lay still, too petrified to move.

'Good morning, Miss Clarke,' said a chirpy voice, familiar in pitch, but the bright cheeriness was something Elinor hadn't heard before.

'I hope you slept well. Oh, and I do hope you like your blindfold. Just to help you sleep, you understand.' Her attacker shifted to a more recognisable, but terrifying, sarcasm.

Elinor remained motionless. Not a nod or shake of her head, even to acknowledge her captor.

'Well, what a fun-packed day we have for you today.' The jaunty tone returned. 'Let me see, what first? No, no, yes, that's it – an anaesthetic-free amputation. That should do nicely.'

A cold chill ran through Elinor Mary Clarke as she lay helpless, unable to forestall what was about to happen to her.

The voice continued, but this time it was much quieter and closer, close to Elinor's right ear.

'But which limb? They all appear healthy. I tell you what, you choose. Shake the limb you'd least like to keep.'

Elinor lay paralysed by fear.

'Oh, go on, don't be a spoilsport. There must be one you're less fond of. Maybe one of your legs that always aches after you've played netball, or whatever it is you do. Or maybe, just maybe, one of your arms that gets in the way when you're lying on your side in bed, trying to get to sleep. No? Oh well, let me choose then. Eeny, meeny, miney, mo, one of you will have to go. Excellent choice, but I know, we'll keep it as a surprise… for you, that is.' The whisper resonated in Elinor's head.

In a wild panic she thrashed around as much as her restraints would allow, throwing her head from side to side, kicking with her feet and yanking at the manacles holding her wrists. She tried frantically to extricate herself from her restraints.

The pain inside her head magnified with the thumping of her ever-increasing heart rate. Fear coursed through her.

It's no good, she thought, *I can't get free, he's going to chop my leg off, I just know it.* She tried desperately to block thoughts and images of her family, who would be desperate to know where she was, but the darkness was like a fresh clear page for the images to sketch themselves on. Elinor's tightly closed eyes welled with stinging tears, carving a salty path through tiny cuts from their outer corners. Her hearing had become ultra-receptive, and she caught the sound of a plug being quietly clipped into its socket and then an item of some description clanging against a surface.

'Oh, silly me, we must adjust your restraints first.' Once again, the voice was laced with mockery.

Elinor felt the shackles on her right ankle loosen, only to be re-attached above her knee. A strong hand gripped her foot tightly and pushed it down hard against the rough wooden bed.

'Now, Elinor dear, brace yourself… or not, it really doesn't matter.'

As a sound of something spinning cut the brief silence, Elinor wailed inwardly. However pointless, she pleaded in her thoughts for her attacker to spare her.

Please don't kill me. Please, please don't kill me…

She tensed her already sore limbs, and as she did,

she felt a cold slicing sensation just above her right knee. She shook her head frantically in a futile effort to stop her barbaric assailant, but the amputation carried on regardless of her protestations. A sharp pain shot up her leg as the blade cut into the bone, and the agony was virtually unbearable, but it was over quickly. Elinor clenched her teeth inside her gag as hard as she could, and despite the severity of the pain, she remained conscious throughout, fully aware and feeling every incision.

A dressing was quickly applied to the open wound, and Elinor's nerve endings transferred every painful moment to her brain. Finally, after what she could only assume was packing and a bandage dressing being tightly applied, then the remainder of her upper leg having something like a pillow wedged under it, it was over. Resigned to her fate, she lay her head slowly to her left and rested. There was a strange feeling coming from the freshly severed limb, a tingly yet intense sensation. She was also convinced she could still feel her toes, and even wiggle them. Elinor allowed herself a subdued cry, half of her relieved to still be alive, the other half petrified of what was still to come.

42

Drew woke early. Morning had come far too quickly and her need for sleep was growing as the case wore on. The investigation was two months down the line and still she felt like they were no closer to catching the maniac. Drew also saw the toll the investigation was taking on Lomas. His usual calm demeanour had evaded him on more than one occasion and she knew without asking that not seeing Heidi and the kids every day was proving hard for him. This was a side to the boss she hadn't seen before. His collected, measured professionalism was one of the things she admired about him. Even when chaos seemed to be reigning all around, Lomas was calm and sure of the next steps to take.

Her involvement in the case, however, was something in which Drew was revelling. It had involved a learning curve steeper than any she could have imagined and the contact she was having with all the families was keeping her focussed on the main objective.

Lomas had told her at the start how easy it was to get distracted by side issues and how her focus should stay on catching the killer. His wisdom, as always, had been absorbed and stored by his young protégé.

A bang on the front door disturbed her thoughts, and she finished a golden piece of lightly buttered toast as she opened the door. No one was there to receive her cheerful greeting as she swung the door open expecting to see a postman. Instead, propped against the wall of the corridor was a plain box. As Drew picked the package up, she noticed writing on its side. In black, very neatly stencilled letters, it said: 'DC Drew Taylor RIP'.

Drew ran to the window of her flat hoping to see who had delivered the box but could see no one. She leapt over a small coffee table and ran through the open door, using the wall opposite the door to change direction as she hurtled down the stairs three at a time. Bursting through the main door to her block of flats, she ran out onto the street, looking in both directions, scanning the area for the deliverer of the box. She saw nothing out of the ordinary. No one was hurrying away, nobody jumping into a waiting car, nothing.

She ran her hands through her red hair, frustrated, and turned back towards the building. Returning to her flat and the waiting package, she went to a work bag and retrieved a pair of latex gloves, snapped them onto her small hands and sat down at a table. She lifted and began turning the box, rotating it slowly, looking for anything which might indicate its contents. Without another thought, she placed the box on the table and called Lomas.

Forty minutes later, Drew's flat was a hive of activity. Grayson Washington and his forensic team, in their customary white suits, dusted the area outside the front of her flat where she'd found the box. Meanwhile, inside, it seemed everyone had looked at the box, which was now laid out on a plastic sheet.

'Aren't we going to open it, boss?' asked Drew, curious to see what was inside.

'Well, if it's from who we think then we'd best take our time and let Sherlock do the opening,' replied Lomas, his gaze unshifting from the wording he had been studying for some time.

'He's not stupid, you know, our man, not at all. Always stencils everything. Must take him ages,' he continued.

Sherlock sat down and carefully ran a blade under the sealed, longer edge of the box, taking great pains not to disturb anything but the glue that held it in place.

'Nearly there,' he said quietly.

He pulled back the two flaps to reveal blood-soaked bubble wrap and an envelope sealed in a plastic bag marked 'Drew'.

'You're popular today,' said Sherlock, glancing up at Drew as he placed the bag outside the box, onto the plastic. He turned back to the main package and nodded to one of his team to photograph the box and its contents. Then he proceeded to slowly remove the wrapping, carefully taking out a raw-looking limb.

As he opened up the wrapping, Sherlock said, 'It looks fresh, Lomas, I'd say not more than a couple of hours, and very neatly cut as usual.'

'Surgical saw?' DI Baxter asked.

'Yep, looks like it. I'll have to get it back and run all the tests, but it looks like your man's handiwork.'

'OK, thanks. Can I borrow some gloves to read this note please?'

'Yeah, sure, they're in my bag,' Sherlock replied, nodding towards a case on the floor.

'Come on then, Drew, let's see what our friend wants to say to you so badly.' Lomas walked to Drew's sofa and sat with DC Taylor beside him. He opened the letter out slowly, faint stencilled lettering already visible through the paper.

He read it aloud.

'Hope you like your present, Drew.
Maybe next time it could be you.
Elinor Clarke is minus a leg,
Next her arms, then her head.'

Drew shivered as Lomas read her name from the note. She put her arms across her chest and rubbed her shoulders as if to warm herself.

'You OK?' asked Lomas

'Yeah, yeah, I'm fine. It just sounds weird having my name read from one of his notes.'

'Yes, I know what you mean,' Lomas said, sighing. He turned and passed the note to Sherlock after dropping it into a plastic bag.

'It's our man all right, but run your tests anyway.' He raised his eyebrows. Despondency filled his voice.

Lomas patted Drew on the knee and then he stood up and walked over to the forensic team busying themselves around the doorway.

'There was a time when none of this affected him.' Sherlock's impromptu comment caught Drew's attention.

'What do you mean?' asked Drew, only too aware of Sherlock's meaning.

'All these girls dying, the time it's taking to catch him, and now this – one of his own directly threatened. You can see it in his face. It's really getting to him, and I've never seen that in all the years I've known him. I've never seen him affected so acutely.'

Drew cast a glance over her shoulder at Lomas. He was crouched in her doorway talking to a man in a white overall, trying to glean any information that might help in catching the maniac before another helpless girl died.

43

'No I will not take DI Baxter off this case, sir!' Marie Carlton slammed her hand on a polished wooden desk in protest.

Superintendent Randolph, her superior, sat behind his desk, chubby fingers crossed together and thumb tips placed firmly against his chin. Bringing his index fingers slowly to a point, he lowered his hands.

'I understand your loyalty, Marie, and heaven knows I have a massive amount of respect for DI Baxter's ability, but I just think that once the Jackson episode gets out, and get out it will, well, let's just say I think it may be prudent to have a new driver on the bus.'

'You mean hang Lomas out to dry as the scapegoat. Blame it all on DI Baxter and let the force save face. Well, sorry, sir, but I don't believe in public sacrifice and I don't believe Lomas Baxter should take the fall, or be removed from this investigation.' Marie had made her anger at Randolph's suggestion clear, and as a result he changed tack.

'Very well I can see you're not going to be swayed, so you have it your way, Marie.' He smiled a smarmy self-assured smile.

'Just remember, you are the one steering the boat,' he continued, changing metaphors.

'And when it comes down to it, the captain either goes down with the ship or brings her home safely. Update me if there's any change, or progress, would you please, Marie?'

Randolph picked up a heavy silver pen from the desk and began to flick through some notes that sat in a neat pile in front of him.

Marie stood, and without another word she walked from his office, bubbling with rage at Randolph's suggestions.

Supercilious arsehole, she thought as she walked away from Randolph's office. She slammed her office door behind her and dropped heavily into her chair. Spinning it around to look out of the window, she slammed her palm on the arm of the chair in frustration. She knew how hard Lomas and his team were working on the case, how many hours and sleepless nights had been committed to it already.

How dare he suggest I take Baxter off the case. He should try getting his arse down here and seeing what's going on, instead of hiding behind his desk, shuffling paper. Prick! Marie's internal dialogue fumed.

Intent on not being 'one of those' senior officers, Carlton gave herself a talking to and then went downstairs to the incident room to talk through the investigation with the team.

44

Louis Matthews held two parts of a pastel green cuff together as he pushed a gold cufflink through both. Flicking the clasp with his finger, he tugged on the fastened sleeve. The cuff protruded slightly from the sleeve of a contrasting grey single-breasted suit. He looked himself up and down in the mirror, vaguely pleased for the first time in weeks at the reflection that greeted him. He wore polished black brogues, with his jacket and his shirt collar open, and for the first time in weeks he was cleanly shaven.

Louis had remained sober for the whole day, as he intended driving himself this evening. He went down the stairs and scooped up an array of credit cards and cash that lay on a small round table beside the front door. With his keys spinning around his finger, he closed the heavy front door, making his way to one of four garage doors. The sun was beginning to fade on what had been a bright day and the smell of the lush grounds surrounding his home filled his nostrils as he gave a quick press on a key fob pointed towards the garage door. It opened smoothly, to reveal a gleaming silver Mercedes convertible with the hood already down. As he took his place behind the wheel and the engine fired into life, Louis recalled how much he enjoyed driving, and a brief vision of Titia laughing beside him as they drove with the hood down on a warm sunny afternoon flickered in his memory. The image went as quickly as it had arrived, as the car stereo came on and snapped Louis into the present. He manoeuvred the car out along the driveway, feeling the temperature change as it moved forwards, he closed the roof.

Once on the open road, he guided the silky-smooth car at speed around familiar narrow country lanes. The black leather seats moulded to him as he toyed with S-bends and long narrow curves bordered by bare hedgerows and fields in a variety of hues, all empty except for a few scavenger birds. Louis crested the top of a steep hill and his favourite view of countryside and a wide expanse of water rolled into sight. He took a sharp right and made his way down a private road, easing the volume down on the stereo as he did. Matthews brought the car to a halt outside Pines Restaurant just as the light was beginning to fade completely.

It was an impressive establishment that boasted celebrity diners of all kinds. Louis and Titia had often eaten here. The food, though a touch expensive, was exquisite and the service impeccable. As Louis stepped from the car, a valet greeted him and whisked the Mercedes away to be parked.

A shocked-looking steward met him at the door.

'Good evening, Mr Matthews. How are you?'

'Fine, thank you, William, you?'

'Yes, yes, fine, thank you. Will you be…' His question trailed off, as if he was unsure how to ask Louis if he was eating alone.

'Dining on my own? Yes, thank you, William,' Louis cut in brightly, saving the young man the embarrassment he could see building in his eyes.

'Certainly, of course. This way please. Your usual table?'

'Yes, that would be fine, thank you,' replied Louis, remaining upbeat. 'Tell me, William, is Georgio working this evening?'

'Yes, I think he starts in about half an hour. Would you like me to send him over when he gets here?'

'Could you, please? I haven't seen him in an age… well, since before my wife was…' This time it was Louis who trailed the end of his sentence, disappearing momentarily within his thoughts. The brave public face gone for an instant.

'I'll get you the wine list.'

'No need, my usual red wine will be fine, thank you, William.'

The young steward left Louis sitting alone at a beautifully covered hexagonal table and went to get him a menu.

As Louis sat mulling over his second glass of red wine, after a sublime dinner, a familiar face caught the corner of Louis's eye, a tall, handsome, smoothly groomed man dressed in a crisp white shirt, contrasted by a jet-black bow tie, black trousers and ebony cufflinks, square and flat. Louis cast an admiring glance over the younger man, taking particular note of his lack of enthusiasm upon seeing Louis sat at the table alone.

'Georgio…' Matthews was first to speak.

'Mr Matthews, how are you?' The question was delivered in a flat and uncommonly downbeat tone.

Louis was confused, a frown furrowing his brow.

'Not too bad considering.'

'Yes, it must have been a trying time for you.'

'I haven't seen you for quite a while. How have you been?'

Georgio glanced around the restaurant and leaned his hands on the table next to Louis's elbow. Then he leaned closer to Matthews and spoke quickly in a quiet, almost whispered voice.

'What do you mean, coming in here all cheerful, asking how I've been as if it's only been a matter of days? Well its been weeks and nothing, not a thing. No word, no text. All I get is to read about you in the paper, worrying what you're going through, if I should call, or if the added attention might drive you to do something more…' Georgio paused. 'Something more drastic than just recluse yourself like… well, like some hermit. It wouldn't have hurt you just to call and let me know you were OK.'

Louis sat back, apparently shocked by Georgio's outburst.

'I-I'm sorry. I had no idea. I didn't think… well, I did think about you, but I didn't realise you'd be so worried.'

Georgio glared at Louis.

'You didn't realise? We were lovers, for God's sake. Didn't that mean anything? I worried from the moment I heard,' the younger man stated through gritted teeth.

Louis placed his hand gently on the back of Georgio's clenched fist, which rested on the elegant white tablecloth. Looking around to check no one was watching, he whispered, 'Meet me later, when you've finished. We can talk then if you want to?'

Then he stood up, dropped some money onto a saucer to cover his bill and a tip, and walked slowly from the restaurant without a glance back at the waiter, who watched him, silently, until he was out of sight.

45

Heavy footsteps climbed wooden stairs, clumping one after the other, slowly, deliberately, upwards. A pause at the top, then on towards a half-rotten dark green door, eaten away by years of uncontrolled mite infestation. The stench of mould-ridden fabric and ageing timber saturated the air. A door swung open to reveal the room that contained Elinor Mary Clarke. But Elinor hadn't heard the heavy footfall slowly thumping up the stairs, nor had she heard the click of the old latch as the rotten green door opened. For where Elinor had lain, enduring days of unimaginable suffering and pain, now lay three neatly severed limbs and a bandaged yet equally precisely removed head. Her torso lay as it had in her final moments of life, strapped down to the splintered, blood-soaked bed.

Manacles were hanging empty, and surgical tools had been strewn around the room haphazardly, most still heavily coated in Elinor's blood.

'What, no muffled screaming today, Miss Clarke? Oh, silly me, you're no longer able, sorry. Well, better get you wrapped up, labelled and boxed. Wouldn't want you to catch a chill and be less than perfect upon delivery. We wouldn't want any dissatisfied recipients now, would we? I much prefer delivering your bits, rather than just dumping them here and there. It's so much more final, don't you think? No? Not convinced? Oh well, we can discuss that some more later. There's work to do now.'

The voice boomed around the room with theatrical, overplayed enunciation, gaps between words filled only by the buzzing of small blowflies laying their larvae in the newly deceased flesh of Elinor Mary Clarke ahead of their inevitable feeding frenzy and subsequent entomologist study.

46

Eleven thirty came and went. Louis sat patiently waiting in his car outside Pines. The occasional sweep of headlights from a car leaving the car park illuminated the front of the restaurant. The door to the staff entrance swung open and Louis's pulse quickened, but for nothing. Two chefs laughed and joked as they walked down the path and past his car without giving it a glance.

Five past twelve, and still Louis sat there, his attention glued to the staff entrance, intermittently flicking across to the main entrance so not to miss Georgio leaving by another exit. He felt like a teenager hovering to catch a glimpse of his latest crush. His car stereo played faintly, soft acoustic tunes, broken by deep vocal tones, and a soft light ebbed from the dashboard.

Louis checked his watch. As he glanced back up his attention was caught by a light inside the restaurant being turned off. He glanced back to the staff door and there was Georgio, tie undone, rubbing the back of his neck with his left hand. Georgio looked up and squinted slightly, trying to make out the shape of Louis Matthews' car. He took his hand from his neck and walked slowly across the car park. Louis watched him as he came over, tall and confident. Georgio opened the passenger door and without saying a word, got in and closed the door.

'You OK?' Louis asked quickly.

'Yes, just tired, it's been a bitch of a night.'

'Look, about earlier,' Louis started.

'Hey, look, I'm sorry I blew up like that, but it was a bit of a shock. Will never said it was you who was waiting for me. He just said it was someone we hadn't seen at Pines for a while.'

'I should have called.'

'Yeah, you should've.'

'My head's been such a mess. What with Titia and then the drunk in the hospital.'

'Yeah, I read about that. I must admit, I was surprised, to say the least, that you had it in you… you know, to beat a guy up like that.'

'Well I'm not particularly proud of it. It's not like I meant to or anything. He just started and wouldn't shut up.' Louis began to sound agitated.

'Hey, calm down, don't worry about it now. It's all done, isn't it?'

'Yes, I think so. I don't think they're pursuing me further for it.'

'So, what now?' Georgio asked.

'I don't know, what do you want?'

'You.'

'Are you sure? I'm not exactly a barrel of laughs since… well, you know.'

'You never were, you miserable bastard,' Georgio said, laughing.

'So, do you need a lift home?' Louis asked.

'No thanks, I've got my car here, and besides I'm knackered. So, what happens next, Louis?'

'I'll call you tomorrow?'

'You sure?'

'Yes, absolutely sure.'

'OK, speak to you then.' Georgio leaned across and kissed Louis, quickly, then got out of the car. Holding on to the top of the door, he leaned back in.

'You'd better call me Louis Matthews.'

'I will, I promise. Goodnight… and Georgio, it's good to see you.'

'Yeah, you too. Goodnight, Louis.'

The car door thudded shut and Louis sighed a huge sigh of relief. He sank momentarily into his seat, eyes closed, hands resting on the steering wheel. He allowed a small smile to creep across his lips as he watched Georgio walk to the far corner of the car park in the darkness. Once the black night had swallowed the retreating waiter, Louis eased himself up in his seat, turned the ignition key, placed the car in gear and pointed it out of the car park towards home.

47

Lomas sat like a chastised schoolboy, his hands clasped on his lap, arms resting on either side of the cold leather chair, his head bent slightly to the left, listening intently.

Marie relayed the conversation she'd had with Randolph blow by blow. However unorthodox or unethical this was, she preferred Lomas to know everything, given the scrutiny they were now both under.

'So the brass want blood,' he said calmly.

'Yes, yours specifically, Lomas, but I told Randolph I wouldn't take you off the case.'

'If you don't, you know how difficult will he make life for you? Marie, we both know how the system works. The super will hang me out to save face and there's very little you can do in the long run to stop him.'

'So what? Give up then? Let him have you as his scapegoat? Is that what you're saying?' Marie's tone was distinctly agitated. Her blue eyes pierced into Lomas, looking for him to defend his position as vehemently as she had when she'd been in with Randolph.

'No, I don't want taking off the case, especially not now with Drew being threatened. Look, Marie, I know I can get him. Doctor Redman says the killer's getting braver, taking more risks, and now he's brought Drew into it… let's just say he's made it even more personal.'

'Yeah, I know,' she said. 'How is she after receiving the package?'

'She's good. I spoke to her half an hour ago and she's even more determined to get him now than she was before,' said Lomas.

Marie looked carefully at Lomas as he spoke. The furrows in his brow looked deeper, his hair seemed to be showing more wisps of grey, and his eyes looked tired.

'You know we should be replacing Drew as well, while we're on the subject – as she's been targeted.' The DCI held up her hand to stop Baxter speaking. 'Before you say anything, I'm not going to yet, but if the threat to DC Taylor increases I will pull her out, Lomas, and there'll be no discussion. Are we clear?'

'Yes ma'am, crystal.' DI Baxter stood to leave.

'Before you go, when was the last time you had a day off?'

'Oh, I don't know, I…'

'Take one.'

'No, I can't, not now. I need to retrace my steps, go back over everything. We've got to be sure we haven't missed anything.'

'OK, if you won't take a whole day then just take the rest of today. Dish out your instructions and go. See Heidi and the kids, do something fun. Do something that doesn't relate to work in any way, shape, or form. Lomas, that's not a request.'

Lomas glanced around the office and then back to Carlton.

She knew how important his family was in maintaining his balance.

Lomas was one of the few police officers she had known who had successfully juggled a bright but demanding career with a wonderful family life. It was something of an anomaly in their line of work. Most were time-served singles or bitter and twisted divorcees with child support payments crippling them. Lomas and Heidi, however, had stood the test of time and were, it appeared, still solid.

'Well, as its an order, I will, thank you,' Lomas conceded cheekily. 'But just this afternoon. First thing in the morning I'm reviewing the case history, interviews and witnesses.'

'Alright, fine, but don't hang around here. See who you need to see quickly, and then go.' Marie smiled. 'Oh, and Lomas, send my love to Heidi and the kids.'

'Will do.'

Lomas closed the door quietly as he left Marie Carlton's office.

Marie, on the other hand, waited a couple of minutes and then headed for Randolph's office.

'This is really going to piss him off,' she mumbled to herself as she walked along the empty grey corridor. One highly polished black shoe clicked in front of the other, the echo reminding

Marie of an old prison movie. Her grey pinstripe suit, conservatively cut, moved freely as she walked to the office of Superintendent Randolph. She stood in front of the door, paused, gathered her thoughts, then rapped firmly just below his nameplate.

'Come…' The senior officer summoned her into his office.

Marie slowly opened the door, and a cool gust of air bit into her as she stood waiting for Randolph's customary wave into his 'space', as he referred to it. Vertical blinds on the open window directly behind him swayed in the chill breeze. He, however, seemed apparently impervious to the cold, wearing a short-sleeved shirt.

He's so strange, thought Marie as she waited to be summoned.

Slowly, Randolph raised a chubby left hand, and with the three fingers he had remaining he waved her forward. His ring finger had been sliced off just below the second knuckle during a fishing trip, when his line had become wrapped around it while attempting to land a blue marlin on a charter, just off the Bahamas. The fish had fought the chubby officer for nearly half an hour, then run with the line and Randolph's finger. The injury was fifteen years ago and he was left with a rather grotesque looking, rounded and scarred stump.

Marie walked into the room and sat opposite Randolph.

He looked her up and down slowly as she sat down, and a momentary smirk passed across his rounded, blush-red face. It was a regular pattern that Marie had witnessed many times before, but also chosen to ignore it. She figured that the tension that would be caused by her calling him out on his unsubtle behaviour would likely lead to her speedy demise from her role, and she had worked too hard and for too long to allow that to happen, especially at the hands of this weasel of a man, to whom she reported. As a result, she took her time before she looked directly at him in order to allow the smirk to disappear from his puffy face.

Bernard Randolph started the conversation with his usual monotone delivery.

'So, Marie, what news do you have for me?'

DCI Carlton decided to opt for a no-nonsense approach. It had always served her well in her dealings with Randolph.

'I'm happy, after speaking at great length with DI Baxter, that he is fully competent to continue spearheading the investigation, sir.' She paused momentarily. 'Therefore, I will not be removing or re-assigning him at this time.'

The corner of Randolph's mouth hinted at a wry smile as he raised his hands towards his head. Clasping them together, he placed his thumbs under his saggy chin.

'Marie, as I said, I support your decision one hundred per cent. I must add that your obvious recalcitrance is trying, but also admirable. So what is DI Baxter planning to do next?'

Randolph's disapproval wasn't a shock. Marie,

however, was determined Lomas wouldn't be hung out to dry to make Randolph look good. For years, she and others had watched Randolph flourish, knowing he wasn't a better or more deserving officer, just one who was better at social climbing. His brown-nosing and buttering up the hierarchy was almost legendary. He played golf, drank and dined with all the right people, and was somewhat of an unashamed master of cringe-making flattery.

DCI Carlton looked directly into Randolph's brown eyes.

'DI Baxter, quite rightly, is going over the entire case with his close team, person by person, lead by lead, and then re-interviewing any key witnesses he thinks are in need of re-interviewing.'

'Good, good – he's doing that as we speak, I take it?' His head tilted forward slightly and his eyebrows were raised in expectation.

'No, actually, I've given him the afternoon off to see his family. It's… been a while, sir.'

'That's what I like about you, Marie, your ability to read your people's needs, to keep them focussed and on track. Good decision.' His words reeked of sarcasm, however well he tried to hide it.

'Thank you, sir.' Marie forced a tight-lipped fake smile. 'Is that all, sir?' she asked.

'Yes, yes, I do believe so, Marie. Keep me informed, would you?' Randolph's attention drifted back to the notes on his desk.

Marie sat for a brief moment, and a feeling of being a young girl, sat alone in church waiting for confession, swept over her. A distant memory of a life which didn't even seem like it could have ever been hers, so far removed was it from the woman she'd become.

Randolph paid her no more attention. In fact, a fly on the wall would think he didn't even know she was there. Then the moment passed and she stood to leave without another word passing between them.

48

Lomas drove for a while, aimlessly turning from one road to the next, his mind a mass of questions with half an answer, of contradictions and hypothetical thoughts. He'd always stood so strong in the face of adversity that he'd seldom stopped to think why he did what he did.

Should I be off the case? Should someone with a fresh outlook take the reins? Someone who hasn't spent weeks chasing the wrong man while innocent girls were being tortured and murdered? These were all questions that he'd never raised before. Not to himself, nor with anyone else. Never had his judgement been questioned to such a degree that he would question himself. His actions and decisions, issues of family, morality, ethics, all appearing as if sent to challenge his inner self.

He stopped the car in the entrance to a park, where high grass embankments rose up to his left, edged by black railings. In front of him was a path winding through the park's many green areas and playgrounds. Birds scavenged for food and ducks sat on a cold uninviting pond. Lomas's glance panned round to his right, and more birds flew up to nests in barren trees, and a woman sat alone, a solitary figure in the centre of a long wooden bench, cloaked in a half-length black woollen coat, jeans and trainers, her head buried in black-gloved hands. She raised her head slowly, her eyes ringed red, cheeks rosy from crying and rubbing her face clear in the cool, brisk afternoon air. She didn't see Lomas sitting in his car, her own stare into nothingness far too intense to notice anything around her. Lomas wondered for a moment what she might be crying about. Maybe a boyfriend or husband had left, maybe a pet had died. It could be any number of things, he thought. Then he thought how free she must feel, free to be able to sit in public in a park and cry, alone, yet exposed to anyone who might chance to walk by. How unconcerned she must be with how the world would judge her for her unfettered expression of sorrow and loneliness. For a moment Lomas envied her, envied her ability to sit as she was, to not care or be concerned. Just for the chance to be free of the constraints of his life. For a moment, Lomas Baxter felt trapped, trapped by life, by emotions, by family, by the expectations of work and the weight of responsibility. He was sure the woman on the bench would think him insane if she were to know, for whatever her problems were had obviously driven her to despair. Nonetheless, envy was what he felt.

His stare broke away and with it his thoughts. Lomas turned the ignition key and started the car. He drove to the gym next as he figured a workout would more than likely rid him of his confusion and clear his thoughts before he headed over to see

Heidi and the kids. As he pulled into the car park, an array of familiar vehicles greeted him. There was always something homely about the gym, even if, through work, Lomas had missed a few weeks. Whenever he went back it was always like going home. A green four-wheel-drive Honda sat in the corner, which indicated that two of the gym's regulars were there. Two international power lifters, Darren and Rob, who were always awe-inspiring to watch train, would have arrived in that. Behind the Honda, there were two small hatchbacks that belonged to a couple of young bodybuilders, and lastly the dark red Transit of Monica Silverman that Lomas had got all excited about earlier in the investigation, thinking it was Jackson's van. Monica had trained hard for years in the gym to help with her shot-put and hammer throwing.

He grabbed his training bag from the boot and shoved the driver's door shut; he never bothered to lock it outside the gym. He headed into the changing room after exchanging pleasantries with the receptionist. Once re-dressed and in his training gear, the problems that were haunting him began to drift away. Instead, his focus shifted wholly to his workout. As he walked through the gym to start his first set on the deadlift platform, he passed Darren and Rob. Darren was wrapping his knees, ready for the gargantuan task he was about to undertake: the 360 kilos that awaited him in the squat rack. A knurled bar was resting on the second pin down, with heavy iron discs loaded almost to the ends of the bar. Lomas stopped a while to watch and shout encouragement, as the monster of a man, with his shaved head and well-trimmed goatee beard, walked towards the rack, legs unable to bend under the pressure of the tight bindings that supported his knees. It stood before him like a medieval torture machine. Most people in the small gym stopped as Darren stepped forward to the rack. Wrapping the end of a wide red leather belt around the upright post on the front of the squat rack, he pulled back, forcing it to contract around his waist, and with his fingers he pushed two steel bars through the eyes on the belt. With his back and abs' supported by the belt and knees wrapped so tightly he could hardly walk, he marched the two steps forward, ducking his head under the bar. He ground the bar against his upper back, settling it into a familiar spot, placing his strong hands, wide, around the barbell. Two spotters stood either end of the bar in case he didn't make the lift, ready to tear the weight from his back. Shouts, almost screams, of encouragement, rang around the gym as Darren stepped back, the bar bending from the huge man's shoulders and dipping at the ends under the extreme load. As he sank slowly down, in a controlled descent, his back was almost straight, head up and eyes burning into the wall in front of him as he fought gravity from pulling the monstrous weight down, deep into a squat position. Then, when he looked as if the weight would carry on driving him down through the floor, he stopped, crouched under the bar, and, with an almighty explosion of power, drove the bar and his body back up towards the start position. His face was nearly purple and his eyes looked as if they were ready to explode. He stood, rock solid, task complete. The massive powerlifter took a controlled step forward and racked the bar as congratulations came in from those watching. As people in the gym drifted away to continue with their own workouts, freshly motivated by the display of strength, they patted the big man on the back as he sat exhausted from his endeavours, removing the wraps from his knees. As Lomas's attention turned from the squat rack, he heard Rob joke that Darren would have to stop taking it easy and try lifting some decent weight for a change.

Over in the far corner of the gym, unaffected by her surroundings, was the solitary, bulky figure of Monica Silverman. Rarely was she seen engaging herself in the gym culture. Instead, she tended to train, speak very little and leave as soon as she'd finished. Lomas watched for a moment as she snatched a huge weight up above her head, with great form, standing statuesque, the weighted bar held aloft, unmoving for a second in a perfect finishing position. Her eyes, always intense, stared directly in front of her, her huge frame unwavering under the enormous weight she held over her. Then, as quickly as she'd ripped it up from the platform, she released the bar, following it down to the rubber matting underfoot. Monica controlled the bounce with the palms of her hands and then turned away to prepare for her next attempt. She chalked her hands, rubbing a large white block over her palms before casting it back into a bag covered in white powder.

Lomas turned away and finally made it to the deadlift platform. After loading the bar with a warm-up weight, he stepped forwards, gripped the cold knurled bar and pulled it up the front of his legs, until he stood upright with the bar, rolling his shoulders back slightly into a lock-out. With the first set complete, he added twenty kilos and carried on into set two. Forty-five sweat-soaked minutes later, Lomas's back and biceps workout was complete. He finished off as always with three sets of twenty-five hanging leg raises and a ninety-second plank, repeated three times, then made his way off to the changing rooms for a shower.

As he left the gym, Lomas nodded to Monica, still training alone in the corner. She wiped the back of her hand across a sweat-soaked forehead, pushing the moisture back into her thick dark hair. Then she nodded and held up a chalky white hand in reply.

Lomas dropped his bag back into the boot of his car and sat behind the steering wheel, his biceps still pumped and totally fatigued.

Thank God for power steering, he thought to himself as he manoeuvred the large silver car out onto the road. The engine purred reassuringly as Lomas made his way to see Heidi and the kids.

His spirits lifted higher the closer he got. He indicated left and turned a familiar corner into the road where his family had been staying for the last few days. The time was approaching four o'clock as he stopped at the end of the sloping concrete driveway, either side of which were plush green lawns edged with evergreen borders. As he turned to lock the car, a loud voice lifted his spirits even further.

'Dad!'

He turned to see Ant bounding down the drive, almost going too fast to stop. He seemed taller, more grown-up, than the last time Lomas had seen him. As his son grabbed him and enveloped him in a huge hug, Lomas could see Eve and Heidi making their way out of the detached bungalow. Eve's pretty face beamed and her blonde shoulder-length locks caught the sunlight, and she too ran down the driveway, stopping him from getting even one step closer to the house. He closed his eyes, kissing their heads, hugging them and taking a deep breath in through his nose, as an animal would smelling their young to identify them as his own. As he looked up, Heidi's gaze and his locked, her warm green eyes welcoming. She looked wonderful, yet not beaming like the kids, who had finally released him from their grasp. Still without a word uttered, he walked up the driveway for what seemed like an eternity, around a small red brick wall to where Heidi stood on the second step up towards the door. As Lomas got within touching distance, he could see Heidi's eyes were welling up with tears, but they weren't quite rolling down her cheeks, as if suspended invisibly, defying gravity. Silently, they wrapped their arms tightly around each other. Heidi sniffed quietly to stop herself from crying and closed her eyes tightly, her eyelids bursting their dam, forcing tears to flow.

'I've missed you so much,' she whispered gently in his ear.

'You too,' came a soft, choked reply.

They stood for a moment, trapped in their embrace by a deep longing to always be together. The forced separation was something they were enduring, but only just, for they were two people who hadn't been apart since they met, except for the odd training course. Lomas had even slept in the chair beside Heidi's bed in hospital when she'd given birth to their children, rather than go home without her.

As afternoon wore into evening, Lomas was bombarded with tales of what the children, mainly Ant, had been up to. They were, and always had been, regular visitors to their grandparents and so had a whole set of friends with whom they could socialise, despite moaning it was boring when not there. Heidi had also collected their best friends from home one evening, accompanied by a police officer, so that they didn't miss out on any essential goings-on. A tutor had been assigned and both children were quite enjoying the exclusivity of private one-on-one education.

Eve commented, 'It's like being the child of a movie star or something, Dad. It's really quite cool.

Everybody's jealous.'

'Dizzy cow,' retorted Ant with sibling mockery.

As ten o'clock approached, Heidi bit nervously on her lower lip. Checking her watch, she looked up to see Lomas looking at her.

'Everything OK?' he asked, with a slightly puzzled look on his face.

'Yeah, fine. I just thought it's time the kids were off to bed.'

'Your mum's right. Come on, time for bed.'

He ushered them off upstairs. At the top of the staircase he gave them each a kiss and a huge hug, as if they were boarding a plane to the other side of the world.

'I'll see you soon. Look after your mum for me, OK?' He said, smiling. 'Now go on, off to bed.' He gestured in the direction of their rooms and stood a while, glowing inside from the pride of fatherhood.

He returned downstairs to Heidi just as she was ending a call in the kitchen on her mobile phone.

'That was Mum. She and Dad are going to stay over with Aunt Suzie. So you can stay if you like?' she said with a girlish smile. 'When will we be coming home, Lomas?' she continued as she walked through to the lounge carrying two glasses of red wine.

'As soon as I can get this lunatic banged up. It's not safe for you to be at home, not yet.'

'I read about that latest girl. Her poor parents must be absolutely heartbroken.' Her tone became more sombre. He moved close to her and smoothed a hand through her hair, catching it behind her ear. The light from a small table lamp cast a subtle glow over his wife's face and the faint smell left over from dinner hung in the air, a homely smell Lomas hadn't enjoyed for a while. He kissed her gently on the forehead and then slowly caressed her lips with his.

'Can we not talk about it tonight? Only, it's the first time I've been away from the case files for weeks and I'm kind of enjoying the break,' he whispered.

Heidi smiled and nodded confirmation of Lomas's request and they sank slowly into the soft leather sofa, wine glasses left untouched on the table beside them.

The next morning came all too quickly for Lomas. He woke a little after 5 a.m. and he watched Heidi sleep for over an hour without her stirring. Not wanting to disturb her, he slid out from under the quilt and headed for a shower. Standing with the water cascading over him, his thoughts turned to work. He'd left a list of instructions the day before, all of which were focussed on pulling the main areas of the investigation together for review, something he hoped the team would have completed by the time he got back to work.

49

Morning for Louis Matthews did not come with the same ease that it had for DI Baxter. Instead, it came abruptly, awakened by hailstones beating on his bedroom window. He opened his eyes slowly. Looking directly up at his bedroom ceiling, he became instantly aware of a hangover thumping in his head. As the numbness of sleep was replaced, limb by limb, with the return of feeling, a short burst of panic shot through him as he could only muster feeling in one arm. Louis turned his aching head towards the centre of his bed, only for his lack of tactile ability to be explained by his entire right arm, from the bicep down, being trapped under a silently sleeping Georgio. Slightly bemused as to how his bed-partner could sleep with an arm tucked under his neck, Louis withdrew it, slowly rolling out of bed so not to wake Georgio.

He allowed himself a moment, while donning a thick white robe, to admire his younger lover, his unusually messy jet-black hair and olive tanned skin tight and toned over a well-trained muscular torso. His skin tone and general appearance was the main reason he got away with calling himself Georgio instead of his christened name, simply George. Louis remembered with a smile when he'd found out, quite by accident one evening, that this suave, well-groomed man wasn't of stallion descent as he pretended, but was in fact from the north of London, with a well-rehearsed Italian accent. As Louis sat at his kitchen table, holding a steaming cup of freshly brewed tea, he recalled his relationship with Georgio. How he had gone to him many times after one or other of his and Titia's numerous fights. How Georgio always treated Titia and her family with professional courtesy when serving them at the restaurant, despite knowing their deepest secrets.

Georgio strolled into the kitchen, holding his head and clad only in hip-skimming white boxer shorts.

'Is there any more tea?' asked Georgio, wrenching Louis from his reminiscence.

'Sorry?' said Louis, only half hearing the question.

'Tea, is there any more tea?' repeated Georgio, dropping two slices of bread into a stainless steel toaster.

'Yes, yes, I'll pour you one.' Louis did so without leaving his chair, as both teapot and cup were already out on the table.

'What a night,' remarked Georgio, stretching.

'Yeah, we haven't been that pissed in months,' replied Louis.

'I thought the taxi driver was gonna crap himself when you rucked him about the fare,' said Georgio, laughing.

'What do you mean?'

'You mean you don't remember? You grabbed him by the throat and told him you were fucked off with them keep ripping you off just 'cause you were pissed. You must remember. You were a fucking' animal, man.' Georgio's fake accent slipped slightly. Even though they were both aware that Louis knew, Georgio still maintained the name and the fake accent consistently.

'I didn't, did I?'

'Yeah, and you only gave him a tenner. You said him and his thieving mates had had the rest already. Then you kicked his door shut and spat on the car as he drove away. It was fucking' mental.' Georgio laughed as he took a bite of his toast, clearly impressed by Louis's drunken antics.

'Anyway, what were you so deep in thought about this early in the morning?' he continued.

'Me? Nothing. I've got a banging headache,' Louis lied.

'Yeah, you were moping about her again. I've told you, you're better off without her.' Georgio's words ate into Louis's conscience over Titia and their many unresolved arguments.

In a flash of temper, Louis snapped back.

'What the fuck would you know? You weren't married to her! You didn't love her!' he screamed.

'No, but you were, and she made your life a fucking' misery. I wouldn't be lumbered with a self-centred bitch like that if you paid me… and another thing, if you missed her so much, what the fuck were you doing with me? You fucking closet case!' Georgio built to a shrieking crescendo, making a series of well-aimed strikes against Louis.

'I don't know what I was doing you with. Maybe I just wanted a bit of light relief, some unchallenging conversation and banal entertainment. But I tell you this, I'd rather have one of her than ten of you any day. At least she could hold her own. You're just chasing the next fucking handout.'

Both men were standing, boiling with rage, their faces flushed with anger, slamming clenched fists on the table as they hurled abuse back and forth.

'How the hell can you stand there all high and mighty, proclaiming your love for your dead bitch of a wife, when you hated her as much as I did? You make me fucking sick, you sad, hypocritical, middle-aged, wanker!' Georgio seethed.

'You hated her?'

'Yes, I fucking hated her. The way she controlled you – "Louis, come here darling." "Louis, do this darling" – Her and her fucking stuck-up family… and you, poor hard done to Louis. Always running when she clicked her well-manicured, pampered fingers. Always there for her every whim, like some fucking subservient puppy. Well, I put a stop to that, and I'm so fucking glad I did.'

Georgio raged, his eyes popping, the veins in his head pounding, sweat breaking out in tiny beads across his forehead.

Louis sat, eyes glazed, like a rabbit caught in

headlights, unable to react for a second, but then, gathering his thoughts, he began calmly, 'What do you mean you put a stop to it?'

'I mean I stopped it, ended it all… but I did it for you, don't you see?' Georgio's tone changed, realising his rant had gone too far.

'You killed her?' Louis's face was still flushed, but with the colour draining fast.

'Yes, but for you. I-I wanted you to be free, free to be with me, don't you see?'

Georgio walked hastily around the table and kneeled before Louis.

'I did it so we could be together without hiding.'

Louis felt Georgio's hand touch his own.

'NO!'

He pushed Georgio away. Leaping up and pushing the chair across the floor, with his eyes fixed on his wife's killer, he scrambled to move away from Georgio, his feet slipping on the polished floor. He had panic, fear and rage all coursing through him. He turned and ran to the hallway, scrabbling in his hanging coat pockets for keys, desperately trying to get out, to get away from the monster whose handiwork came back to him night after night in his dreams – visions of Titia laid bare in the morgue.

Georgio chased him from the kitchen, grabbing his arm to turn him.

Louis didn't want to hear any more. He flung his arm back, casting off Georgio's grasp.

'You must listen to me,' Georgio pleaded.

'Listen, listen to what? Are you going to tell me how you mutilated my wife? How you cut her up, carved her into pieces like joints of meat… or are you going to tell me it was all a mistake? That you didn't mean to cut her arms and legs from her body. What, Georgio? What can you possibly have to say that would explain any of this?'

Louis's mind was awash with emotion, hot tears streaming down his face, tears of betrayal, of remorse, of shame. For weeks he'd wanted to come face to face with Titia's killer, only to find that her killer, her torturer, was his own lover.

Once more he pushed Georgio, but harder this time and he fell to the floor, where the younger man stayed, sobbing, pleading for a hearing, like a condemned man begging for clemency. Louis could bear to hear no more. He ran to the garage, leapt in his car and was gone in a cloud of scattered pebbles and hailstones.

50

Dr Redman, Sherlock, Grayson, Drew, Peter and Nick all awaited DI Baxter's arrival. They had all been summoned to go over, in detail, the case history so far. Each was needed for their own differing but equally valuable viewpoint. All of them had already made significant contributions to the investigation.

A newly charged and revitalised Lomas bowled through the door, exactly on time, not one minute late nor early.

'Morning, how nice to see everyone, and all looking so cheerful,' he greeted them sarcastically, as they all had faces longer than a coal barge.

'Right, people, the order of the day is to retrace our steps. We'll go over the entire investigation. I want to know if your opinions are the same now as they were earlier, or if they have changed, and why, given the recent developments. DC Taylor, now a possible target, has been given permission to leave the investigation but wishes to stay, I think to her credit. Now, Dr Redman, you've had the opportunity to study the movements and patterns of the killer. What are your thoughts?'

The room sat in silence for a second or two. Then Dr Redman spoke in his slow monotonous drawl.

'As I predicted, he is without a doubt getting better at his work. The shift from dumping body parts at first, to labelling and mailing, or delivering them, would indicate a growing confidence and an evolution in his behaviour.'

'A growing confidence in his ability to evade capture?' Drew interrupted.

'In your inability to capture him, yes, Detective.' The change of emphasis was strongly highlighted by his deliberate speech and was not lost on the team. He continued.

'He probably now thinks he can strike whomever and wherever he wishes at will, and that there is little if anything you can do to stop him. He displays a high degree of precision and knowledge of both medical and police procedures. The use of stencils and, I think, as the learned Mr Washington and his team have discovered, ' – he motioned towards Grayson – 'mass-produced pens to avoid forensic or handwriting detection, demonstrates a well thought out plan and a level of premeditation. The girl you freed – Christina Marley – will no doubt be intended to be the subject of a later attack, but I think that's likely to be when our killer needs something to entertain him, rather than a driving need to finish the job. As our killer must already know, Miss Marley poses no threat to his freedom due to her lack of information. I firmly believe that, unless he is captured, he won't stop. Instead, the time between capture and kill will reduce, as he evolves, eventually becoming frenzied, chaotic even.'

The doctor hung onto the last few words of his analysis as if trying to drive his point home to his respectfully silent audience.

'Thank you, Dr Redman,' said Lomas, breaking the short silence.

'Sherlock, how about an overview from you?'

Sherlock sat, hands clasped together in front of the lower half of his face, as if praying for answers to unspoken questions.

'Well, since you called yesterday, I've gone over every file, autopsy report and all the physical evidence we have, and there are a couple of things which concern me.' He paused

'Yes, go on,' Lomas prompted.

'I don't think what I'm going to say is going to be particularly popular, but I think we are looking for two killers.'

The room fell to a new depth of quiet, as if a mute button had been pressed, silencing the whole team in unison. Then, once more, DI Baxter broke the hush.

'Two killers?'

'Yes, I don't quite know how I missed it before, or even if I just overlooked it as not ringing true, but there is one victim who stands out from the rest, although tortured while alive and dismembered likewise. There remain more than a few aspects which don't fit the pattern, for one of the victims.' Again he paused.

'Victim three, Titia Matthews, was the last victim to be dumped in pieces outdoors, nothing unusual there. However, on re-inspection of the photos I took of her limbs… may I?' he asked Lomas, pointing to some enlarged photographs he had brought with him.

'Yeah, sure.' Lomas nodded, grabbing the photos indicated by the forensic specialist and handing them over.

As Sherlock passed everyone colour copies of Titia's severed body parts and close-ups of wounds, faces around the room paled. The visual, graphic illustration of why they were all sat around this table, stared them in the face. They were almost unrecognisable as pictures of a human being, such was the angle of focus.

'If you remember, Lomas, I said at the time that the fact the limbs were severed by a single blow, with a sharp object, like a meat cleaver, knife or similar, was not too much of an issue. This was because victim one, Sarah Rosewood, had had both legs removed the same way, but, when we go further and compare the wounds on Rosewood and Matthews, if you look at pictures three and four, marked in the bottom corner with their names, you will see that the angle of entry, here and here, are different. Upon closer inspection, I'm so confident they're different that I will state that Sarah Rosewood was dismembered by someone who was right-handed, but Titia Matthews' killer was most certainly left-handed.'

Sherlock cast his gaze around the room. Everyone except Lomas was staring at the pictures in front of them. Lomas, however, was looking directly back at him. This was the reason Lomas and the others held Sherlock in such high regard. If and when he stated something as fact, then it was beyond doubt or question.

'You're absolutely sure about this?' Lomas queried unnecessarily.

'Yes, without a doubt. Like I said, I knew it wouldn't be popular, but there you have it. We have not one but two killers. Both capable of horrendous acts of mutilation and torture.'

'Based on what you've just said, are all the other victims still related to our original suspect, Doctor?' Drew asked insightfully.

'Yes, I believe so Drew. I have examined all the evidence as if it were the first time I'd seen it, but I found nothing else new except for this.'

'With that in mind, boss, I think we should be looking closer to home for Mrs Matthew's killer – would you agree?' She looked to Lomas for confirmation.

'Yes, why don't you pull the Matthews' file, as you're the most familiar with it? Pete, if you could help Drew please? I want every member of her close and extended family, friends and neighbours, pulling back in and starting from scratch. Drew, Pete, as if we'd just found her, you understand? Don't make any allowances for what you think you already know.' Lomas turned to face Grayson.

‘Do we have the reports back yet on the note Drew received?’

‘No, not yet.’

‘OK, I want them today.’

‘I’ll do my best.’

‘Good, thank you. Dr Redman, I know you’re officially a consultant, but if you would, I would appreciate you sitting in on the Matthews’ interviews and doing some psychological analysis of the family, the way they interact, respond to questioning, the whole piece.’

‘Certainly DI Baxter. Always pleased to help in any way possible.’

‘Great. Well, this was meant to go on most of the day, so has anyone got anything else by way of new information, or would our time be better served following up our new leads?’ Lomas paused and looked round the room, giving each member of the team an opportunity to voice a fresh opinion. No one spoke.

‘Right, let’s get to it then.’ He turned on his heels and was first out of the door.

51

DCI Marie Carlton sat patiently and listened to a refreshed, more energetic Lomas than the one she'd seen the day before, as he explained their findings, plan of action, and detailed exactly the assistance he needed from her in the way of search warrants for Louis Matthews' house. On top of this he wanted one for Ben and Coline Carter's, plus the additional manpower required to search the residences. She watched him with a certain amount of envy for the enthusiasm he maintained, even after all these years he still buzzed from the chase. Her days were filled instead with petty bureaucracy and meetings with stuffed shirts like Randolph, who had long forgotten that police work was more than a PR exercise, but was about what was actually happening on the streets of their allotted divisions and stations. As she listened, Marie congratulated herself on her steadfastness, for not biting the bullet and offering Lomas as a sacrificial lamb to be slaughtered by the press and public alike. With his newfound resolve, she was sure he was the man to catch both killers, as it now appeared. She also knew the focus of the superintendent would be on the team missing this information the first time round, not that reviewing every piece of evidence in an effort to uncover the smallest detail might help them stop a prolific murderer.

She turned her chair to face the window, then spun it back to face Lomas.

'So, how are the team feeling about the new information?'

'They're as motivated as ever and determined to track both of these monsters down, and I know they will not rest, or leave any stone unturned until they have. They are the finest team of officers I think I've ever worked with, ma'am. They're bright, intuitive and driven.'

'You're confident then?'

'Yes, ma'am, yes I am. I know we've had some setbacks, and God knows it's taken too long and too many people have been hurt, but it feels like we're moving in the right direction.'

'OK, Lomas, I'll have your back. I'll go upstairs and take the flack, but we need a result, and quick.'

'I know, Marie. I won't let you down.'

'I know.' Marie smiled and nodded.

Baxter turned and headed for the door.

52

A young, fresh-faced officer stood just inside Drew's flat. Over the road were two more police officers in an unmarked car, photographing anyone who went into the building. The surveillance teams had been changing shifts outside Drew's for the last couple of days, and so far the most interesting thing they had seen was a drunk pissing himself because he was too inebriated to remove his dick from his trousers in time. To their great amusement he continued to expose himself, only to shake it and put it back into his wet, piss-stained trousers and then stumble off down the road.

At 10.35 a.m., the postman strolled towards the doorway leading to Drew's flat. In addition to his normal bag he carried a box, approximately eighteen inches square, sealed using parcel tape printed with 'Fragile' and 'This Way Up' and with arrows pointing towards to the top of the box.

'Have a quick chat to the postie will you, Graham?' said a crackled request over the young officer's radio as he stood patiently inside the flat.

'Yeah, sure, why? Anything in particular, or just the weather?'

'No, smart-arse, he's got a box. Just see what it is, who it's for.'

'Will do,' he replied.

Looking through the spy-hole, PC Graham Farmer waited until the postman was about four feet away, then opened the door.

'Morning, what have we got this morning for DC Taylor then?'

'A couple that look like bills, oh and this,' he said, removing the box from under his left arm.

The officer took it from him, careful not to turn it the wrong way up.

'Where's this from? There's no postage.'

'Some big bloke a few hundred yards back give it me. Said it was for Drew Taylor, this address and could I deliver it or he'd miss his train.'

The young copper's heart quickened.

'What did he look like?'

'I don't know, mate. He had a scarf up round to his nose and a woolly hat on.'

'What was he wearing?'

'A checked shirt and black tracky bottoms, why?'

'Never mind, stay there.'

The officer bolted down the stairs, not thinking to radio across the road to the waiting car. Breathless from running and bouncing with adrenalin, he blurted the news to the two waiting officers.

'A few hundred yards away, you say?'

'Yes, in the last four or five minutes,' Farmer replied, still breathing heavily.

Hastily, the older of the two got on the police radio. Within seconds, he and all the cars in the area were being barked at by Lomas to close off all roads within a five-mile radius of Drew's home. No one was to get in or out of the immediate area. PC Farmer was ordered to stay put and, more importantly, not to open the package until Lomas arrived.

Within minutes of receiving a call for support, a police helicopter was airborne and searching from the air with high-tech surveillance equipment, scouring the area for the mystery man.

Officer Farmer waited patiently, as instructed, inside Drew's flat, accompanied by a rather uneasy-looking postman.

'Have I done something wrong, mate?' the postman asked worriedly.

'No, no, it's just that, because you took the parcel, my DI will want to talk to you. He's good at getting you to remember things that you normally wouldn't even know you've seen.'

'What d'you mean?'

'Well, say you're walking down a street and a woman pushing a pram walks down the same street, but on the other side. Now, you may think that a quick glance over the road is all you took, but in fact you've not only seen her, her pram and the clothes she was wearing, you'll have also seen the cars driving down the road, ones parked by the kerb and any number of other things at the same time.'

Farmer grinned, pleased with his simplistic explanation of peripheral vision and subliminal recollection, all of which had been explained to him by Lomas one day the previous week.

'Oh right, I see, so this DI of yours gets all that out of you when he talks to you,' he replied, only half understanding.

They sat in silence for the next few moments, a silence which was broken by the bustle of Lomas Baxter and his entourage approaching the flat.

In trooped a whole host of people, including Lomas and Drew. A series of brief greetings were exchanged between the arriving officers and PC Farmer. Then they all gathered around Drew's dining table, in the centre of which was the parcel.

To Drew, this whole experience was slightly surreal. She was in her own home, but it was filled with her colleagues, all of whom were working. As she looked around her, she felt as though her belongings looked alien, like those of any other crime scene she'd ever attended, taken out of context by the bustling team of officers that were beginning to fill her flat. Drew found herself looking on her home as a crime scene, and it was at that moment she decided she had to move – not to evade the attention of the murderer they were tracking, but to give herself space, space of her own. A place the whole station hadn't trudged through in the line of duty.

Lomas donned a pair of thin white latex gloves, to go with the white disposable suits they'd all put on upon entering Drew's home, before sliding the box towards himself and simultaneously motioning to a forensic officer to come over to open the square box. Slowly, carefully, the forensic specialist sliced a fine line through the tape holding the lid together. Placing the blade carefully on the table, he pulled the box flaps aside, revealing a shallow recess and a note, below which was another lid.

The note, in the instantly recognisable stencilled lettering, simply read:

Heads you lose, tails I win.

Lomas picked the note up and placed it inside a waiting evidence bag and sealed it to avoid any potential for contamination before it reached the lab.

The DI looked back to the individual standing next to him and nodded for him to continue. Retrieving the knife, he patiently sliced the second lid, taking care not to let the blade penetrate too far beneath the surface of the tape.

As he pulled the box open, a gasp slipped from everyone around the table. Two or three of the officers looked away in an attempt to stop themselves regurgitating whatever they'd eaten so far that day. DI Baxter closed his eyes briefly in disbelief at the sight within the cardboard cube.

A severed hand, removed at the wrist, bloodied and stained, with chipped broken nails, held the decapitated neck and chin of Elinor Mary Clarke's head in its palm. The head was battered and bruised, one eye was completely closed from countless blows, and the whole of the face was hideously discoloured. Her one open eye, which was bloodshot, was staring directly up from the box like it was glaring directly at Lomas as he stared down into the container. Ritual engravings were scored deep into the once pretty forehead, all of which were framed by blood-soaked, matted curly hair.

'Jesus fucking Christ!' There was a stunned outburst from over Lomas's right shoulder. The postman.

While crowding round the box the officers had forgotten about the postman, and while they were unprepared for what was revealed when it was opened, he was totally untrained for what his natural curiosity had led him to view. PC Farmer and Drew quickly spun round to face the shocked postie and ushered him over to the sofa, well away from line of sight of the box. Stunned, he stared at the floor, shaking his head, unable to comprehend what he'd seen.

As Lomas looked at the head, studying the work of the monster he was tracking, he noticed something. Protruding from behind the swollen bottom lip was the corner of a small piece of paper.

'Drew, can you pass me some tweezers please?'

Drew did as requested.

Without moving Elinor's lips, Lomas pinched the tip of the tweezers onto the fragment of paper. As he withdrew it, it unfolded from its concertinaed position inside Elinor's mouth. It was stained with blood, but legible nonetheless. As Lomas opened it up, the stencilled wording confirmed how sick and twisted their killer was. Lomas read the five words aloud, and the officers around the room, some with more time served than Lomas, cringed, some shivered, but all were horrified.

'I guess it was heads.'

'Sick bastard,' muttered one of the younger officers, his eyes welling up, unable to move his gaze from poor, poor Elinor's head.

53

At the same time, but in a far more affluent part of the city, Louis Matthews was cautiously placing his key into the shiny brass lock on the right-hand side of his front door. He glanced over his right shoulder, casting an investigative eye down the long driveway leading up to where he stood.

His caution was due to his increasing uncertainty as to how he would react the next time he saw Georgio. Given that less than a year ago he was appalled by most forms of thuggish or violent behaviour, events had overtaken him and he found himself unable to accurately predict his own behaviour, or his reactions to stressful situations.

I've beaten a man unconscious and assaulted a taxi driver for trying to overcharge me. What the hell will I do to Georgio? Louis thought as the key clicked in the lock.

You probably won't do anything... but he did kill my wife. His internal voice continued its dichotomous conversation. The last few words, summarising what Georgio had done, were eating Louis up.

It was more than twenty-four hours since he'd stormed out and driven away in a fit of rage, disgust and disbelief. He had stayed overnight in a cheap, rather dingy hotel by the side of the road somewhere about ninety miles away. Not because he had driven there purposely, but just because that's how far he'd had to drive before he started to calm down. The distance he travelled hadn't taken long and Louis had spent the day in Seaton, walking by the sea, sitting on a park bench surrounded by pigeons for hours, finally whiling away the evening in the hotel restaurant and bar, engaging in occasional two-or three-word conversations with the staff. Mostly though, Louis had thought. Thought long and hard about the dilemma in which he found himself.

His boyfriend, and long-time secret lover, had murdered his overspending, over-opinionated wife, apparently in a premeditated act of jealousy. A wife who had walked out on Louis after finding out he had been sleeping with her sister, of all people.

God knows what she'd have done if she'd found out about Georgio, he thought.

Not only had he murdered her, but dismembered her in such a way that the very recollection of Titia's pieced-together corpse, laid out on the mortuary slab, had made Louis physically sick on more than one occasion during the day.

All of this was spinning and turning in Louis's head like a fully loaded cement mixer, churning and mixing and throwing up all kinds of moral dilemmas, all of which Louis Matthews had decided would have to be faced.

Should he report Georgio to the police? It was a

question he'd posed to himself in various states of drunkenness as the evening wore on. Even at one point blurting out to a poor bewildered waiter, 'Yep, I should report the loser,' as he downed another scotch and soda.

Louis had come back from his overnight trip with more questions than answers. A mixture of constantly spinning questions hammering around in his head, like a small child on a waltzer. This, combined with copious amounts of alcohol, had finally sent Louis off to an unsettled sleep on an uncomfortable, poorly made bed.

He had woken, un-refreshed and unprepared for the day ahead. He'd taken double the amount of time to make the return journey and now found himself pensively opening his front door.

As the door swung open, the whisper of a draught excluder on the floor was the only sound Louis Matthews heard. He stepped slowly over the threshold as he had done many times, but he'd never paused as he did now. Stopping just inside, he listened: nothing.

A bird chirped outside on a nearby tree, but inside, nothing.

'Hel—' He coughed, clearing his throat. 'Hello.'

The only thing that greeted him was silence, and it filled the house, thick and heavy. Louis moved quickly through to the lounge, then the kitchen. Still nothing.

Georgio was nowhere to be found. A wave of relief passed briefly over Louis as he stood at the top of the staircase.

He came back downstairs and registered a red flashing light on his answering machine. He pressed the play button.

'You have two messages,' said the automated voice.

'Message one…' Beep.

'Hi, it's me. Look, I know you're pissed off, but we need to talk, I tried your mobile but it was off. I'm not going into work, and my mobile will be on. Please call.' Beep. Georgio's voice was low, lower than Louis had ever heard him.

The answering machine cut through Louis's train of thought.

'Message two…' Beep.

'Mr Louis Matthews, this is Detective Inspector Baxter. We have some developments on your wife's case that I would like to discuss with you. If you could call and let me know the earliest you're available, I would appreciate it.' Beep.

Panic shot through Louis as if he'd just been shot with a tranquilliser gun. He began to shake, his hands began trembling first, then his knees and legs. He made his way quickly to the kitchen and sat down.

What does he know? Louis thought.

Surely he doesn't know. Maybe Georgio's turned himself in?

Maybe he's told them I helped him.

His internal dialogue rose to nearly a shout, booming inside his skull. Beads of sweat popped on his brow. He rubbed an anxious hand over his forehead and back through his hair.

'Georgio, I must phone Georgio,' he muttered to himself.

He grabbed the phone from beside the answering machine and punched in the familiar digits of his lover's mobile phone number.

As the phone rang, a swarm of conflicting thoughts were flying through Louis's head like a plague of locusts, chaotic and unyielding. The ringtone beeped in his ear for what felt like an eternity.

'Come on, come on, answer the fucking phone,' he whispered impatiently.

Midway through a ring, a voice interrupted the monotonous tones and, with the uncertainness of someone who had just woken, croaked, 'Yeah, hello, who is it?'

'Georgio, it's me, Louis.'

Suddenly the voice on the other end of the line changed, a fresh, alert tone replacing the sleepy, uninterested one.

'Hi, how are you? Look, we—'

Louis interrupted Georgio in mid-sentence. 'Listen, the police have phoned saying there are some new developments on Titia's case. Have you said anything to anyone?'

'No, not a soul,' replied a panicky-sounding Georgio.

'Well, DI Baxter wants to see me as soon as.'

'What are you gonna tell him?'

'What do you mean?'

'What the fuck are you going to tell him, Louis? Have you said something? You better not fucking grass me up, Louis Matthews!' Georgio was almost shrieking down the line.

'I don't know what I'm going to say yet, do I? I don't even know what he wants me for.'

'OK, OK, I'm sorry. I'm just scared, Louis. I'm so, so scared.'

'So you fucking should be, you psychotic bastard.'

'Is that all you phoned for, to hurl insults and abuse, 'cause if it is—'

'No, no, no… that's not why I phoned. I don't know why I phoned. I just thought—'

'Thought what?'

'Nothing, I-I don't know anything any more.'

Click.

Louis replaced the handset and in a bewildered daze picked it back up and redialled.

Click.

Georgio looked at the phone in disbelief and then slammed the dial pad with the side of his fist. Enraged, he jabbed at the speed dial button that held Louis's number.

'Engaged, why the fuck are you engaged? You fucking jumped-up wanker!' he shrieked at the phone.

As he perched nervously on the edge of his bed, nervous energy surged through his legs, down through the balls of his feet and into the floor, the laminate wood surface feeling cold on the soles of his feet.

Time and again the speed dial was answered by an engaged tone. Georgio became more and more anxious, with beads of sweat running down the sides of his face, his whole body was becoming covered in the cold sweat of fear.

He recalled briefly feeling similar just after he'd killed Titia, as the stench of her freshly mutilated body hung in the air, warm and thick. A wave of cold sweat had covered him in an instant, chilling him to his core.

He remembered standing over her dismembered corpse as a shock wave of realisation had hit him. Not because he'd killed her, but because of how he'd gone about it. Scaring himself with the level of depravity he'd sunken to, yet he'd stood and admired his work for a good hour before beginning to bag her up for disposal.

The pictures, so vivid in his mind's eye, transported him back to the night he'd decided she must die.

Titia had breezed into Pines at about eight thirty in the evening and seated herself at the Matthews' usual table. Without waiting to be approached, she had summoned Georgio with an arrogant click of her well-manicured, pampered fingers, followed by a beckoning wave.

It was a warm evening and she was wearing a sheer white vest top of fine woven silk and a fitted grey Armani skirt with a pale stripe. The ensemble was completed by a pair of high sling-back Gucci shoes and a matching clutch purse. Her jewellery, he remembered, was uncharacteristically sparse. A small pair of diamond stud earrings, a thin, silver necklace and bangle was all she wore.

Most male eyes in the restaurant had glanced at her as she made her entrance. However, those who knew Titia looked away again after admiring her beautifully shaped, tanned legs and gorgeous dress-filling figure. Mrs Matthews' reputation as a stunningly attractive, yet extremely repellent women preceded her. Very few regulars in Pines ever spoke to Titia, except for a courteous acknowledgement.

As Georgio reached the table, Titia looked up at him with her magnetic, deep blue eyes, a contemptuous look painted across her face.

'Has that useless husband of mine been in here yet tonight?'

'Mr Matthews has not yet been in, Mrs Matthews,' replied Georgio, managing to hold his tongue and his accent.

'Oh wonderful,' Titia continued with mock euphoria. 'Well hopefully I'll be gone before the snivelling bastard arrives. Now, be a darling, would you, and fetch me a large vodka Martini… oh, and some of those lovely filled crackers the chef does so well.'

Again Georgio kept his thoughts to himself, burying them deep inside and, as only a true professional can, he smiled graciously and turned away.

As the evening wore on and the vodka Martini's flowed, Titia's polished, collected demeanour fell away.

Louis didn't come in that night. Had he done so, maybe things would have gone very differently.

But as it was, Titia's analysis of their marriage – Louis's shortcomings as not only a husband and lover, but also as a man – became increasingly public.

Georgio's disgust grew as he listened to her crowing, slating Louis to anyone who would listen.

Three very well-dressed businessmen from the same party all tried to sit and impress the beautiful Titia. All were cut down in a similar fashion by the blonde lawyer, like a praying mantis, drawing them in with her alluring looks and then biting their heads off one by one, devouring their egos with a relentless appetite.

'I don't want to talk to you. If I wanted to listen to an overdressed, impotent, underachieving failure, I'd go home. Now piss off, or make yourself useful and go and buy me a drink. Either way, go away you boring wanker.' That was how the third charmer was dismissed.

The final straw for Georgio came when he cleared away four empty glasses, all of which Titia had insisted on staying on the table. As he placed his fingers into the drinking vessels, Titia spoke, quite softly at first.

'Of course, if I didn't know better, I'd say that poor, blubbery, pathetic Louis was compensating for something. In fact, if he wasn't such a beer-swilling, football-mad arsehole,' she slurred, 'I'd say that shagging my sister was just another attempt to cover up for something…'

Titia sniggered and put her index finger to her lips. With her free hand she tugged at Georgio's shirt, pulling him closer. Then she whispered, 'You don't suppose he's gay, do you?'

'What?' exclaimed the waiter.

Titia sniggered again. 'Shh… I said, you don't suppose Louis is… queer, gay… for fuck's sake, Georgio, gay. I bet that's it. I bet all these years that wanker's been hiding behind affairs and football drinking sessions with the boys, that would explain a lot.'

The sound of her voice ate at him. When Titia Matthews said his name, Georgio's skin crawled, his stomach churned and his fists spontaneously clenched. It was then, right there at the table, that he decided to kill her. He would have done it right there and then if he could have got away with it. The temptation to drive her pretty blonde head crashing down against the thick redwood dining table almost overwhelmed him, as he stood glaring at the drunken wife of his secret lover. A wife who had spent the whole night tearing the name of her husband to shreds and unknowingly uncovered his most secret of all secrets. Georgio decided Titia Matthews must die. He also knew how.

He'd been reading all about the two girls who'd been hacked to death by the murderer the tabloids had dubbed 'The Hatchet Man'.

That's how I'll do it, he thought. *No one will suspect me when there's already two dead.*

He remembered reading that both victims had probably been dismembered while still alive, but had been tortured for days before.

'No problem,' he muttered to himself.

The images and sounds of the night he killed her came flooding back to him, as if watching it being replayed on a cinema screen, each phrase and emotion prickling with realism.

He remembered walking her out to her car. She was really drunk by the end of the night and needed Georgio's arm and shoulder to steady herself.

This was what he'd told Lomas and Drew, when they'd interviewed him following the discovery of Titia's body and learning that the Pines was the last place she may have been seen alive.

What Georgio hadn't told them was that in the shrouded darkness of the cold night, he'd punched Titia full in the face. As they stood in the darkened car park beside Titia's Mercedes, her body had crumpled instantly from the blow. He'd caught her and positioned her unconscious body into the passenger seat, then he'd jumped in behind the wheel. He drove for miles, out along the coast road to a secluded cabin, long since derelict and unused. It was remote and undisturbed, hidden from view down a long, winding road.

Louis had taken him there once. He'd told him it belonged to his grandfather and that one day he would renovate it to its bygone splendour.

Georgio had stopped to lock the gates on the private road that led to the cabin and driven with the bare minimum of lighting. Then road led up a winding trail, which was canopied by mature, overhanging trees that surrounded the run-down shack. In the seat next to him Titia hadn't stirred. She sat, slumped, her forehead pressed against the passenger window. Her breathing was shallow, misting the glass immediately in front of her mouth, the stench of alcohol oozed from her, filling the small car.

His fury and hatred for the woman slouched beside him hadn't abated during the long drive. If anything, it had done quite the opposite. Driving her plush, well-equipped car, smelling the freshly treated leather and her expensive perfume mixing with the alcohol in the air like a rich cocktail, had done nothing to calm him. It had just made him more resolute to carry out his premeditated act. To rid Louis of the rude, arrogant, ungrateful bitch.

He stopped the car sideways-on to the porch steps. They were wooden and rickety and rose four tiers to an equally unstable balcony-style porch, complete with swinging chairs. Georgio opened the door on the passenger side of the Mercedes and wrenched her out by her left arm. Falling like a battered old rag doll, Titia crumpled to the floor insensible. Adjusting his grip on her left arm, Georgio squatted down and hoisted Titia up and over his shoulder. A sudden gasp of air was forced from her body as it settled into position with her abductor's shoulder pressing into her abdomen.

Georgio remembered thinking how light she felt, even as a dead weight.

He kicked open the half-closed, decaying door, and it swung back unimpeded. Georgio stepped inside and dumped his victim down onto a large kitchen table, it creaked a little under its first load in many years. The surroundings were dusty, and dark, thick grey cobwebs dominated the corners of the room, layered from years of web-building, snares from which no flying insect would be able to free themselves. The room was lit only by shafts of moonlight, piercing the numerous holes and cracks that riddled the walls and dust-covered windows.

Georgio didn't care how dusty it was. It suited his purpose perfectly.

He bound her ankles to the table using the strap from a handbag he'd found in the Mercedes on the journey, Titia's wrists he shackled down with his own belt and a torn strip of old curtain that was lying on the floor near a grimy window.

There, that'll keep you still, you fucking bitch.

Over the next couple of hours Georgio paced the creaky floor of the cabin, tirelessly marching back and forth across the room as he tried to plan his next move, interrupted only once by a soft groaning from Titia, which he responded to by punching her as hard as he could, sinking her back into a drunken, unconscious state. He was piecing together all the news clippings about the murders in his head. He knew the girls had been dismembered, everyone knew that, and that they'd had engravings on their foreheads. Beyond that and reports of severe bruising, he couldn't remember much.

Georgio decided that he knew enough to try to link Titia to the other two, leaving him in the clear. A quick call to Louis to set up where to meet him later formed his alibi. If asked, he decided he would just say he went home from work and called Louis using his mobile – perfect. He concluded the phone call to Louis just as Titia began to stir. He put on a pair of gloves as he walked over towards her and beat her around the face.

Unaccustomed as he was to physical violence, his feelings towards Titia made it easy for him to deal out blows from the back of his hands, inflicting a torrent of pain on his captive. Even in her semi-conscious state, the sting of the gloved hand and dull thud of knuckle on cheekbone penetrated her mind. She struggled against the makeshift restraints that bound her to the table. Titia was becoming more sober and aware with each blow, her dark surroundings starting to come into focus and then a solidly connected fist ploughed into her temple and she slipped once more into darkness.

Georgio lifted her head by the fringe of her hair, opened her mouth and slipped two sleeping pills onto her tongue. Then, still holding her hair, he flicked up the sports cap on a bottle of water from his pocket and squeezed a jet into her mouth, flushing the pills down her throat. When he was sure her mouth was empty, he released his grip and watched her head bounce onto the table.

'That'll keep you out until tomorrow. Then the fun really starts, you stuck-up slag,' he raged. His carefully played Italian accent had gone in his anger, replaced by his natural tones.

Georgio spat a mouthful of water onto Titia's unconscious face, checked the bindings were secure and then left the cabin to get cleaned up and meet Louis.

Georgio's night with Louis was everything he wanted it to be, a night of pure unbridled lust. Everything he had done was to spite Titia. They even discussed her briefly, between several acts on her bed. Georgio had told Louis that Titia had been in Pines earlier, sober at first, but drunk and abusive by the time he saw her leave.

He remembered Louis had become slightly upset, but a blowjob had soon cured that, distracting the older of the men from thoughts of his wife.

Georgio returned to the cabin early the next morning, catching a train to a station four miles away and jogging the rest of the way to see how his prisoner was getting on. As he jogged, he decided what he would etch on her forehead: Prisoner. He figured she would spend her last living moments as one, but he also thought about how Titia had kept

Louis a prisoner of a loveless, bitching, moaning marriage for long enough.

'Yes, that'll do nicely,' he muttered under his breath as he jogged up the driveway towards the cabin door, hardly out of breath after the four-mile run.

He slipped a pair of thin black leather gloves on before opening the door. As soon as he stepped foot inside the cabin he heard a shuffling noise coming from the table where Titia was bound.

'So the bitch is awake, cool.'

Titia looked across at him through bruised, battered, terrified eyes.

'Georgio?' she croaked, as he stepped closer.

'Yes, Georgio. Now shut the fuck up, you self-centred bitch.'

'But why, what are you—?'

'I told you to shut up. Now fucking do it or I'll kill you now!' Georgio yelled, sweat rising on his forehead. This wasn't what he'd planned. He didn't want to talk to her. He just wanted to kill the bitch.

Titia did as she was instructed. Her words ceased, but the startled rabbit look in her eyes remained.

A gag, Georgio thought. *I need to find a gag to shut this cow up.*

He looked around the room, searching. Nothing, not even a bit of rag to roll into a ball, just a length of string about two feet long that he hadn't noticed the previous night when fixing her bindings. He returned to Titia's side, and she was still silent, staring and afraid. Georgio pulled a retractable knife from his pocket, opened it with his left hand and grabbed the hem of Titia's fitted Armani skirt with his right. Titia tensed as he snatched at her skirt. Georgio held it clear of Titia's shapely legs and slashed a two-inch split in the bottom edge. Then, dropping the knife on the table, he grabbed the garment with both hands and ripped it in a line up to her waist. She was wearing a tiny white lace thong, see-through and barely covering her neatly trimmed pussy. Georgio looked for a second and wondered what the fascination was to straight men, he included Louis loosely in this thought, which he dismissed as rapidly as he'd thought of it. Deciding that the thong was too small to roll and gag her with, he proceeded to remove a long strip from Titia's skirt. He noticed the fear in her eyes as they darted quickly, following him around as he moved, but as instructed she remained silent. He rolled the freshly cut cloth and stuffed it, with some difficulty, into her mouth and secured it with the piece of string he'd found.

'Silence at last,' he mocked, smiling at the woman lying on the table before him.

'Now, it's about time I made life a bit easier for myself. So, Mrs Matthews, I've decided that I'm fucked if I'm going to carry you back out of here kicking and screaming, so… the gag has taken care of the screaming, and this.' He paused. Ducking down and reaching under the table, Georgio grabbed the handle of a sharp, shiny, new axe, which he'd carried with him in a rucksack in preparation for the task ahead. He stood back up, towering over the bound and gagged Titia, whose eyes widened as Georgio raised his left hand high above his head, brandishing his weapon of choice.

'And this… well, this should take care of the kicking.'

The axe fell with the power and determination of a well-trained henchman, except Georgio wasn't. He was a waiter, a waiter who found it surprisingly easy on this day to take the life of his lover's wife in a way which before would have seemed unthinkable to him. The barbaric, precise manner in which Titia's body split into more manageable-sized sections surprised Georgio as he wielded the axe time after time.

At first there was a muffled scream from Titia, muted by the gag. This was coupled with some struggling and disbelieving, fearful eyes, but the pain, together with the shock, proved too much for Titia and her final, agonising moments were short.

54

The forensic team, like the investigating team, were grappling with their own basic feelings of disgust and empathy. Disgust at the final acts of mutilation and carnage, which they were duty-bound to not only view, but probe and investigate, to try to find some vital clue to the identity of the individual carrying out the horrific slayings. Empathy, because as human beings they empathised with the families, friends and loved ones of all the victims, some taking a minute amount of comfort from the fact that the families involved had rarely had to witness the scenes that they as police officers had to endure.

Sherlock, especially, was feeling the mounting pressure to find something, anything, that Lomas could use, but, no matter how many times he went over the evidence, reports, or autopsy records, he could find very little to offer. The search of the cottage where Christina Marley had been found gave them nothing. Every tool, blood sample and stain had been tested and re-tested by Grayson's team, but the killer had left them nothing, no fingerprints or DNA traces.

Frustrated, he turned his attention to the latest body part to grace his lab.

Elinor Mary Clarke's head was discoloured and had distinct signs of rigor mortis, with bruising and other marks sustained during her last few days apparent all over the surface of her once pretty face. Her forehead bore the familiar shapes and patterns, which, it had transpired on further investigation, were not of pagan origin, but were actually random etchings that had subtle similarities to pagan ones.

'The Phantom of the Opera' played quietly in the background, just masking the sound of a ticking clock hanging on a far wall. Sherlock began to inspect the severed neck, checking the cut, determining that the method and angle of removal were synonymous with the killer of all but Titia Matthews.

He probed the tainted flesh, recording his findings into a small Dictaphone on his table, methodically tracking a path around the skull in a well-practised route he had taken many times over the years. When he reached the front of the young woman's face, he gazed at her lifeless eyes.

'I'm sorry we didn't get to you in time, my dear, we are working as hard as we can to try and stop him, trying to prevent another you.'

A small tear welled in his eye, and he didn't hear the soft footsteps making their way across the lab, the highly polished floor offering no resistance or friction to the soft leather soles as they approached behind the forensic examiner. The shadow of the figure approaching was cast back and away from Sherlock by the angle of the lights overhead.

Suddenly, an acute sense of not being alone pricked Sherlock's consciousness. He turned quickly, his heart beginning to race.

A quiet, tearful-looking Drew stood less than a metre behind him.

'Drew, are you OK?' Sherlock asked quietly, rubbing his forehead with the back of his hand, relieved by the sight of the young officer.

'I'm not sure…' Her lower lip was beginning to lose shape and tremble.

'What is it, what's wrong?'

'It's this,' she replied. With tears starting to flow, Drew took a plastic bag from the pocket of her pale grey hooded top.

Inside the bag, Sherlock could clearly see a letter of some type. It was small and white and folded neatly. He removed his gloves and grabbed a fresh pair from a box on his desk, stretching them over his hand.

'Did it arrive in the bag, Drew?'

Drew shook her head, which was half hidden by the hood of her top.

'OK, pass me the bag and take a seat.' He motioned to a stool on his left. Drew did as instructed and, sobbing softly, she released her grip on the bag.

'It a-a-arrived about fifteen minutes after the last officer left my place. I told him that I'd be OK, and h-he could go. Th-then there was a knock at the door, and when I opened it, that was on the floor.'

'All right, Drew. It's OK, you're safe here. Have

you touched the letter?'

'No, I used the gloves your guys left at my place.'

'OK, good, let's have a look then. Have you called Lomas?'

'Yes, he said to get it to you and meet him here.'

Sherlock opened the letter and began to read.

'You're next, you're next
You fucking ho,
You and your DI
Are just too slow.

Miss Clark's young face
Is in a box,
With her severed head
And her matted locks.

They left you
On your own to sleep.
No rest for you,
While a watch I keep.

You'll never get me
In the dock.
Time is ticking
Tick tock, tick tock.

Your body toned
And fighting fit,
Will be an easy

Corpse to split.

I'll deliver you,
Both far and wide,
Or maybe dump you
At high tide.

So rest assured
Your time is soon.
Here's to going mad
Inside your room.'

Sherlock glanced sideways at Drew as he finished reading, although his voice had become quieter as he worked his way through the twisted, intent laced rhyme. DC Taylor was still weeping softly, she looked up and caught his glance.

'He's going to try to kill me, isn't he? I'm next and there's nothing we can do. He says so right there.'

'Now, Drew, you know we won't let that happen,' Sherlock said in an attempt to placate her.

'We said that about Anna-May Appleby and Elinor Mary Clarke and look what happened to them. We have surveillance on my flat and he can still deliver this unseen, why did they not see him? What chance do I have?' Her hysteria was building.

Sherlock stood up and awkwardly embraced a shaking, bewildered and petrified Drew.

'Come on now,' he said softly. 'You know that's not true. We didn't know before the other girls were taken that they were targets, but with you, we have a chance to stop him, and we will. You can't blame the guys watching your flat for not seeing him, he's well practiced at avoiding attention, and you know we'd have had a camera outside your door if there'd been enough light for it to work. Now, let me call Lomas and see if he's nearby so we can show him this.'

Lomas studied the note long and hard, his furrowed brow conveying his thoughts. No words were necessary to know that the contempt he felt for the killer was growing by the day. As was his frustration at their apparent lack of leads. Grayson Washington had joined them, alerted by Loams on his way in of the new evidence that would need testing.

'If there's anything on this, Grayson, anything at all, I'd appreciate it straight away.'

'Of course, goes without saying.' Washington had everyone in his department working and re-working the evidence they had collected for any forensic clue or the slightest detail they might have missed on earlier examination. All the body parts were still being preserved, with most undergoing their fifth or sixth round of analysis by Sherlock.

Drew sat in Lomas's office with her knees drawn up in front of her chest, hands clasped tightly around them. Her intense stare was burning with both fear and rage. She had bloodshot eyes from the bitter salt tears, which were unyielding. Even as she began to calm, the soft droplets still tricked slowly down her reddened cheeks, forming two damp patches on her light grey sweat top. Pictures of Lindsey Demitri's pieced-together body lying on the clinical slab of the morgue flashed through her mind. Yet, unlike the true vision her memory had stored, this one had her own head superimposed on the corpse of Lindsey, the second victim, and in this half daydream, half nightmare, Drew's own eyes flickered open, staring at her with the same intense glare. Then, in her own voice, the jigsaw cadaver spoke, taunting her.

'*They weren't quick enough. They weren't there. They left you on your own and he came. Came and got you. This is you. This is me. This is how we end up. Time is ticking. Tick tock, tick tock.*'

Drew jumped from her waking nightmare as Lomas burst into his office. She sat, terrified, looking around the room, reassuring herself she was still alive.

'I've got Louis Matthews in Room One waiting to be interviewed. Are you going to be all right here on your own for a while?'

'No!' she snapped. Then quickly she corrected herself. 'Yes, I-I mean yes. I'll be fine.'

'Well stay here until I come out, then I'll take you home.'

Lomas breezed back out, and before the door had clicked obediently onto its catch, he'd disappeared down the corridor.

Alone, Drew once more pulled her knees up in front of her and clasped her hands tightly around them. Like a chastised child, she sat, curled up as much as her limbs would allow. Everything in the office seemed alien. She thought this must have been how people being brought into the station for the first time must have seen it. Trays of filing neatly piled up on top of grey metal filing cabinets. Crime reports awaiting reading on one corner of the desk, a phone and clock on the other, next to a picture of Heidi and Lomas's kids. Drew could pick out no specific noise from the buzz of the busy station beyond the closed door of the office. However, her ears did connect with the solitary sound of the clock, its gentle tick, tick, tick getting louder, progressively driving deep into Drew's mind, as if it was being gently hammered deeper and deeper into the depths of her skull. Soon her head was echoing with a symphony of clocks, all ticking, second after second, louder and louder until she could hear nothing but the deafening crescendo as even her own pulse became one with the orchestra of sound. Drew raised her hands to her ears, covering them. With her eyes closed tightly, she began to hum in a vain attempt to distract herself from the unyielding tick, tick reverberating in her head. It was to no avail, for although the vibration she felt in her lips told her she was humming, the sound couldn't penetrate the endless noise inside her pounding skull.

55

The sound of the interview room door opening made Louis jump nervously as Lomas burst in, flanked by Dr Redman.

'Hello, Mr Matthews.'

'Hello.' Louis got halfway to his feet, awkwardly leaning forward as he shook the hands of both men.

His hand was cold and clammy and Lomas could see tiny beads of sweat on Louis's forehead. The information was mentally noted as they took their seats. A young officer stood by the door. Lomas commenced with the formalities of the recorded interview, and then, with no build-up of any kind, fired his first question at Louis. Like a rock thrown at full force into a still lake, Lomas threw it and watched for ripples.

'So, Mr Matthews, what *do* you know about the murder of your wife?'

A stunned Louis rocked back in his chair, seeming totally unprepared for the immediate assault and the phrasing of the question. Trying to compose himself, he closed his eyes briefly and clasped his fingers together, drawing in a deep breath and began.

'Look, DI Baxter, I don't quite know what you're trying to imply, but I can assure you I don't know any more than I've already told you, which, I'm sorry to say, obviously wasn't much help, seeing as the monster that killed my wife has done so again and is still on the loose.'

'Well, yes, the killer of your wife is still on the loose, as you quite rightly say. But I have information which suggests that you didn't quite tell us everything when we discovered your wife – you know… skeletons in closets, Mr Matthews?'

This was, as far as Lomas was concerned, a fair bluff to tag onto the first question, as almost everyone had skeletons and very few people opened their closets to the police, especially where murder was involved.

Lomas didn't have to look too carefully at Louis. He began to shake, ever so slightly, only noticeable at first because his fingers were still clasped, and then he began twitching nervously. Then he looked directly at the table in front of him and followed up by glancing around the room.

Lomas knew something was going to give. Louis was folding and unfolding his hands, rolling the backs of his fingers against each other, eyes looking nervously around the interview room. The sweat on the interviewee's brow was becoming more noticeable and so far Louis had avoided wiping or dabbing to remove the beads that rose to the surface of his skin. Instead, he shifted restlessly in his chair.

DI Baxter had seen this reaction many times over the years, and he timed his next move differently each time, depending on his subject. He was now sure Louis was guilty, guilty of hiding something, but somehow he still didn't believe he was a murderer. He just needed to work out which button to press.

Louis opened his mouth to speak, elevated his head slightly. Then, without a word, he dropped his focus once more towards the table.

Their game of cat and mouse continued in silence for what seemed like an eternity. Lomas staring directly across the table at Louis, Matthews firing glances across the table and then around the room, working hard to avoid eye contact.

Biting on his lower lip, Louis raised his head again and for the first time looked Lomas in the eye.

'I do know why she left me, if that's what you mean?'

Lomas, studying Louis, sensed there was more, and a poorly thrown decoy such as this wasn't enough to put him off the scent. Louis's physiognomy was such that Lomas knew instinctively he was hiding something, something bigger than why Titia left him. Maybe they were linked, the reason and the bigger picture. But the bigger picture was where Lomas wanted to get to. Like a bloodhound with the first real hint of a scent caught on the breeze, he pursued his goal, shrugging off Louis's offer of information.

'No, Mr Matthews, I believe – in fact, I strongly believe – that you know far more about your poor wife's brutal, savage, and let's face it, motiveless murder than you've told me. Don't you, Mr

Matthews!'

Lomas slammed the palm of his hand on the table. His voice was raised just enough to drive his last four words home with an impact that made his interviewee jump slightly.

Louis's bottom lip, released from between his teeth, began to tremble, his chin wrinkled and eyes screwed up, tight. Louis pressed his open hands over his closed eyes, as if he was trying to keep his entire world of secrets and lies pressed inside his head. Lomas saw the torture eating at Louis. His hands pressed over his eyes were not only beginning to shake, but his fingertips were digging into his forehead, nails drawing blood where his fingers clamped hard onto his skull.

'Come on, Louis, tell me what it is. I know you didn't kill her. I know you never intended for her to end up pieced together like a jigsaw on a slab in the morgue, did you?' Lomas's tone was softer, more sympathetic as he began to turn the screw, winding Louis tighter, all the time watching carefully.

'Help me, Louis. Help me get the person responsible. Someone is responsible. Someone deserves to pay. Pay for mutilating your beautiful wife. Sure, you argued, she walked out, but she didn't deserve to die. No one deserves to die like that. Help me make it right. Help me make them pay, Louis. Make them pay for what they've done to Titia, to you, to your future together.'

His words bore into Louis, at first just breaking

the surface, but as he spoke, as he began to justify and rationalise, the words worked their way in deeper, deeper into Louis's conscience, until the gentle taunting struck a nerve, a tingling, painful, hidden nerve. Louis Matthews could take no more. No more lies. No more hiding behind his grief.

A voice inside his head shouted, *You know you'll have to come out if you tell him. The papers are bound to find out. They'll find out and they'll splatter your picture over every paper that carries the story.*

Louis didn't care. He had to free himself of the burden of guilt that he'd carried since he'd found out. No, since he'd started sleeping with Georgio.

What about Georgio? shouted the voice. *He'll go inside for sure. Crime of passion or not, he'll go inside, and you know what they do to woman killers inside. That'll be your fault, Louis. You might even join him as an accessory.*

Now bright red with frustration and shaking, Louis shouted, 'Enough!'

'Enough, I've had enough. I can't carry on. I'm so tired of it all.'

His sobs and yells filled the room. Lomas glanced towards the recorder, making sure it was running.

'It's all right, Louis, in your own time,' he said calmly.

'I know,' blurted Louis. 'I know everything. I know why, and who. But, before I tell you, what's going to happen to me?'

'I'll do all I can to help you, Mr Matthews. Please, tell me what you know.'

'I'd been seeing one of the staff at Pines Restaurant,' Louis began. 'Titia didn't know, but that's not why she left. He's one of the waiters there.'

'He?' Lomas's eyes widened and his eyebrows rose at this latest admission of promiscuity, adding to his cheating with his wife's sister.

'Yes, *he*, DI Baxter. I'd been seeing him for a while and things were getting quite serious. You've got to believe me. I didn't know he was going to do it. I didn't prompt it and I didn't take any part in it. I only found out it was him a few days ago.'

'Please, go on, Mr Matthews.'

Louis extended his pause, attempting to gain some level of composure.

'He said she was too controlling and that she was taking advantage.'

'Of you?'

'Yes, of me. Apparently she went into the restaurant one night and spent the entire evening bad-mouthing me. Georgio listened to her all night and he said that by the end of it he'd decided to kill her.'

'What, just like that? She bad-mouths you, so he kills her? Is Georgio… you did say that was his name?'

'Yes, DI Baxter, you heard correctly.'

'Georgio?' Lomas paused, questioningly.

'George Davis. He calls himself Georgio to make himself sound more exotic. It works as well.' Louis cracked a brief smile.

'As I was saying, is Georgio given to impulsive decisions, fits of rage, temper tantrums Mr Matthews?'

'No… well, not really.' Louis's answer reeked of hesitancy and untruth.

Louis continued, recounting when and how he'd found out about Georgio's sordid secret, disclosing how his lover had abducted, tortured and eventually murdered his wife in the secluded cabin, as well as revealing a few sordid secrets of a more personal nature.

He also gave a thorough recounting of his sexual and emotional exploits, the details of which Lomas skipped over as he described the remainder of the interview to Pete when they caught up in his office.

Marie Carlton also joined them, keen to know the latest developments as far as Louis Matthews was concerned. Relief flooded across her face as Pete explained that his checks had brought up all the details they needed on one George Henry Davis.

'So an arrest is on the way then, Lomas?'

'Yes, ma'am, as soon as I can assemble the team. We're going to send one team to bring him in and a forensic team to the cabin Louis Matthews told us was the location of the murder.'

'I'll convey the good news upstairs. Well done, Lomas.'

Marie smiled warmly at Lomas, relieved as much for herself as for Lomas. She knew that a result on this case would not only make her life easier with Randolph, but also that the heat on Lomas would ease, for a while at least anyway.

56

Louis Matthews sat in his cell on a cold hard bench that doubled as a bed, for those who were unfortunate enough to end up taking part in an enforced sleepover. The faintest smell of its previous occupants wafted up as a draught of air blew under the heavy grey steel door.

A shiver ran down his spine as he clenched his fingers over the front edge of the seat. The longer he sat, the tighter his gut knotted, nervous and frightened of what would happen when Georgio found out – found out that he, Louis, partner and friend, had betrayed him. Louis closed his eyes for a second and could almost hear Georgio shrieking at him, his fake accent dropped, replaced by every insult and curse that he could muster. Louis's eyes flicked open as a door on a nearby cell slammed shut.

Was that Georgio? he thought. *Surely they couldn't have picked him up this quickly?*

His heart raced and stomach tightened as he strained to hear a sound, any sound, from the next cell. Hampered by the rain which had begun drumming on the window, he detected a faint cry, the pitch of a muffled moan which Louis decided couldn't be Georgio. His thoughts returned to the can of worms he'd opened not an hour previously and the wrath he would face from his lover the next time they met.

The wall against his back was cold and hard, and he wondered if this was how he would be forced to live, if he would be charged as an accessory, or whatever it was that people who withheld information about murders got charged with. The smell of urine once more clung to his nostrils and the rattling of keys against his cell door dragged him out of his daze. With a metallic thud of the lock and a slow squeal, his cell door swung open and a sombre-looking DI Baxter stood there. His stare locked onto Louis's eyes like a homing beacon locking onto its target.

'Mr Matthews, come with me please?'

Lomas turned to walk away and was replaced with a young uniformed officer who took Louis by the arm and led him down the familiar corridor, past a row of grey steel lockers, towards the interview rooms.

A feeling of turbulence hit Louis's stomach, and his mouth began to salivate in readiness to vomit at the thought of more questioning to come. All this, and the events of the past few months, struck Louis Matthews like a charging bull. As the salivating in his mouth intensified, his stomach rolled upward like a growing tidal wave, the morsels he had consumed exited his body and a surge of thoughts ram-raided his brain. Louis Matthews saw black as he crumpled to the floor.

57

The address that Lomas and his assembled squad descended on was 36 Easter Street.

'OK, you three around the back, cover the door and any exits on the rear of the building. You two, to the side by the fire escapes. Pete, stay close, we're going in through the front door.'

The five officers in the other two groups disappeared from view as Lomas led the way up the four large steps to a red panelled door. The smooth grey concrete surrounding the door was cracked and weathered with age, and the paint on the door itself was flaky and dry. A badly pitted, round brass doorknob stood out from the centre of the door at chest height.

'A far cry from the salubrious home of Mr Matthews, don't you think?' Lomas remarked quietly. Pete nodded and then flicked a glance towards the intercom entry buttons to the right of the door. Lomas followed Pete's glance.

DAVIS Flat B, it said beside the middle button.

'Team Alpha in position.'

'Team Bravo in position,' crackled two almost identical, robot-like voices over Lomas's radio.

'OK, hold your positions. If he makes a run for it, he's yours. Be careful, we don't know quite how this guy's going to react.'

Lomas pushed hopefully at the heavy old door, and it swung effortlessly back on its hinges. He turned to Pete and motioned for him to be quiet as they began their ascent up the staircase. As they turned one-eighty degrees on the first-floor landing, the brown carpet twisted under Lomas's feet. Dimly lit and with peeling water-stained wallpaper, the staircase stank of mildew and old newspapers. They continued upwards, creaks from the odd step sounding a hundred times louder than they actually were. With the second flight of stairs behind them, they stood before a plain white door.

'Ready?' Lomas asked quietly.

Pete nodded confirmation.

Lomas raised his right fist and knocked three hard, purposeful knocks.

Inside, George Davis was standing in his kitchen, which was small but functional, holding a black silicone spatula. He had just poured an omelette mix into a heated pan and cursed as he heard the knock.

'Shit, always when I start something. It better be you, Louis, with an apology,' he yelled as he walked quickly across his compact flat. He snatched at the handle and pulled the door towards him.

With the words 'George Henry Davis?' and the sight of two men who must have been police, standing at his door, George Henry Davis's life went into slow motion. A feeling of almost drunken bewilderment hit him full on. Then, in an instant that felt like an age, panic replaced bewilderment, one like no panic he had ever experienced before. A raw, savage, fight or flight panic. Still seeing his life in frame-by-frame nanoseconds, he turned on his heels and launched himself into a sprint. Dropping the spatula to the floor, he turned, and with both hands and all the effort he could muster, George threw the door back into its frame.

Lomas threw his left forearm up and his foot out to stop the door from slamming shut on him.

'He's running. I repeat, he's running!' Lomas shouted into his radio as he burst through the door after George.

George ran, and after a short burst across the room, he jumped, arms covering his face and with his knees up, straight at the tall, wide, and luckily rotten-framed sash window.

Two officers in the alley to the side of the building watched in disbelief as George crashed out of the window, sending glass cascading down over them in a shower of razor-sharp shards.

George was stopped dead by the fire escape railings. From the force of his leap, his body smashed against the cold iron uprights. He screamed in agony as his right forearm snapped with the impact. As he landed on the moss-covered platform he could see the imposing figure of Lomas closing in just metres away. Davis scrambled to his feet, tucking his injured arm into the side of his body, adrenalin pumping through him, fuelling his desperation to escape. He began a sprint, ignoring the pain of a thousand glass splinters that were ripping the soles of his feet open. As the blood began to seep from the torn skin, George ran down the fire escape.

Lomas climbed hurriedly through the smashed window and the two officers below realised they were safe from the falling glass. All three began hurriedly closing in on George.

The two cops on the ground caught George's eye as they began to move in. He stopped momentarily on a platform halfway between the two officers below and Lomas above.

He glanced down at a communal bin store that had a fence separating it from the two cops out on the path. Then he looked round, checking on Lomas's progress. Gripping the top of the flaky black railings with his left hand, and with his right arm pulled tight in against his chest, he sprang up and over the railing. Some two and a half metres down, Davis hit the floor, hard. He screamed out loud and his head wrenched backwards, face contorted in agony, as his open wounds were split even more by the sharp tarmac driving the splinters of glass that were lodged in his cuts deeper into his feet. His agony was cut short by the sound of Lomas clattering down the fire escape and the two officers on the path closing in. George stood upright and resumed his desperate sprint to the front of the building. In front of him was a thick hedge. He curled himself up in mid-air as he leapt at full sprint through it.

'He's going for the street!' Lomas yelled to the two officers in the alley.

DI Baxter catapulted himself over the railing, rolling as he landed in the way a parachutist might. Up quickly and unhurt, he continued to give chase with Peter close behind.

George Davis winced as the branches of the hedge ripped at him. It was as if every obstacle he encountered wanted to inflict some injury, no matter how small. His bare arms took the brunt of the attack as he scrambled through the thick shrubbery. Behind him he heard the shouts and yells of his pursuers, still chasing hot and on his heels.

'He's through the hedge. Don't lose him!'

The hammering of shoes and boots on the hard unyielding ground seemed to grow louder. George glanced to his left. The leading arm of a pursuer appeared from behind the hedge. Directly behind him, the same hedge rustled as Lomas jumped into it, following him through. George turned to his right and dug in deep, dragging out every ounce of energy, calling on all his reserves of mental strength and ran, ran for all his worth, ran for his life.

Still he heard his pursuers.

Cut through the alley, he thought quickly. He darted left, off the pavement. Then he heard a screech of tyres, a locking of wheels and a bang, noises which eight officers and one car driver would never forget.

George's legs folded sideways under the impact, his knees giving way, his shoulder and already broken right arm hitting the shiny black bonnet, closely followed by the side of his head. His body slid up the bonnet at pace, and with all the muscle tension released, he was limp, like a huge rag doll smashing into the centre of a clear hard windscreen. His head, torso and hips bounced off the leading edge of the roof and George Davis's body was flung high in the air and over the back of the car, then dragged back to earth, as gravity smashed him into the cold hard road.

'No!' yelled Lomas, raising his hands to his head.

As George Henry Davis lay on the road, twitching his final involuntary movements, a tearful, shocked and shaking Coline Carter sat behind the wheel of her battered black BMW, utterly unaware of the ironic twist of fate that had just befallen her… her, and her sister's killer, who lay dead in the road behind her.

58

A large figure slipped into the shadows, disappearing through bushes that lined the driveway. Far off, a street lamp cast a yellow glaze over the rain-kissed street, and the fresh smell that comes with a sharp winter shower filled the air as thick clouds spread to leave star-spangled gaps in the night sky.

DI Baxter drove quietly onto the hardstanding at the front of his house, a house that had been without the noise of his family for too long. Exhausted from his day, Lomas closed and locked the car. Turning to walk up the driveway towards his house, he scuffed his right shoe against something in the darkness. He reached down between the car and the thick evergreen bushes and found a long, thin box. Lomas's heart sank and his mouth became dry as his fingertips pressed against the box sides. The corners were moist from the rain. He quickly placed it back, as near as possible to the spot from where he'd taken it and turned back to his car. Sitting back inside with the light off, Lomas closed his heavy, weary eyes and rested back in his seat. Letting out a deep sigh, he pressed speed dial three on his mobile phone.

'Sherlock… Lomas. I know it's late and it's been a hell of a day, but I need you and Grayson's boys over at my place again.'

'OK, sure, no problem. What is it?'

'Another delivery from "parcel express", I think. On the drive this time. He obviously wanted me to find it straight away.'

'OK, we're on our way. Do you need anything?'

'No, I'm fine, thanks. Well, apart from being bloody knackered, but sleep can wait, I guess.'

'Well don't go to sleep on the drive. The parcel guy might come back and ask you to sign for the package.'

'Yeah, thanks, mate.' Lomas smiled.

Sherlock chuckled a low, amused chuckle and hung up.

Lomas reclined his seat slightly and eased back to wait for Sherlock and Grayson to arrive.

The street was silent, no passing cars, no people waiting. Lomas sat wondering what gruesome gift was awaiting them in the latest box, and why had it been delivered to him, here, at home.

It makes no sense, he thought. He mulled over the previous deliveries, including the one he'd received personally, but arrived at no answer, no conclusion, other than he was chasing a sick bastard.

DI Baxter stepped from his car to greet the team as they donned their familiar overalls and gloves. A few knowing glances were exchanged and the team swarmed over the front of Lomas's property like bees hungry for nectar on a summer day. Spotlights were positioned and lit, whitewashing the area in a bright clinical light.

Lomas watched as one of the team, who had just asked for his keys, eased Lomas's car from the drive and the others began their floodlit inspection of the damp ground. His thoughts were spinning, locked in a tangled web of theories and supposition, bouncing backwards and forward from the first grisly findings to this most current delivery. The loss of innocent life was eating its way into him, digging into tiny cracks in his belief that he would catch the killer before any more life was lost, a belief which he himself had continually drilled into his team for what felt like an eternity.

The box was plainly visible under the bright white lights. It leaned against the bushes displaying the exact same stencilled lettering that all previous boxed deliveries had had.

DI Baxter
Private and Confidential

'Do you want me to do the honours?' enquired Sherlock, glancing from Lomas to Grayson.

'Yes, go on, let's get it over with,' said Lomas.

As Sherlock eased a short, sharp blade along the clear tape holding the box lid together, all around drew breath. He then slit the length of one side, eased the package open and held it as one of his team took pictures of the open box. Taking great care not to disturb the contents, Sherlock pulled the front of the box further still to reveal a neatly severed pair of slender shaved legs, removed precisely from below the hip and above the ankle. They were packed, opposite-ways, tightly into their wrapping. There was no sign of either foot, and various bruises and cuts were apparent at first glance.

'Bag and tweezers please?' Sherlock motioned to a team member.

From behind the calf of one of the legs, Sherlock withdrew the item they had been expecting. A note stained with blood. He placed it into the waiting bag and sealed the top.

'We'll read that in a second, if that's OK with you, Lomas?'

'Yeah, fine. I'll go in and make us a coffee while you boys finish up out here.'

With plastic covers over his shoes, Lomas made his way into his empty home. Flicking on the kitchen light, closely followed by the kettle, he rattled around in the cupboards, his thoughts drifting momentarily to Heidi. The day had been long and hard. Not having her there when he got in made things even worse. His reflective spell deepened as he realised they hadn't spoken for two days, something he never did. Lomas glanced at his watch. *Too late to call now*, he thought as the sweeping hands indicated it was just past quarter to two in the morning.

As the water in the kettle bubbled to boiling

point and beyond, the switch clicked. Almost simultaneously, Grayson walked into the kitchen holding an evidence bag with the note inside and a larger plastic sheet. He laid the plastic over Lomas's kitchen worktop and placed the sealed evidence bag onto it.

Lomas passed Grayson a cup of coffee, Sherlock followed closely behind and took another cup from Baxter, and together they stood round and read the note, through the plastic, in silence.

Delivery, delivery
For Baxter, DI
To view and behold
With your own eyes.
A pair of legs
But look, no feet!
From poor, dead Elinor
A girl so sweet.
She's gone now, and
It's all your fault,
You've failed you see
My task to halt.
Who next, you ask,
Mmm, DC Taylor?
Or maybe Heidi
Your wife, or jailer?
Your ball and chain
Yes that'd be fun,
Shall she be next
Is she the one?

You'll soon find out,
All in good time,
While you waste yours
On these 'clue-filled rhymes'.

'Bastard! Is he so arrogant that he thinks he can take Heidi or Drew? I'll see him burn in hell before he fucking gets his hands on either!'

Lomas raged, slamming his coffee cup onto the worktop, snapping the handle off in the process and spilling some of the contents.

'Who the fuck does he think he is?'

'He's sick, Lomas, very, very sick, and obviously in need of some serious help. Now, take a second and decide how you're going to handle this.' Said Sherlock.

'What do you mean?'

'What I mean is, is there any way he could know where Heidi and the kids are, or is he bluffing? Drew's under twenty-four-hour surveillance now, so she's fine, but what about Heidi, how safe is she?'

Lomas picked up the phone, infuriated by the thought that the killer could be targeting his own wife.

'Hello?' A groggy, sleepy voice greeted him. Heidi sounded as though she was warm and safe in bed at her mother's house. He paused for a moment, a feeling of relief flowing over him. He decided not to panic her by telling her of the night's events.

'Hello, sorry it's really late. I just wanted to hear your voice and check you were all OK. It's been a hell of a day.'

'Are you OK, honey?'

'Yeah, yeah, I'm fine. Just dog-tired and missing you like crazy.'

'I miss you too.'

'OK, you go back to sleep, we'll talk tomorrow. I love you.'

'I love you too honey, goodnight.'

The receiver at the other end clicked down. Lomas sat for a moment holding the silent phone against his ear, then returned it to its cradle.

Re-energised by his brief chat, Lomas sprang from his chair and turned his attention to Grayson Washington.

'Grayson, I need your help, now more than ever. We have got to nail this son of a bitch. I won't let him get to my family, or to Drew.'

'Whatever I can, Lomas, you know that.'

'I appreciate it, just do what you do.' Grayson nodded in confirmation and turned to start packing up the evidence with meticulous attention to detail, avoiding any possible contamination.

59

A shrill ringing woke Lomas from a broken, restless sleep that seemed like it had been only minutes since he'd closed his eyes. Reaching out, he located his phone.

'Yes, hello?'

'Lomas, it's Grayson.' His tone was excited and his speech rapid, causing Lomas to shake himself awake as he listened.

'We've found something, something quite unusual on the note from last night and the one from Drew's last parcel.'

'Go on, what is it?'

'Well, on the reverse side of both is a small amount of magnesium carbonate, just a slight dusting, but enough to pick up a sample for testing.'

'Why does that sound familiar, Grayson?'

'Well, the amount of years you've been pumping iron, Lomas, I hope it does sound familiar. Magnesium carbonate, otherwise known as chalk – weightlifting chalk, that is – you know, for improving grip?'

'Yes, yes, I know what it's used for. Are you sure? I mean, really sure?'

'A hundred per cent, Lomas, no doubt in my mind.'

That was as much as DI Baxter needed.

'Do me a favour, let Marie Carlton know, and I'll see you in half an hour.'

'OK, no problem, will do.'

'Oh, and Grayson, well done, great job.'

Lomas was up, out of bed, dressed and in his car in no time at all.

On his way to the station he passed the gym where he trained, and inspiration hit him like a bolt from the blue. A hundred, logically sequenced, well-ordered thoughts flooded his brain, and a buzz of excitement rushed through him. He was on to something, he knew it – all he had to do was prove it.

He was greeted by Grayson and Marie Carlton. No sooner were they through the door than Lomas was articulating his thoughts and orchestrating all those around him to turn his ideas into reality.

'I've got it, ma'am. I need three search warrants and I need them as soon as you can. Grayson, I need your findings and evidence together and ready to present to the team as quickly as you can, please.'

'Done it,' the forensic specialist replied instantly.

'Good. Now, I need to get the team together. We've got a lot of work to do.'

'How sure are you, Lomas?' enquired Washington.

'A hundred per cent, no doubt in my mind.' Grayson smiled as he repeated his earlier line.

Marie Carlton accompanied Lomas, Grayson and Sherlock into the briefing room.

'Pete, round everyone up. I don't care if they're in bed, been on double shift, shopping with Gran, or feeding their pet chimp. I want everyone in here, ready to go in forty-five minutes.'

'Yes, sir, no problem.'

'Oh, and Pete,'

'Sir?'

'That includes Drew. Get her and whoever's minding her here too.'

'Yes, boss.'

Lomas shot a quick glance at Marie. She nodded her approval, still unaware of exactly where Lomas was heading but behind him all the way.

'DI Baxter, could we speak in my office please?'

'Ma'am.'

Lomas followed Marie to her office and behind the closed door he explained exactly what, why and who he wanted. His rationale as always was sound, and as always, she felt compelled to go the distance with him and hurriedly did what she had to, to secure his search warrants.

60

The team were assembled as ordered, with five minutes to spare. In a crowded briefing room, some unshaven and hurriedly dressed, they stood awaiting the arrival of the man who had guided them this far through the most horrific murder investigation any of them had ever witnessed. Inquisitive whispers and a hubbub of anticipation gave the room a buzz of anticipation. Then, on the stroke of the forty-fifth minute, the door swung open and in he walked.

Detective Inspector Lomas Baxter stood before them with an increased air of confidence. Casting his eye over the room and stalking the width of it with the prowess of a dominant male lion surveying his pride, he began.

'Thank you for getting here so quickly, and at such short notice, and thank you for your massive efforts on this investigation so far. I need you to know that every one of the victim's families and friends will want me to let you know how much they appreciate how much you've each invested in tracking down every lead and following up on each thread of evidence.' He paused briefly.

'I know we've worked long hard hours and witnessed some hideous and traumatic things. I've brought you here to let you know about some new evidence that our forensic team has brought to light, and to let those of you who don't know that the killer delivered a box to my home in the early hours of this morning. From this package, which we believe contained the legs of Elinor Mary Clarke, we discovered another note. Nothing unusual there you may think. However, on the reverse side of this note, and, on the reverse of the note delivered in the box to DC Taylor, forensics have discovered a trace of magnesium carbonate, also known as weightlifting chalk, which is used to improve grip during lifts and opens up a whole new line of enquiry, because now we're looking at people who train with weights. I want to go one step further and present to you a new prime suspect.'

Lomas nodded to Marie Carlton, who flicked off the lights in the briefing room and clicked on a laptop mouse, which in turn flicked on a projector. An image was cast onto a large whiteboard. It was a bulky, dark-haired weightlifter holding aloft a mass of iron at either end of a thick bar at the completion of a gold medal winning clean and jerk. The headline above the newspaper picture read:

Monica Silverman lifts gold

A tumultuous buzz of conversation exploded in the briefing room. Lomas stood patiently and waited for the noise to abate, then calmly continued.

'Monica Silverman is not only a gold medal winning weightlifter, shot-put and hammer thrower, but she is also the medically trained daughter of one Dr Thomas Silverman. She resides and trains locally and is immensely powerful, giving her the ability to not only deliver tremendously damaging blows, but can also, no doubt, carry out the detailed medical procedures and amputations that our victims have all endured. I also happen to know that she holds a particular loathing for slim, petite "Barbie dolls", as I've heard her call them. In addition, Miss Silverman drives a dark red Ford Transit van. Ladies and gentlemen, this is our killer. I would stake my life on it. Monica Silverman is the vicious, sadistic murderer we've been hunting.'

Again the room erupted in spontaneous conversation, and again Lomas waited.

'To be clear, Monica is not stupid, is most certainly not to be underestimated and she's not going to be easy to catch – we know that from experience – but, we have three search warrants coming. One for her home, one for the gym where she trains, and one to impound and search her van. This won't be easy. In whichever of these places she is found, we've got to bring her in. I want two teams. I'm going to head one. DCI Carlton is going to head the other.' Lomas smiled a reassuring smile at Drew and continued.

'My team will take the gym. DCI Carlton's team will take the house. Now, Monica trains at various times of the day, but the guys at the gym tell me that today, Saturday, she nearly always trains at about midday. Her workouts last for between sixty and ninety minutes, so here's what we're going to do. At 12.30 p.m. we hit both places simultaneously. But only if one team has sight of Miss Silverman or her van. I don't want any have-a-go heroes on this. She's strong and she's dangerous, so a team effort is essential. You go in together, take her down together and restrain her safely. It's the only way we'll get her in custody, and if she puts up a fight, be careful, follow the lead officer and cover each other's backs. Look at this picture, remember the face, remember all the work you've done, and if I'm right, remember what she's done. Be careful, good luck.'

61

At precisely 12.30 p.m., both teams rendezvoused at their positions. As Lomas and his team pulled up in two cars a hundred yards from the gym car park, they could clearly see Monica's Transit in the car park only feet from the doorway of the gym.

Lomas radioed through to Marie Carlton that they were in position and had visual contact with the suspect's vehicle.

He sat for a moment contemplating his timing. Then he gave the signal and both parties descended rapidly on their targets.

Lomas's team drove both cars through the entrance to the car park and pulled up close behind Monica's van, blocking it in completely. Six officers, including DI Baxter, quickly alighted the cars and followed him into the gym, Nick Swaine standing square-on by his side. As they entered they could see Monica in the far corner of the gym, locked out in the same position she had held in the picture. Her focus was complete, her concentration unwavering. At first she didn't even register the presence of six plain-clothed officers entering the gym. As they approached, she glanced to the right and instantly recognised Lomas. She calmly lowered the relatively light training weight to the floor. Then, without a pause, she snapped it back up to shoulder height.

Lomas motioned for the team to spread out but stay back as he watched Monica. He then waved to the other gym members to leave.

Clothed in grey sweatpants and a thick black T-shirt, pulled in at the waist with a wide belt, Monica Silverman repeated another repetition. As she lowered the bar to rest across the front of her shoulders, she looked once again at Lomas.

'Can I help you, DI Baxter?' Her voice was cold, calm and with a hint of sarcasm.

'You know why we're here, Monica. Why don't you come along with me to the station so that we can have a little chat?'

'Whatever would you want to chat to me for, Detective? You haven't said any more than ten words to me in as many years of training here.'

'Come on, Monica, don't make this difficult. I want you to come to the station and I also want to have a look in that van of yours, because I don't think you've just been carrying your gym bag in there, now have you?'

Monica Silverman's look changed at the mention of her van, and an evil, narrow expression came over her.

'You want to take me to your station? You'd better have brought more backup than this bunch of pussies, Lomas.'

With that, Monica launched the bar, which had

sat across the top of her chest, forward with both hands, sending it hurtling through the air and crashing into Tim and Dave, the two youngest of Lomas's team. Bowled over by the force of the bar, they crumpled to the floor.

Seeing this, Nick Swaine shot forward from Lomas's side, and with one hand on his cuffs he grabbed for one of Monica's wrists. Spinning her left hand over his right she grabbed his forearm, and reaching into the breast pocket of her T-shirt with her right hand she produced a stainless steel scalpel, which she drove down into the top of Nick's chest, just short of his collarbone. Nick let out a scream as he folded at the waist, clutching at the scalpel, his face contorted in pain.

The two remaining members of Lomas's team attempted to seal off Monica's only escape route from behind a large squat rack where she had backed herself with one huge step. Enraged and screaming like a wild animal, she grabbed at some loose weight discs that lay on the floor and hurled them like discus at the two officers. They slipped and ducked to avoid the barrage of flying iron. Philip, the bigger of the two, misjudged the flight path of one disc and it connected squarely with his right kneecap. He fended off the following discs with his arm in a desperate attempt to stop one cracking his skull.

Lomas saw a ten-kilo barbell on the floor. Seizing the opportunity, he grabbed it.

Monica was still throwing small discs of various

sizes at Philip and John and didn't see Lomas make his move.

With the bar held across his waist, Lomas tucked and rolled in front of Monica and drove the end of the bar into her gut. She gasped for air, and a shocked expression temporarily replaced her rage. In an instant, Lomas dropped the bar, stepped in and drove his clenched fist into the bridge of Monica's nose, following quickly with a sharp right hook to the side of her jaw. Monica wobbled, dazed and unsteady. Once again, Lomas seized the chance offered by the let-up in Silverman's onslaught, swept his leg and kicked her feet out from under her. As she fell to her knees, Tim and Dave rushed over, forced the bulky weightlifter to the floor and cuffed her hands quickly behind her back.

They struggled to raise Monica, and with an arm each, they led a dazed Monica Silverman out towards the parked cars. But as the fresh air hit her, so did a fresh burst of energy, and with it she spun the two young officers, still clinging to her arms, round in a full circle. Then, as their head's swam, disorientated, she slammed them backwards against the wall of the gym, driving back with the full force of her muscular frame. She took half a step forward and then slammed them once more into the brickwork. Their grip eased momentarily and she ran for the gap between the rear of her van and the two police cars sealing it in.

Lomas, who had been following a few paces behind, emerged from the gym doorway and saw

Silverman bolting for the road. He launched himself into a sprint, darting through the same gap that Monica had taken. He was covering the ground much quicker than the handcuffed weightlifter, and within a few rapid steps he was closing. He then threw himself, arms outstretched, at Monica's back, catching her in a perfect rugby tackle. They crashed to the floor, the air driven from the cuffed woman's lungs as she landed between Baxter and the floor.

Jumping to his feet, Lomas tugged at the restraints, forcing Silverman to stand. With a strong grip on the cuffs, Lomas turned Monica round and forced her back towards the gym and the waiting cars.

Lomas stopped her at the rear doors of the dark red Transit, holding her in situ. Monica's head bowed as Lomas flung open the rear doors to reveal a boarded, heavily bloodstained prison, on the floor of which was a pair of black leather gloves and a red-and-white checked shirt.

DI Baxter had his prisoner.

The End

Acknowledgements

A special thank you to Hilary Woodward who turned my hand written scribbles into something I could work with.

Also to Elinor Mary Clarke who worked at The Titchfield Mill and whose name I asked to use for a victim.

Thank you for buying and reading Prisoner, I hope you've enjoyed it. Your support means a lot.

If you could find the time I'd really appreciate it if you could leave a brief, honest review on Amazon.

Heath

Want to know what's next?

Read an excerpt from Khan over the page. To be released in 2020 !

Khan - Coming in 2020

Khan - Chapter 1

The sleek black Range Rover slowed in the humming evening traffic, at the same time the tailgate eased open. A tightly wrapped cloth bundle was pushed from the rear of the 4x4, slamming unceremoniously to the black tarmac. As it hit the road it rolled directly into the path of a dirty white van. The driver of the van saw the bundle drop and locked the brakes, but the gap was too short and the van skidded over the cloth mound, snagging it with the underside of the engine cover and dragging it along for forty feet. No sooner had the front of the van ensnared the bundle, than the Range Rover tailgate closed, the suspension dipped and it accelerated away through the busy mass of cars.

Fourteen days earlier

Inzamam Khan slammed his iPhone onto the thick, white cotton table cloth and shouted at the top of his voice.

'Fucking Sons of infidels, they have less sense than they were born with, do I have to do everything myself? Is there no one around here with an ounce of initiative?'

‘What is it boss?’ a bearded Indian youth scurried forward, whilst in the background, a pair of scruffy looking white men in their early twenties leaned against the doorway to the kitchen of Inzamam’s restaurant. The good looking Asian businessman looked beyond the vocal one and over at the loitering pair with disdain; they were a necessary evil, a means to his ultimate end and as such he tolerated their presence, humoured their feeble attempts at wit and paid them handsomely for their endeavours. They on the other hand thought that they were in with ‘The Man,' that’s what they referred to him as when they were disrespectfully sniggering at a safe distance, but when in his domain they hung back until called, held in place by fear of the ramifications they had observed others befall at the hands of Inzamam.

Seeing the two youths reminded Khan of a recent incident they had witnessed…

Another youth had challenged Khan over the size of his cut. Inzamam had not reacted to the young man’s verbal taunts, nor to the obvious racial tirade which accompanied his ill-informed attempt at increasing his payment.

‘Come on you fuckin’ thick Paki, I’m due more than that, I’d get more than that in tips waiting in this fuckin’ shit-hole of a restaurant!’ he had yelled across the kitchen. Inzamam had stopped checking the takings, turned calmly and walked across to the three youths without uttering a word, or changing his expression. As he had got within arm's length of the gobby one, his hand had shot out and grabbed the youth by his throat contracting his fingers around the windpipe of the young man as he pulled him close; the loiterers had eased backwards, leaving their accomplice alone in the clutches of the businessman. Gobby, tried to struggle but Inzamam grabbed a handful of hair on the back of the youths head. As he did so he simultaneously released the lad's throat and slammed his face down onto a stainless steel worktop at such pace that he had bounced the face of the youth off the counter three times, before a large silver-coloured pot had fallen off the end, clattering to the floor. With the third strike the youth's body had gone limp and Inzamam had released the grip on his hair, dropping him to the floor, his legs spasming as his crumpled form hit the ground. He'd turned his attention to the loiterers who both turned to run.

'Stay there gentlemen,' he had said quietly. The pair had frozen to the spot as the Restaurateur walked around them slowly until he was standing before them, staring intently. They'd glanced over their shoulders at their acquaintance, who was sprawled motionless on the floor, fear filling their eyes they turned back to face Khan.

‘Are either of you unhappy with your level of remuneration?’ They’d looked at each other briefly and silently shook their heads.

‘Good,’ he continued quietly, ‘then this conversation will not need repeating, will it?’ Again both shook their heads, neither uttering a sound.

‘You know where the door is, you may leave.’ They both glanced round at their associate again.

‘Oh don’t worry about him, I’ll take care of him.’ With no need for a second instruction the pair had run out of the back of the restaurant. No repeat performance had ever been required by the two.

Inzamam snapped out of his recollection.

‘Get me a coffee Raj and none of that cheap filtered crap we serve up to the monkey’s who come in here.’ He shot a glance at the Asian youngster. Well over six feet in height, with a thin beard and an athletic build, Raj was a regular visitor at the kitchen and a regular recipient of the verbal abuse Inzamam chose to dole out at will. As well as being Khan’s right hand-man, gifted with a great technical knowledge, he spent his days running errands for the older Restaurateur, from picking up dry cleaning, to covering for Inzamam when his wife called the restaurant to speak to her husband who was invariably in the office with one of the many young waitresses he employed; usually based on looks, age and vulnerability, which, as with most people in his life he then exploited. As ever Raj complied with the order from Khan, without complaint or argument, Khan watched him as he made his way silently to the rear of the kitchen and set about brewing a fresh pot of the expensive, rich-fragranced coffee in the meticulous way he always did. Khan smiled and moved his attention to the loiterers, who, upon noticing his shift in attention, shifted their weight off the door frame and stood straight.

'So, what are you two doing here? Hopefully it's good news, I've heard enough shit for one day.'

'We, we've run out boss,' the skinnier of the pair stuttered, blinking furiously as he did.

'Run out, really? What of everything?'

'Everything except the green boss, we had really busy night in town last night,'

'Yeah the coke went really quick.' Interrupted his partner, a mop-topped chav attired in a knock off Adidas tracksuit and high top Nike basketball boots. He had a round chipmunk-like face with cratered skin from clawing at acne in his early teenage years.

They were a useful, if not overly bright pair and Inzamam supplied them both with a free to use mobile phone so that he could get hold of them day or night, a privilege he made frequent use of. He also knew that the loiterers were using the phones to call premium rate sex lines to satisfy their sexual desires at his expense. Inzamam viewed their perverted needs as a further example of infidel weakness and considered the phone bills a small price to pay, when compared to the income the pair generated. The two low level thugs served their purpose and epitomised the picture of an inferior race that Inzamam Khan had been cultivating since his youth, one which he had used to fuel his business empire.

As a boy Inzamam had spent much of his time in the company of his Father, Malik, who he idolised and despised in equal measure. Malik Khan had been a middle ranking commander who had helped set up and run an al-Qaeda training camp near Kandahar, Afghanistan. The elder Khan had oversight of training for impressionable young recruits in the use of small arms, explosives and orientation among other subjects. The syllabus was delivered within the framework of the Taliban's interpretation of sections of the Qur'an and their plans and endeavours were underpinned by their belief that they were messengers of God's will and if they were successful it would be due to their actions being ordained at the highest level, with Inshallah (God willing) accompanying directions given to the freshly initiated.

Whether the enemy was the Russians as in the 1980s, or later, the allied forces of the USA, UK and others, the local's who fought retained their mantra, that the infidels were weak, they surrendered to their greed and debauchery, availing themselves of alcohol and were promiscuous in nature. From an early age Inzamam had questioned the logic of fighting these forces with bullets and bombs, convinced that the preaching of his father and his brethren were misguided, short-sighted and un-ambitious and whilst he agreed with the cause, he found it difficult to believe that they would ever truly overthrow these super-powers, without first infiltrating their lands and destroying them from the inside. It was then, as a teenager that he began to formulate his plan, his contribution to the Jihad.

The epiphany came for Inzamam one day whilst sat sharing a meal of spiced goat and potatoes with some of the young trainees. They were descended from farming families and as the conversation unfolded, Inzamam learned that their fathers had changed their crops almost without exception to the opium poppy. As an inquisitive child Inzamam had asked questions, keen to know more. The farmer's sons bragged about how their families had forged great business arrangements with district officials, warlords and drug traffickers who targeted the greedy western infidels with their high quality opiates. A lightbulb moment had occurred for Inzamam that day, and from that point onwards he had developed a carefully crafted plan. The central part of which was to supply the finest Afghanistan product to the masses of Western civilisation. As a lever to realising this vision, his main focus quickly became convincing his father to move the whole family to England, for which he sold a heavily researched concept of a better life for his brothers and sisters to his parents, the pivotal part of his plan being demonstrating, in private to his father, how their move would enhance the progress of the Holy War against the weak British fools. He explained in great detail to the elder Khan how he would use their connections in Afghanistan and Pakistan to flood England with opiates. A flood which he would orchestrate by using the infidel's own sons to market and sell their products to the weak minded, addiction-driven non-believers.

He also outlined, using an intricate, but well drafted business plan, how they would establish and run a chain of high quality restaurants, serving their native dishes to the paying British public. This was the only aspect of his plan that had been altered once they reached English shores and discovered the nation's hunger for basic, hot and spicy curries generalised as 'Indian' food. Because of the English obsession, the Khan's restaurants became generic Indian, fronted by the father and son duo of Malik and Inzamam, who quickly became pillars of their local communities, commended for their charitable giving and community spiritedness, with their eateries becoming the well managed front, for what speedily became the largest drug trafficking and dealing business in the south of England.

Inzamam called on his side-kick once more to restock the grubby looking pair.

'Raj, get these two sales machines some more nose candy,' the loiterers nodded at each other proudly, not understanding the sarcastic, back-handed nature of the compliment.

'How about the smack, how's that been going?'

'I done most of mine.' The bony one retorted quickly. Silently Khan shifted his stare to Chipmunk who blushed and shifted his weight uneasily from one high-topped trainer to the other.

'I've not moved much boss, sorry boss, I've tried, but the peeps they just want the coke init.' He wiped his flat nose on the shiny sleeve of his track suit top and sniffed in a lung full of curried air. Inzamam Khan moved slowly to the side of

Chipmunk, who leaned towards his associate's bony shoulder. He placed an arm around the back of Chipmunk's shoulders, griping a handful of track suit in his strong hand, feeling the youth shake in his clutches. He smiled a broad menacing smile, perfect straight white teeth glinting at Chipmunk, who could feel the Asian's warm breath on his cheek.

'Don't worry, Raj will get you more coke and you can sell double the amount of nose candy to the clubbers, while your racing snake friend here can wind some more smack into the junkies, can't you Darryl?' Bony gulped, he'd thought his speedy shifting of junk would keep Khan's attention on Chipmunk, not make their sales a joint effort.

'Yes boss, course I can.'

'Good a joint sales force. You boys are going to have more cash than you know what to do with soon, if you keep sales up at this rate.' Inzamam knew of course they couldn't keep up their newly found momentum due to both being too keen on sampling the product themselves, but this was an accepted consequence of using junkies as pushers. The pay off was worth the cost and Inzamam was making plenty off the back of the two scrotes.

Thank you again for buying and reading Prisoner, your support means a lot.

If you could find the time I'd really appreciate it if you could leave a brief, honest review on Amazon.

Heath

Go to www.heathgunn.com and join

The Gunn Club and I'll update you on new releases.

Or chat to me on

Instagram - heathgunn1

Twitter - @Heathgunn

Facebook - Heath Gunn-Author

LinkedIn - Heath Gunn

ABOUT HEATH

Heath was born in Sheffield, grew up in Rotherham and left home at eighteen to join the Royal Navy, as a Helicopter Engineer.

He has lived in Hampshire, along the South Coast ever since, as he loves being near the sea.

Heath is the CEO of Hampshire based disability charity, Enham Trust; and alongside a varied and colourful career to date, Heath has written stories of various lengths, poetry and Childrens picture book stories, for years.

Prisoner is the first in the DI Baxter series, with more gripping stories on the way in 2020.

He'd love to hear from you, either through his website or social media channels, mentioned earlier.

Printed in Great Britain
by Amazon

56123075R00234